**STILL IN SHOCK . . .**

Rob sat immobile, face oyster white, eyes shadowed in their sockets and staring off into space.

"Rob?"

He turned his head slowly and looked up at her.

"What's going on?"

"Something happened."

Gracie sat down next to him. "What happened?"

"There was a fight."

"A fight? When?"

"More than a fight."

"When was this?"

"Up there. On the trail. I can't quite . . . someone . . ." He massaged his forehead with his fingertips. "I remember . . . trying to get away."

"To get away from someone? From who? Do you remember?"

"It's all a fog. I remember a lot of . . ." He stopped, frowning.

"A lot of what?"

He looked straight into Gracie's eyes. "Blood."

Goose bumps walked ghostly fingers up Gracie's arms and made all the hair stand on end. "Blood."

He nodded. "I remember a woman screaming," he said, his eyes never leaving Gracie's. "I think I saw someone die. And I think someone tried to kill me."

# ZERO-DEGREE
## MURDER

**M. L. ROWLAND**

BERKLEY PRIME CRIME, NEW YORK

**THE BERKLEY PUBLISHING GROUP**
Published by the Penguin Group
Penguin Group (USA) LLC
375 Hudson Street, New York, New York 10014

USA • Canada • UK • Ireland • Australia • New Zealand • India • South Africa • China

penguin.com

A Penguin Random House Company

ZERO-DEGREE MURDER

A Berkley Prime Crime Book / published by arrangement with the author

Berkley Prime Crime Books are published by The Berkley Publishing Group.
BERKLEY® PRIME CRIME and the PRIME CRIME logo are trademarks of
Penguin Group (USA) LLC.

For information, address: The Berkley Publishing Group,
a division of Penguin Group (USA) LLC,
375 Hudson Street, New York, New York 10014.

ISBN: 978-0-425-26366-2

PUBLISHING HISTORY
Berkley Prime Crime mass-market edition / January 2014

PRINTED IN THE UNITED STATES OF AMERICA

10  9  8  7  6  5  4  3  2  1

Cover art by Dominik Michalek/Shutterstock.
Cover design by Diane Kolsky.
Interior text design by Kristin del Rosario.

*For Mom and Dad,*
*my role models.*

*Adventurers in their own way.*
*Models of integrity. Lives of service.*

## ACKNOWLEDGMENTS

A heartfelt thank-you to:

Nancy Chichester, Jo Colwell, Sergeant Trace Hall, Steve Kennedy, L. Lee and Norman Lapidus, Barbara Law, Kathleen Law, and M. Scott Nash.

My editor, Faith Black.

Anne McDermott.

And, of course, my live-in encyclopedia, my fellow adventurer, my source of never-ending support, encouragement and love, my best friend, my husband, Mark.

And to all the Search and Rescue volunteers who routinely risk their lives.

# CHAPTER

## 1

**T**HE body hung upside down in the truck, suspended by the seat belt, sun-bleached hair skimming the roof of the cab.

Gracie Kinkaid and Ralph Hunter crouched side by side atop a granite boulder, looking down through the shattered passenger window of an F-150 pickup, which lay upside down at an oblique angle amid a jumble of rocks and vegetation. The stark white light from Gracie's LED headlamp merged with the beam of Ralph's mag flashlight, illuminating the cab and the body of what appeared to be a young man inside.

"At least this time the body's in one piece," Gracie said. "I can handle 'in one piece.'" She tugged open her radio chest pack and picked out a pair of purple latex gloves. As she snapped them on, she added under her breath, "At least I hope I can."

Ralph tugged on his own gloves, slid off the boulder onto a wide triangle of open ground next to the truck, and handed the mag flashlight back up to Gracie. "Light it up, will ya?"

Gracie grabbed the heavy flashlight and swept the cab interior with its beam. "Not a lot of blood," she said. "He didn't bleed out."

"Blunt force trauma probably knocked him out," Ralph said. "Hanging upside down in the seat belt probably killed him."

Gracie nodded. "Traumatic asphyxia. First time I've seen someone die from wearing a seat belt."

"Dead for sure without it." Ralph turned and looked up at her over the top of his glasses. "You okay with this, Gracie girl?"

"I better be, dammit," she said. "Or I need to find something else to do with my stupid-ass life." Knowing that with any other team members around, Ralph would never ask her that question, she added, "I'm good. Thanks, Ralphie."

"Okay," he said, reaching up to pat her foot. "Let's open 'er up then." He leaned down and tested the handle of the bashed-in door. It didn't move. Bracing himself against the side panel, he hauled on it with both hands. "Nope," he said finally. "Not gonna happen." He swept away the remaining glass shards with his sleeve and stretched in through the window to place two fingers on the carotid artery of the young man's neck.

Gracie counted off the seconds to herself until Ralph said in a low voice, "Nothing."

He grunted as he heaved himself even farther inside the cab.

"Careful, Ralphie," Gracie whispered.

A mumbled curse and another grunt later, Ralph wormed his way back out of the window. "ID," he said and tossed a thin leather wallet up to Gracie, who snatched it out of the air with one hand.

He leaned back inside again, elbowed aside the deflated balloon that was the deployed airbag and sifted through the papers and trash scattered throughout the cab.

Muffled voices and bursts of laughter filtered out from

the forest of Joshua trees behind Gracie—the rest of the recovery team hiking in with the Junkin litter, the sturdy plastic basket in which they would transport the body. "Ralph," she said. "Litter's here."

Wedging the mag flashlight in place between her feet, Gracie opened the wallet and zeroed the beam of her headlamp onto the California driver's license inside. A bright young face smiled back at her.

*Shit.*

She snapped the wallet closed and shoved it into a side pocket of her fleece vest. She looked up, breathing in the pungent pine and sage perfume of the high Mojave.

The sky, a deep rose in the west, dissolved to teal overhead, then indigo in the east, where, one by one, stars, bright and unwinking, unveiled themselves for the night watch.

Anxiety knotted Gracie's stomach. She forced herself to take slow, even breaths in through her nose, out through her mouth. "Don't you dare get sick," she whispered. A smile tugged at one corner of her mouth. "You barf all over Ralph's boots again and your ass is grass."

Ralph hauled himself up onto the boulder and took the mag flashlight from Gracie. Together they slid off the other side and stood watching the litter team approach, headlamps bobbing like tiny Chinese lanterns in the near darkness.

Four men scrunched into view and up to where their teammates stood. On a count of three, they bent as a single unit to lay the litter in the sandy dirt. "Howdys" and "Heys" rumbled throughout the group.

As the men unclipped from the litter and sipped from water bottles and hydration packs, Ralph brought them up to speed. For reasons that weren't immediately obvious and which might never be determined, a Ford F-150 pickup had shot off the winding gravel Forest Service road above their heads, cartwheeled down more than three hundred feet, and finally come to rest upside down with the sole occupant still inside. Deceased.

"Who is it? Do you . . . we know?" asked Lenny Some-body, burly, pink-cheeked, barely twenty-one, and so new to the team Gracie didn't even know his last name. His voice was incongruously high and timid. It was his second SAR mission, his first body recovery.

"Uh, that would be my cue," Gracie said, withdrawing the wallet from her pocket. Keeping her thumb firmly pressed over the face, she focused her headlamp beam on the driver's license. "Bradford, Joshua D. From down the hill. Long Beach. He would have been seventeen . . . next Monday."

Silence enveloped the group as all descended into their own morose thoughts of how, in a matter of seconds, a young life can be snuffed out by an error in judgment or too many beers.

Steve Cashman broke the mood by scrambling up onto the boulder. He held his flashlight shoulder high, focusing the beam down into the cab of the battered pickup.

Gracie noticed that, characteristically, Steve wasn't wear-ing a helmet, in direct violation of team policy.

The rest of the group climbed up onto the boulder and stood in a semicircle, necks craning, headlamp and flash-light beams converging on the truck.

Kurt, wearing gold-rimmed glasses, his long sandy hair pulled back into a ponytail, stood on Gracie's left. "We waitin' for the Coroner?" he asked.

"Negative," Ralph answered. "Coroner's still a couple of hours out. We'll litter the body out to the road. She'll pro-nounce him there."

"We can do a litter raise," Cashman said, sweeping the rocky hillside above the truck with the beam of his flash-light. "Haul 'im up, right up there to the road."

"Risk outweighs any advantage."

"We brought some of the ropes shit," Cashman said. He gestured toward the rope coils and jumbles of steel carabin-ers and pulleys piled in the litter. "It's in the—"

"Negative," Ralph said. "Decision's been made. We're littering him out."

Cashman swung his flashlight around, shining the beam at Ralph. "Who made the decision? You and Gracie?"

"Watch Commander. Get that light out of my eyes, Steve."

Cashman swung his beam back down to the truck.

"That's it then, right?" Lenny asked, his face a shade paler than before. "'Cuz if the Watch—"

"Come on, Hunter," Cashman said with a smile. "Don't be such a pu . . ." He glanced across at Gracie, then back down at the truck. ". . . Spoilsport."

Ralph lowered his voice an octave. "Decision's been made, Steve."

Kurt leaned in toward Gracie and said so softly that only she heard, "Shut the hell up while you're ahead, Cashman."

Gracie took a deep breath and jumped into the fray. "We need to figure out how to extricate the body."

Crouching down for a better angle, Kurt said, "Gonna be a sonofabitch."

"Through the door?" Lenny asked.

"It won't open," Gracie said.

Cashman jumped down next to the truck and tugged on the door handle.

Lenny jumped down next to him. "Through the window then?"

"We can cut the door off," Cashman suggested.

"That would require—" Gracie began.

"Take too long for extrication equipment to get here," Warren, the fourth member of the litter team, said. The older man was so stolid and quiet, half the time Gracie forgot he was there.

Lenny crouched down next to the hood. "How 'bout through the windshield?"

"It's too—" Gracie said.

"Too smashed in," Kurt said. "Too narrow."

"How 'bout the window?"

Several rescuers shook their heads.

Gracie tried again. "He'd be—"

"Truck looks kinda teetery," Lenny said. "Can we rock it onto its side so it's more level?"

"It's—"

"We could build a three-to-one Z-Rig," Cashman suggested. "Hoist it up."

Eyes focused on the truck, Ralph stood several feet away from the rest of the group, remaining silent, letting all present have their say.

Gracie smiled to herself and gave up. She should have known better than to try to get a word in edgewise. She had learned a long time ago that it took a lot less energy to stand back and listen, to speak up only when she felt a pressing need to step in and be heard, usually when someone's safety—especially her own—was at stake.

Not to mention that her legs had already morphed into wobbling stalks of wilted celery as they did every time she spoke more than monosyllables in front of a group, even her buddies on the team.

She stepped from boulder to boulder around to the opposite side of the truck and looked down at it from that angle. Fishing a piece of strawberry bubble gum out of her pocket, she popped it into her mouth. Blowing bubbles, she shone her flashlight at and around the truck and listened to the alpha males jockey for dominance in the team hierarchy under the guise of volleying extrication ideas back and forth.

It really shouldn't have mattered how long it took to decide how to remove the body from the truck. They weren't, after all, in a tearing hurry.

Except Gracie had shed her heavy fleece jacket for the half-hour drive out from the town of Timber Creek. She had left it behind in the Search and Rescue unit when she and Ralph had slipped and slid down the steep hill to the truck. All she was wearing was a black, lightweight fleece vest over an orange cotton shirt, and a pair of army-surplus desert camo pants. A pair of short, black gaiters were Velcroed over the tops of her hiking boots to keep out the dirt and desert pricklies. Hastily braided hair was mashed up beneath a black ball cap with *Timber Creek Search and Rescue* embroidered on the front.

Carrying the litter out would generate body heat and warm her up. But now, standing around, she felt the chill of a late November evening at sixty-five-hundred-feet elevation. Goose bumps tickled up her arms and legs, soon to be followed by chattering teeth and shivering.

*If you don't get moving, Kinkaid, the body the team hoofs outta here is gonna be yours.*

The discussion on the other side of the truck had deteriorated into the telling of morbid jokes.

Gracie shifted her weight to the other long leg and cracked her gum like a rifle shot, not caring how obnoxious it was.

No one took the hint.

"Can we make a decision already?" she asked.

The current joke Cashman was telling continued unabated.

Gracie's patience circled the drain. She flicked away her gum. "All right, listen the hell up!" she barked across the truck.

Dead silence.

Gracie's legs trembled. "This is what I propose. First, we stabilize the truck with rocks and logs so if it settles at all, nobody gets squished to death. Then someone—Cashman—crawls beneath the bed on this side. There's enough room." She retraced her steps around the ring of boulders to the other side of the truck. "Someone else—Kurt—crawls beneath on this side. And Lenny . . ." She pointed a purple finger at him.

The young man took a step backward.

". . . climbs in through the passenger door window,

which, by the way, would be too small to get the body through since rigor has most likely set in and we're dealing with a stiff in the true sense of the word." She softened her voice. "Lenny, you cut the seat belt with your knife." She raised her voice again. "And the three of you—Cashman, Kurt and Lenny—take the body out through the rear cab window—it's big enough—and hand him off to me, Ralph and Warren, who will put him into the litter. Then all six of us lift him up onto this big flat rock." She stomped her foot. "We put him in the body bag and package him in the litter. *Then* we all hoof him back out to the road and wait for the Coroner to get here. Any objections?"

Four men stared at her.

She looked over at Ralph, who was watching her, eyes crinkling with amusement. "Works for me," he said. "All in agreement?

Some nods. Some shrugs.

"Okay, then," Ralph said. "Let's get moving!"

# CHAPTER

## 2

THREE men and a woman hiked along a narrow winding trail carved out of the side of a mountain.

On their right, gunmetal gray cliffs jutted sharply upward toward a cloudless sapphire sky. On their left, the mountainside fell away in a rugged free fall of granite boulders, leafy mounds of manzanita, ponderosa pines and white fir, then rose up again across the gaping divide. Successive mountain peaks receded from forest green to hazy mauve. Along the horizon line in the distance stretched the biscuit-colored flats of the Mojave Desert.

Rob hiked in the lead. Dressed head-to-toe in black, he was tall and long limbed, his strides long and fluid. His cheeks were pink with cold. His chest heaved with exertion, yet he maintained a steady pace up the trail. "Keeping up then, old man?" he said over his shoulder to Joseph hiking directly behind him.

Joseph was a bull of a man with fleshy cheeks and a square jaw. Heavy eyebrows formed a straight line above deep-set blue eyes. His silver beard was full, yet carefully

trimmed. The desert-camouflage bandana covering his head
was tied at the back of his neck. Even though he was older
than Rob by twenty-five or so years and shorter by half a
foot, he was having no trouble maintaining the pace up the
trail. "Any closer behind you, my friend," Joseph said, "and
*my* head would be up your ass instead of your own."

Rob threw back his head and laughed, the sound echoing
throughout the canyon.

Several yards behind Rob and Joseph hiked the woman
and the third man.

Diana was petite and small-boned to the point of appearing frail. But she was fit and strong, able to keep up with the
men hiking ahead of her. Her eyes were large and dark against
flawless skin. Shoulder-length hair, almost black, was tucked
up beneath a multicolored knit hat. While warm enough from
hiking, she was thankful for her long coat, which shielded
her from the icy wind pushing her up the trail.

Close behind her, Tristan hiked on long spidery legs.

As she hiked, Diana struggled to ignore Tristan. His
open, congenial nature and startling blue eyes were appealing enough. But the man talked incessantly, babbling on and
on about himself, trying to impress her, trying, she knew,
to get her into bed.

Hiking uphill at altitude had winded Tristan and he had
finally stopped talking, allowing Diana to focus her attention
on the man hiking several yards ahead: Joseph—a personal
coach for Rob Christian, the British star of the movie they
were shooting in Timber Creek.

When Joseph Van Dijk had arrived on set the previous
week, Diana found something hauntingly familiar about the
man, but couldn't put her finger on exactly what it was. She
searched for opportunities to observe him from a distance
and gathered information about him from other crew members and fellow actors. She learned that he held himself apart
from everyone but Rob and revealed nothing of a personal
nature. And while he appeared friendly enough, sometimes

joking and laughing with Rob, his smiles never seemed genuine, rather a baring of yellowed teeth.

The more Diana watched and learned about Joseph, the more convinced she became that she had seen his face somewhere before and that he wasn't who he pretended to be. But his true identity eluded her, remaining just out of her grasp, fleeting, like a nightmare that, vivid in sleep, fades upon waking.

All of which was why, repelled as she was by Tristan, she had accepted his invitation to go hiking along with some of the crew and other actors staying in town over the holiday weekend, welcoming the opportunity to observe Joseph even more closely.

Tristan patted Diana's shoulder from behind. "Doing all right then, love?" he said, panting.

"Fine," she answered over her shoulder.

"How much farther are you planning on going then, Rob?" Tristan called up ahead.

Rob glanced back over Joseph's head at the two laboring a short distance behind. He stepped out onto an expansive promontory of rock jutting out from the trail and turned back. "You two ready for a breather?"

"For a mile at least," Tristan said.

Rob glanced down at his watch. "We probably ought to head back. Don't want the others to worry."

"Christ, no," Joseph said, walking past Rob onto the level outcropping. "Turn a walk into an international incident."

Diana stepped past Rob and Joseph and sat down on a large concave boulder at the far end of the outcropping. The high-altitude sun warmed her head and shoulders even as sharp gusts of bitter wind bit into her bare cheeks and whipped the hair around her face. She tugged her hat down farther over her ears.

Tristan sank down on the boulder beside her. "About bloody time," he muttered and blew out a long breath. "Shouldn't have drunk so much bubbly at lunch."

"We still have the hike back," Diana said. She took a sip from her water bottle, then clipped it back onto her belt.

"Don't remind me."

The two rested side by side, watching Rob and Joseph who stood in middle of the promontory.

Joseph was showing Rob the curved fang of a knife in his fist. "This is how you hold it, my friend," he said. "So it is hidden. Then you strike. Low. Like this." He jabbed his arm up in a fake punch to the other's midsection. "Then up, so you cut as many organs as you are able."

"Jesus," Rob said.

"It is how it is done," Joseph said with a shrug.

Rob clapped Joseph on the shoulder and lowered his knapsack off his back and onto the ground. He pulled a water bottle out of a mesh side pocket, took a swig, and turned to look out over the view. "Amazing up here," he said.

Joseph swung down onto a boulder on Diana's left.

Diana shifted uncomfortably in her seat and resisted the temptation to stand up and move away from Joseph. He was too close. She had hoped to remain a passive observer, not an active participant.

Joseph reached inside his jacket and pulled out a pint bottle of blackberry brandy. He extended the bottle toward Diana.

When she shook her head, he held it out toward Tristan.

"Why not, right?" Tristan said, swallowing the *t* at the end of the word. He reached across Diana to take the bottle. She leaned back so his arm wouldn't brush her breast.

Tristan took a swig of brandy, then reached across Diana again to hand it back. "Thanks." Still leaning forward he said, "Your work is impressive, Mr. . . . Van Rijk, is it?"

"Van Dijk. Joseph." The man's voice was rough and deep with the trace of an accent Diana couldn't place.

"You fight very well," Tristan said. "Fascinating to watch."

Another shrug. "It is what I am hired for." He took several long swallows from the bottle.

"Where'd you learn to fight like that?"

Instead of answering, Joseph looked at Diana and asked, "So, miss, how are you enjoying the walk so far?"

"It's very beautiful up here," she said, giving the man a quick smile, then looking away.

Joseph pulled a pack of Camel non-filter cigarettes from his pocket. He tapped the pack on his open palm, then extended it out to the pair. "Smoke?"

Diana shook her head.

Tristan drew out a cigarette. "Trying to quit actually, but what the hell?"

Joseph put a cigarette between his own teeth, lit it, and shoved the pack back into his pocket. He dragged the smoke deeply into his lungs and blew it out directly into the wind, which carried it away over his shoulder. He took another swig of the brandy, then looked over at Diana again. "Where are you from, miss . . . your last name, please?"

"Diana," she answered, eyes forward. "I live in L.A."

"And you are . . . an actor?"

Diana shrugged and nodded.

Tristan leaned forward again with his elbows on knobby knees. "Don't let the modesty fool you, right?" he said. "She's brilliant. They don't know what they have here."

Diana shot Tristan a tight smile.

Joseph took another casual drag from the cigarette. "You enjoy this?" he asked, exhaling the smoke with his words. "Working on this movie?"

"Yes, it's—" Diana began, but Tristan cut her off, gesturing expansively.

"Diana Petrovic. The next bloody . . ."

"Tristan," Diana hissed.

"What?" Tristan asked, feigning indignation.

"Petrovic," Joseph said in a mild voice. Diana stiffened.

". . . the next bloody Meryl Streep," Tristan finished.

"Petrovic," Joseph whispered. He inhaled deeply from the cigarette and blew out the smoke.

Fear flickered through Diana like flames at dry, dead timber. She stood up. "I . . . I think we should go back," she stammered to Tristan, who stood up next to her. "The others will worry." She moved on unsteady legs back across the outcropping toward the trail.

Rob laid a hand on Joseph's shoulder "Before we do . . ." he said to Diana, then to Joseph, "show me that release one more time, will you then? The one from yesterday."

For a moment, Joseph didn't move. He simply watched Diana, who stared at the ground, hands deep in the pockets of her coat. Then he flung the cigarette, still lit, into the dirt and stood up, rocking for a moment on his feet.

Tristan appeared next to Diana. "You all right then, love?"

It was all Diana could do not to shrug off the arm he put around her shoulders. "I want to leave," she said. She stepped away from Tristan and out onto the trail. "I want to go back to the others."

"It'll only be a second, right?" Tristan turned back to watch Rob and Joseph grappling in the middle of the out-cropping.

Joseph had Rob in a headlock. Then, so fast Diana hardly saw him do it, Rob thrust an elbow into the other man's ribs, knocked his hands apart, and twisted around to wrap an arm around his head.

"Good, my friend," Joseph said with a grunt, then flung an arm around Rob's waist.

Evenly matched, the two men strained against each other until, without warning, Joseph threw himself to the ground. Rob stumbled to keep his balance and Joseph broke free.

Rob's jacket zipper snagged the bandana on Joseph's head, pulling it askew.

Kneeling on the ground, Joseph pulled the fabric back into place.

But it was too late. Diana had already seen.

Joseph had only one ear.

Like a curtain thrown open to reveal the painful glare of the sun, the pieces of the puzzle snapped into place. Recognition punched a gasp from Diana's lungs. She stared in horror at the evil standing only ten feet away.

Time had been unkind, adding pounds to his stocky frame and flesh to his cheeks and neck. And the beard he wore hid his face somewhat. But Diana knew without a doubt that the man's name was not Joseph Van Dijk.

Her mind flashed to stories she had heard and read, pictures she had seen. Of slaughter. Men killed in front of their wives. Children in front of their parents. Diana's own uncle murdered along with his three sons.

The man standing a few feet away was a Satan among lesser demons, his calling card the disembowelment of his victims while they still lived.

Believed by the entire world to be hiding somewhere in Europe.

But he was here. *Here*.

He was Radovan Milocek. He was "The Surgeon."

Rob held a hand out to Joseph, who still knelt on the ground, and hauled him to his feet. Then he clapped the shorter man on the shoulder again and smiled down at him. "Good one, man. Thanks." He slung his knapsack onto his back and said, "Give me another second though, will you?" With a wave of his hand, he trotted up the trail and disappeared around the curve of the mountain.

Joseph straightened and turned around. He looked directly into Diana's eyes and saw the horror there. The recognition.

With flat, expressionless eyes, Radovan Milocek smiled at Diana—a baring of short nicotine-stained teeth.

# CHAPTER
# 3

"**W**HAT peckerhead told me three aspirins with orange juice would 'absofuckinglutely' prevent a hangover, so 'have another shot of Cuervo'?"

Gracie lay in the living room, stretched out on the sagging couch wrapped up in her favorite purple fleece blanket. "Had to be Cashman," she mumbled into the cushion pressed beneath her cheek. "Yeah, it was definitely Cashman. Peckerhead."

Outside, a harsh wind blew down the long valley, whistling around the corners of Gracie's one-bedroom cabin and rattling the windows and shutters like an unseen specter trying to gain entrance. Inside, where Gracie lay, only the ticking of her great-grandfather's mariner's clock on the fireplace mantel intruded upon the silence. Gnarled branches of a piñon pine growing outside the front picture window churned a marionette of shadows on the hardwood floor.

The litter carry the evening before had been a muscle-straining danse macabre even with six rescuers sharing the load—an arduous, meandering mile of sliding down into sandy washes, scrambling up rocky embankments, and plowing through dense cholla and yucca lying in wait to stab spines and spears through thick pant legs and into tender skin.

When the recovery team reached the dusty Suburban parked on one of the myriad dirt roads crisscrossing the desert flats, Ralph and Warren stayed behind and waited for the coroner to arrive and pronounce the body. The four remaining team members drove back to town and blew off a little steam with a four-hour marathon of karaoke and tequila at the team's watering hole, the Saddle Tramp—the diviest bar in Timber Creek.

Gracie cringed as she remembered one particularly unfortunate incident that had occurred sometime after midnight. "Oh God!" she groaned into the cushion. "Did I really fall down on the stage with Cashman?"

She wiggled onto her back, trying to find a more comfortable position on the lumpy Salvation Army couch.

"You're too old to be singing karaoke and closing out smoky dive bars, Kinkaid. Have I said that before? Yes. Am I talking out loud to myself? Yes. Do I do that too much? Yes." She covered her eyes with an arm. "But it's the only way I can get intelligent conversation," she added and snorted at her own joke.

The day's activities so far had consisted of shuffling from the sleeping bag on a narrow camp mattress upstairs down to the living room with a detour through the bathroom for a quick shower because the smell of stale cigarette smoke in her hair was tripping her gag reflex. Breakfast was a giant panda mug of double-strength Folgers Instant washing down her morning-after remedy of two Tylenol and two Motrin.

She stretched a hand out from beneath the blanket and picked up the panda mug from the ancient sea chest that served as a coffee table and which, along with the couch, were the only pieces of furniture in the cavernous room.

Gracie took a sip of coffee.

Lukewarm. "Ick."

She slid the mug back across the chest.

For the past two hours she had lain on the couch, unable to move, scabbed-over pinhole reminders of cactus itching on her legs. Even the mood-enhancing Baroque adagios playing softly in the background had hurt her head, so she had turned them off.

It was no use trying to blame the body-numbing malaise solely on too many Saddle Tramp shooters. She had been hung over often enough to know better. It was Joshua Bradford's bright, young face recurring in her mind's eye that made her body feel heavier than an old mattress. And the pervasive marrow-deep exhaustion that comes with three SAR callouts in two days.

The first search for two sisters, ages six and eight, had had a happy ending when the girls walked out of the woods behind their house on their own. Gracie had just pulled into her driveway when her pager beeped again to look for a man who had become separated from his female hiking partner. While Gracie and two other SAR team members searched far into the night scouring a boulder-strewn area north of the valley, the man, who had hiked out on his own and not bothered to call anyone, had spent the afternoon and evening drinking and playing pool at a bar in town.

The third callout less than twelve hours later was the body recovery.

"Maybe it's finally time to admit you can't cut the mustard," she said. "Whatever the hell the mustard is." She burrowed deeper into the couch. "Yeah, right, Kinkaid. Quit the team." She snorted. "And do what else with your scintillating life?"

Sunlight arced a buttery reflection across the glossy wooden floor, steeping the entire room in a warm amber glow. Outside, the wind fussed and moaned. Inside the sanctuary of the cabin, it was still. And church-mouse quiet.

Gracie's eyes closed.

# CHAPTER

# 4

**T**ERROR thrust Diana down the trail, a lion at her back, propelling her blindly forward. Her hands, their multi-colored gloves black and wet with blood, were outstretched in front of her.

Her heart sledgehammered in her chest. The harsh cold air stabbed steel knives into her lungs with each breath. She wasn't going to make it all the way back to the trailhead.

She skidded to her hands and knees on the hard-packed dirt.

*Get up!* her brain screamed. *He's coming for you!*

Diana staggered back to her feet and left the trail, scrambling up the steep incline on all fours. Hands clawed at the dirt and pine needles, grabbed at branches and rocks, anything to pull herself up from the trail, away from the living, breathing demon who pursued her.

Only fifty feet up the slope, the burst of energy faded and Diana was unable to climb any farther.

*Find someplace to hide! Where?*

She swung around in a full circle. Eyes wide with panic

searched the hillside until she spotted a space between two massive boulders. She ran over and wedged herself down in between them. Trembling, silent, wary as a fawn in the brush, she crouched and waited. "Please don't let him find me," she prayed over and over. "Please don't let him find me."

Five minutes passed. Ten. Twenty. An infinity.

Where was he?

Then she heard them—footfalls coming down the trail. Fast.

Diana squeezed her eyes closed, held her breath, listened.

She imagined him stopping, seeing where she had left the trail, climbing up the rocky incline on velvet lion's paws to find her.

But he didn't stop. He passed directly below her on the trail, so close she could hear his hoarse gasps for air.

The footfalls faded away.

Silence.

# CHAPTER

# 5

*B*EEP! *Beep! Beep!*

Shrill tones slapped Gracie awake from a deep, dreamless sleep. Unable to pry her eyes open, she fumbled around on the sea chest. Her hand closed around a warm black banana left over from breakfast four days before and jolted her wide awake. "Dammit!" She wiped yellow mash onto her sweatshirt and scrabbled though the detritus on the table, in the process knocking a teetering stack of last week's newspapers and mail off onto the floor.

Her fingers clutched the cool plastic receiver. She dragged it to her ear. "Grace Kinkaid," she croaked into the mouthpiece. Dial tone.

Pager.

She tossed the receiver in the vicinity of its cradle and unclipped the Search and Rescue pager from the waistband of her sweatpants. She squinted at the postage stamp–sized screen and read the neon green message: LOST HIKERS. ASPEN SPRINGS. ALPINE CERTIFIED ONLY. MANDATORY RESPONSE.

Shit. Another search. The last thing she felt like doing.

Gracie fell back on the couch and considered setting a personal precedent by not responding when she didn't have a good excuse. "Let someone else show up for a change," she complained to the ceiling. "And what does 'mandatory response' mean anyway? We're volunteers. What if we have jobs? What if we have families? Oh, screw it. None of those apply to me, so what the hell? Just do the damn job."

She retrieved the dangling receiver and punched in the phone number for the Sheriff's Office squad room. She hacked like a veteran smoker to boost her voice from bass to tenor and announced, "Grace Kinkaid," to the deputy on the other end of the line. "ETA twenty minutes." She plunked the receiver back down. "Wishful thinking."

She swung her legs over the side of the couch and sat up with a groan. Elbows on knees, she examined the garage-sale rug beneath her feet and noticed for the first time how its nauseating pea green and orange color scheme didn't match anything else in the entire cabin. Not even close.

"Grace Kinkaid to the rescue," she said to the rug. "Now if only I can stand up."

# CHAPTER

# 6

**A**NTICIPATION bubbled up inside Gracie's chest as she kicked the mudroom door closed behind her and dropped an enormous duffel bag onto the kitchen floor.

The adrenaline rush that came with every callout had blasted the lethargy to oblivion.

She knelt on the bare linoleum and unzipped the bag filled with meticulously maintained and packed search clothes and gear. She lifted out a pile of clothes folded neatly at the top of the duffel and stepped onto the tiny braided rug in front of the sink. She mentally assessed the upcoming search while stripping off sweatshirt, pants, and socks and hauling on lightweight fleece long underwear.

The Aspen Springs Trail. Up on Mount San Raphael. Had it snowed up there yet? She didn't remember seeing white on the mountain's barren crown the last time she drove down the hill. But that was the week before last. It had rained in Timber Creek since then. Rain in the valley might mean snow on the mountain four thousand feet higher.

Gracie plowed through the morass that was her memory

of the night before and remembered a buxom weather lady
on one of the Saddle Tramp's televisions predicting a large
front swooping into Southern California from the north.
Heavy rains were expected to reach the coast the middle of
the following day, and the mountains that night with the
possibility of up to a foot of snow. The afternoon's heavy
winds could be heralding a storm. A glance at the mini
weather station on the kitchen counter told her the barom-
eter wasn't dropping . . . yet.

She sat down on one of two mismatched kitchen chairs
and stretched on knee-high polypropylene sock liners followed by heavy wool socks.

There was little chance the search would still be ongoing when the storm hit. Still, prudence dictated she add
winter mountaineering equipment to her Search and Rescue
pack.

She groaned out loud at the thought.

Some searchers, usually enthusiastic rookies, carried
SAR packs as heavy as fire trucks with a junk-drawer full
of accoutrements and high-tech toys swinging from the outside loops. Gracie knew that while her gear was her lifeline,
she didn't need to carry a Hilton on her back, only enough
to survive in the wild for a night, two at the most. Comfort
wasn't the goal. Survival was.

Team members were required to carry a host of items in
their packs, the majority of which Gracie had never used.
Since, much to her disgust, physical strength and stamina
had proven to be an issue, she had refined, whittled down,
packed and repacked her equipment into the lightest, most
compact system of anyone on the team. Even then, her summer pack weighed a hip-bruising thirty-four pounds. Winter
alpine gear of ice axe, crampons, snow shovel, and a
vacuum-packed bag of extra heavyweight clothing, socks,
and gloves would weight the pack even more.

The telephone on the counter rang, jangling Gracie out
of her presearch routine. She pulled on a pair of midweight

fleece pants and counted off the rings until the answering machine picked up.

"Happy Day, Turkey!" The screech of her half sister's voice jarred her like a Black Diamond Jeep trail.

Gracie's eyes whipped to the Sierra Club calendar hanging from a magnet hook on the refrigerator. "Crap. It's Thanksgiving." Her mood ratcheted back down a notch.

She buttoned up a neon orange fleece shirt as she listened to Lenora's voice shrill against the background clamor of a houseful of adults, offspring, her mother's yappy wiener dogs, and Hortense, the canary: "You live only three hours away and haven't been to see us yet," Lenora scolded. The sharp edge to her voice told Gracie the tongue lashing wasn't altogether playful. "You really need to make the effort."

"The highway flows both ways, Lenora." It came as no surprise that her older half sister—with whom she shared her mother, but not her father—expected Gracie to drive a hundred miles to see her. It would simply never occur to Lenora that she should be the one to schlep across all of the Inland Empire and up the mountain to see Gracie.

Her sister signed off and her mother came on the line. "Happy Thanksgiving, Grace dear," Evelyn chirped. "It's your mother."

"As if I didn't know your voice, Mother dear." Gracie stuffed shirttails into black Gore-Tex zip-up-the-side pants and Velcroed the waist tabs closed.

"I really wish you had decided to come," Evelyn continued. "Seven hundred fifty dollars really was a fab price for a last-minute L.A. to Detroit ticket."

Gracie rolled her eyes at her mother's obliviousness to her current state of unemployment. Two weeks before, during one of their monthly telephone conversation, Gracie had divulged that she was, once again, out of work. She had left out the part about how she lost her most recent executive job delivering Domino's Pizza because she told a belligerent tub-o'-lard to stick his penny tip up his fat, hairy ass.

That was last month and Gracie hadn't gotten around to looking for another quality job.

"You haven't seen these darling babies in so long," Evelyn cooed.

Gracie sighed and stood to stomp her heels down into heavy mountaineering boots. "Lenora's spoiled rotten kids can hardly be considered babies. And they're most assuredly not darlings."

"Or Harold either," her mother continued. "And . . . and . . . Oh, here he is—"

There were several seconds of muffled argument and next on the line came her half brother toward whom Gracie felt not one ounce of sisterly affection. Hard to cuddle up cozy to an iceberg.

Harold's voice, normally oozing with lawyerly pomposity, sounded forced with good cheer as he wished his little sister a Happy Thanksgiving.

Hmm, Gracie mused as she sat back down again to cinch tight the boot lacings. Perhaps Wife Number 3—what's-her-name—was about to become Ex-wife Number 3. Her brother had a nasty habit of sleeping with his future wives while he was still married to the previous ones.

Gracie listened to several seconds of silence until Evelyn came back on the line and warbled, "We miss you. We love you," followed by a loud kiss into the phone.

A chorus of voices yelled, "Happy Thanksgiving!" and "Wish you were here!" followed by a cacophony of "Bye!"

The call ended abruptly, plunging the room back into silence and leaving Gracie feeling even more hollow than before.

That Morris, Evelyn's third husband and Gracie's stepfather, had been present for the holiday feast in his own palatial home in Grosse Pointe Farms was a given. That, once again, he had refused to wish his stepdaughter "Happy Thanksgiving" should have been expected. Somehow it always managed to catch her off guard.

Gracie leaned forward, elbows on knees, staring at the yellowed linoleum beneath her feet. She could envision the entire scene in excruciating detail. Her mother—crisp lace apron over smart Pendleton sweater and slacks—gently prodding her husband. "Mo Mo, can't you at least say, 'Hello?'" Morris's refusal to budge from his La-Z-Boy in the den—one hand clenching the chair arm, the other moving only at the elbow to bring his ever-present Johnnie Walker Blue to his lips, granite eyes never leaving his beloved Detroit Lions on the flat screen.

"Can't really blame him." Gracie sighed. A smiled tugged at the corners of her mouth. "I wouldn't want to talk to me either."

She leaned back and frowned down at the shapeless blob that was her body. As always, when she finished dressing for a winter search, especially after adding her radio chest pack, Day-Glo orange helmet and Gore-Tex parka and gloves, she looked like some goofy hybrid of something-or-other and something-else. "Hieronymous the Hippopotamus meet . . . Michelin Woman," she grumbled and pushed herself to her feet.

# CHAPTER
# 7

**R**ADOVAN Milocek crouched behind the giant trunk of a ponderosa pine and surveyed the parking lot below him with a hawk's eyes. Sweat dried on his temples, and his chest heaved with the exertion of jogging all the way down to the trailhead from the rock outcropping.

The scene before him was unremarkable, tranquil. The parking lot contained only Rob Christian's motor home and several cars—one of them his own. Not a single person was visible.

Milocek sucked the cold mountain air in through his nose and blew it out through his mouth to slow his breathing.

He had anticipated overtaking Diana quickly. But the more distance he covered with no sign of her, the more certain he was that she had hidden somewhere along the trail and he had passed her by.

Milocek ground his back teeth. He had taken too long finishing the business at the outcropping before following Diana down the trail.

He would have to go back.

But he was confident he would find her.

He remembered that farther up, past the outcropping, the trail split with one leg leading up to the top of the mountain and the other winding for miles through the wilderness area. There was only one way out and that was the trail down to the parking lot.

He stood between Diana and escape.

He eyed his own little car parked next to the motor home and calculated how long it would take him to run across the parking lot and climb inside.

Why not simply drive away, south, to Mexico, then Central, even South America?

He shook his head. Never again would he run. He would die first.

The thought of death brought with it a curious sense of release, of calm.

He physically shook the thought away like a dog shaking water from its fur.

Milocek backed away from the tree on hands and knees. He pushed himself to his feet, jumped silently down onto the trail, and trotted up the way he had come.

## CHAPTER

# 8

"**C**OME on! Let me in! I need to go!"

Gracie kneaded the steering wheel of her rust-pocked Ranger pickup. As far as she could see in both directions, a train of cars, minivans, and sport utes snaked bumper to bumper along the Boulevard, the main thoroughfare running the length of the valley.

Thirty million people within a three-hour drive of Timber Creek. And this weekend it seemed that every single one of those thirty million had negotiated the mountain roads up to the little resort town with the sole purpose of hindering Gracie's progress to the Sheriff's Office.

She sagged down in the seat, chewed a piece of grape bubble gum, and waited.

The town's normal population of twenty thousand often ballooned to more than one hundred thousand for long holiday weekends. Which was precisely why Gracie normally hid out in her cabin the entire time, a reluctant box turtle emerging only in emergencies like a search or a craving for a venti Double Chocolaty Chip Frappuccino from the Safeway Starbucks.

Gracie popped a purple bubble and leaned over to crank up the London Symphony on the radio. She sank back in the seat and watched the traffic through half-closed eyes.

Sixty teeth-clenching seconds went by until finally a miniscule space opened up between a Ford Expedition and a white minivan that had slowed to a stop.

Gracie stomped on the gas. The pickup rocketed onto the Boulevard, then screeched to a standstill an inch from the Expedition's bumper.

"Thank God for six cylinders."

She laid her head back on the headrest and blew another bubble.

The Bavarian-style village of Timber Creek lay as a jewel in the mountains one hundred miles east of Los Angeles, six thousand feet higher and a world apart. In a single hour, one could drive the curving, precipitous highway up the mountain, leaving behind housing tracts, office buildings and strip malls, palm trees and labyrinthine freeways, breaking out of yellow air into azure skies and evergreens.

Gracie eased her foot off the brake and the Ranger inched forward.

Willow thickets hugged both sides of the road in a rich blend of yellows from brilliant cadmium to dull ocher. Christmas lights draped along fence posts and railings added glowing polka dots of red, blue, and green to the lengthening blue shadows. Gracie craned her neck and just caught a glimpse of the sparkling silver bracelet that was the lake itself. Beyond, the sun hovered, a golden glowing eye in the west.

Up ahead, a station wagon dragging a muffler turned left, suddenly clearing Gracie's lane for the final quarter mile to the Sheriff's Office.

She mashed the accelerator to the floor. The speedom-

eter lunged to the right. Fifty. Fifty-five. She slammed on
the brakes, turned into the Sheriff's Office parking lot, and
screeched to a stop. "What the—?"

The parking lot overflowed with reporters, cameras,
lights, and television vans. Channel Four. Channel Seven.
Channel Nine. KTLA. They were all there.

Gracie gaped at the spectacle until a car turned into the
driveway behind her, nudging her out of her stupor.

Duly appreciative that someone had the foresight to cor-
don off a parking area for incoming search personnel, Gracie stepped on the gas and roared into an open space.

# CHAPTER
# 9

TIMBER Creek Search and Rescue operated under the auspices of the County Sheriff's Department and functioned out of the Sheriff's Office—a long, two-story building painted bone white and trimmed in dark brown paint and pink stone.

Gracie shoved open the heavy reinforced-steel Employees Only door and clumped in, her heavy boots echoing down the narrow hallway leading into the bowels of the building. She pushed in through the door of the multipurpose squad room that served as the Search and Rescue briefing room.

Walls the color of vanilla pudding were crammed full of maps, bulletin boards, deputy cubbyhole in-boxes, and multiple doors leading to hallways, supply closets, and evidence storage. A chalkboard covered one entire wall and a waist-high shelf serving as a desk ran along three walls. In the center of the room was a twenty-foot-long conference table surrounded by a dozen butt-flattening wooden chairs.

The squad room's only occupant was Ralph Hunter, who

sat at the conference table reading a days-old L.A. *Times*. Behind half-moon glasses, the blue-gray eyes slid in her direction. "Hey, Gracie girl," he said and winked at her.

Gracie beamed back at him. "Hi, Ralphie." She leaned across the table to scribble her name on the callout roster, "Long time, no see."

Ralph's hair was silver, worn bristle-brush short, yet his heavy eyebrows were black. He was lean and fit, a good six inches taller than Gracie's five foot eight, and, at forty-eight, twelve years older. His skin was the color and texture of well-worn saddle leather from too many days without sunscreen in the California sun. Gracie found him undeniably sexy.

As ever, Ralph looked immaculate—clean-shaven, uniform shirt Martha Stewart perfect, with every crease ironed to a razor's edge. His bearing—chin and shoulders back, spine ramrod straight—hinted of a past military stint longer than a single tour of duty. The one time Gracie had seen him without a shirt, she had noticed several oddly shaped scars on his neck and shoulder, and one, about six inches long, running down one side of his abdomen. She had never dared ask him where he had gotten them and he had never volunteered the information.

After the death of his wife, it had taken two years for Ralph's eyes to crinkle with humor if something amused him, five for him to actually chuckle at one of Gracie's lame jokes. But even before Eleanor's death, Gracie had never heard him laugh outright. It hurt her with a physical pain to see such indelible sadness in his blue-gray eyes.

Gracie tossed her gum into the nearest wastebasket and dropped into the chair at the end of the conference table closest to Ralph. As the only woman on an eleven-member team, she grabbed the psychological advantage whenever she could.

Ordinarily ten men to one woman might be a to-die-for

ratio. But more often than not, Gracie found working in close proximity with so many Manly Men for so many hours, often days at a time, took its toll on her. She could take only so much crotch arranging, and fart and blond jokes before she began to crave a bubble bath or painting her toenails petunia pink.

"Missed you for turkey and dressing," Ralph said, folding the pages of the newspaper back. "Eleanor's sister outdid herself this year."

Gracie sucked in a breath between her teeth. "Sorry. I really meant to come."

Ralph looked at her over his glasses.

"I did! It's just . . ." She stopped. "Okay, I should have called. Will you tell Eleanor—shit—Eleanor's sister I'm really sorry I didn't call?"

"Gracie, it's not a problem. We just didn't want you to be alone today."

"I . . ." *Wanted to be alone* is what she almost said. She stopped because she wasn't in the mood for another lecture. She eased the subject toward more comfortable territory. "So what's all the hoopla outside?"

"Rob Christian got himself lost on San Raphael."

"Who?"

"Rob Christian."

Gracie made a face and shook her head.

"Rob Christian. Actor. Movie star."

"Rob . . ." Gracie said. "Vaguely familiar." Comprehension dawned. "Ohhhh, yeah. A Brit, right? Way too cute for anybody's good?" She grimaced as the information sank in. "That's who we're looking for? Hell's bells." Gracie slumped down in her chair. So. They were searching for one of the biggest movie stars in the country, maybe the world, and the sum total of her presearch grooming had been waving a dry toothbrush in the general direction of her teeth and smoothing her hair back into an elastic. Period.

She leaned forward again. "Who else called in?"

"Cashman."

"That's it?"

"That's it."

"Everyone else who stayed up the hill either called in or was called?"

"Everyone."

Before Gracie had time to groan, Steve Cashman burst into the room.

At thirty-one years old, the man's personal hygiene ran neck and neck with a five-year-old's, with the five-year-old pulling ahead. As usual he appeared as if he had stepped out of bed and right into the squad room. His blaze-orange uniform shirt was as wrinkled as aluminum foil that has been wadded up and reflattened. Greasy blond hair stood out in porcupine-quill spikes. Darker beard looked as if it hadn't been trimmed since *last* Thanksgiving. And Gracie never got used to the sight of his fingernails—permanently oil-stained and longer than hers.

But hygiene wasn't really the issue. Five years on the team with Steve Cashman had proven to Gracie that, if left to his own devices, the man could single-handedly screw up a perfectly good search.

Cashman slid into the chair on Gracie's left and leaned in toward her. "Hey, beautiful."

Gracie leaned way right, resting her cheek on her open palm. "Hey, Steve."

"Guess who the MisPer is."

"Rob Christian."

"Not just Rob Christian. *The* Rob Christian! I can't believe it!" He pounded his fists on the table, making Gracie jump and almost forcing her to strangle him.

"Cashman, get me a refill, will you?" Without looking up, Ralph slid his coffee mug across the table. "Four creams. Two sugars."

"Sure!" Steve leapt to his feet, sending his chair skidding back to crash against the wall. Snatching up the mug, he bounded out of the room. The door slammed, fluttering memos pushpinned to a nearby bulletin board.

Gracie laid her cheek down on the table's smooth cool surface. "Thanks."

"Anytime."

"Three out of eleven," she said. "Pretty pathetic turnout even for a holiday. Most people will have finished eating by now. Maybe they're too stuffed to show up. Or maybe they've had too much to drink. Or maybe I'm just jealous that they have lives."

Ralph's response was another look over the top of the glasses.

"Don't say it." Gracie grabbed the Sports section of the *Times* and glanced down at the page. Instantly bored, she flipped it back onto the table. "Rush, rush, rush to get here. Then sit on your hands and wait." She picked a piece of gum from her shirt pocket, unwrapped it, and tossed it into her mouth. She flicked the wrapper into the wastebasket. "Two points."

The room felt close and warm. Gracie was dressed for a nighttime expedition at altitude in late autumn, not for sitting in a stuffy room in an overheated building. She unbuttoned her shirt cuffs and shoved the sleeve layers up her arms. "Hot in here."

She drummed her fingertips on the tabletop and blew a giant bubble, popping it loudly and drawing yet another look from Ralph. "Sorry," she whispered and tapped her toes inside her boots instead.

Normally before a search the squad room was an ant farm of activity—team members copying maps, strategizing, assigning teams and radios, readying vehicles and equipment. "What's going on?" Gracie asked unable to sit still and be quiet any longer. "What are we waiting for?"

"Briefing," Ralph said.

"Really. It must be downright nippy in hell," she said and was pleased to receive a crinkling of the blue-gray eyes.

The squad room door bumped open and Cashman crept in, balancing a coffee mug filled to the brim with what looked like beige mud. He eased it onto the table in front of Ralph.

"Thanks, Cashman."

"Sure thing, Hunter." Cashman skipped around behind Gracie to drag his chair back up to the table and drop into it. "Hey, Gracie—"

The squad room door banged open again and Gracie swallowed her gum.

Three backs straightened, three pairs of eyes tracked Sergeant Ron Gardner as he strode around the table to the opposite end from where the team sat.

Gracie's toes curled at the sight of the man. Six-foot-two. Porcine facial features. Buzzed red hair. Beefy, hairless arms. Putty gray uniform shirt filled to overflowing by a barrel chest. If she had tried, Gracie couldn't have invented a better caricature of a grade-school bully all grown up. There wasn't a doubt in her mind that, as a kid, Ron Gardner had shoved the littler kids into rain puddles and picked the wings off butterflies. As an adult, he was belligerent and condescending. From the first instant she had laid eyes on him, Gracie hadn't liked him. And she had more than a sneaking suspicion that the feeling was mutual.

"Captain Harter would like to acknowledge the sacrifice you all are making by being here today," Gardner announced too loudly for the enclosed room.

*All three of us*, Gracie thought and resisted the temptation to plug her ears.

"As you may know, a film is being shot in the valley," Gardner boomed. "A lot of the cast and crew stayed up here over the holiday weekend. Apparently a lot of them are English or some other kind of foreigner and don't celebrate Thanksgiving."

*Neither do some Americans.* Gracie drew a pencil and little spiral notebook from the breast pocket of her shirt.

Out of the corner of her eye, she saw Cashman glance over at her, then pull out his own little notebook.

"From what we can tell, Mr. Rob Christian—with whom no doubt you are very familiar . . ."

Gracie stared straight ahead.

". . . and an undetermined number of others of the cast and crew went hiking this morning from the Aspen Springs trailhead. San Raphael Wilderness Area. At some point, the group had lunch, then separated. Most of the group returned to the trailhead while others, Mr. Christian included, elected to continue up the trail. It should be noted that during this time an unknown quantity of alcohol was consumed. Only physical description we have so far is of Mr. Christian. Age thirty-three. Six-three. One ninety. Blond over brown."

Three pencils scribbled down the information.

"When the smaller hiking party failed to return by the original rendezvous time, the group at the trailhead waited another hour or so, then drove down to where they had cell phone reception, at which time they called their producer, who then called us. That's it."

"Number of MisPers?" Gracie asked.

"Undetermined."

"Aviation up?" Ralph asked.

"Too windy. The responding deputy is interviewing the RPs." Reporting Parties. "I want trackers up there yesterday."

"Oh, goody," Gracie whispered.

"Hunter. Ops. Set up a command post at the trailhead."

"Roger, Roger," Ralph said.

Gracie's eyes slid over to meet Ralph's. He knew she found it amusing that higher-ups found it necessary to order the team to do things they did countless times when those same higher-ups weren't around.

Ralph kept his eyes front and center.

"Cashman, Kinkaid, Tracking Team One," Gardner said.

Gracie sagged back in her chair. Even though she should have anticipated being paired up with Cashman, whatever enthusiasm she had for the search crashed and burned at the prospect of working with the man for the entire evening. Searches could be exhausting in themselves. But the yank and pull of preventing Steve from bungling an entire operation could just plain wear her out.

"Cashman, Team Leader," the sergeant announced.

Gracie's cheeks flamed. Ralph's exaggerated clearing of his throat was the only thing that stopped her from snapping her pencil in two and hurling the jagged pieces at Gardner's head. By all rights she should be the team's leader. She had more seniority and more experience than Steve, and she possessed a State of California certification in tracking, which Cashman did not. But there was one thing Cashman had that Gracie didn't: testicles. To Ron Gardner, that made all the difference.

One time in her Search and Rescue career, Gracie had gotten sick and hadn't been able to complete a mission. No matter that it was a recovery from the charred remains of a plane crash where the only recognizable portion of the pilot's body was a pristine pair of hands. No matter that she had proven herself on every other mission before and after. She was a woman and she hadn't carried her weight. In Gardner's eyes, nothing Gracie could do would ever make up for it.

"Shit pot of reporters out there," Gardner continued as he walked back around the table. "No one talks to the media. We have a PIO for that." He grabbed the door handle.

Three chairs scraped back.

Gardner turned around. "Hear me, people," he said.

Three searchers froze.

"Get in. Find the MisPers. Get out. I want it fast. I want it clean. Anything else and this will turn into a goddam media circus. Sew it up by midnight. *Comprende?*" His eyes bore down on Ralph.

"Copy that," Ralph said in the calm, steady voice to which Gracie aspired.

"Get out there," Gardner said. He pulled the door open and strode out of the room.

With cheeks still burning, Gracie hauled a heavy HT—handheld transceiver—from a Pelican case lying open on the conference table. "Ready for the HT ID?

"Stand by one," Ralph said, grabbing up the sign-in sheet. "Ready."

Gracie read the numbers from a label on the side of the radio. "One zero four two nine one."

Ralph scrawled the ID next to Gracie's name on the form. "I'll bring up the CP," he said. "Take the Suburban and get up there."

Gracie turned to leave.

"Gracie," Ralph said.

She turned back. "Yah."

Ralph winked at her. "Go get 'em."

Gracie's anger melted away, no doubt the intended effect.

"I'll drive," Cashman announced, grabbing a set of keys from a pegboard near the door and preceding Gracie out of the room.

"Fine by me," Gracie answered as the pair double-timed it up the long, empty corridor. The novelty of commanding a Sheriff's Department unit fully equipped with lights and sirens had worn off years before.

But when Cashman also offered to take the radio, Gracie balked, stopping in the middle of the hallway. One relinquished a certain amount of status and control when not carrying the HT. She could care less about status, but on a search the radio was her only link to the Command Post and the outside world. Without a radio in the field, she felt as vulnerable as if she were dangling over a hundred-foot cliff without a belay line.

Cashman stood in front of her with his hand outstretched. Gracie almost told him to go get another radio. They would each carry one. But the heavy HT could literally be a pain in the neck and she was already carrying a heavier than normal pack. She unsnapped the elastic band that held the HT in place on her chest pack, lifted out the radio, and handed it to Cashman.

"I'll grab maps and be right out," she said and turned down another hallway. Behind her she heard Cashman say, "I'll get the Suburban."

Gracie grabbed a rolled-up set of laminated maps from a back office and walked out the back door of the station.

Blinding studio lights lit up the parking lot like a movie set. News cameras homed in on Cashman already loading gear into the Suburban that sat parked and running in front of the Sheriff's Office. As soon as Gracie emerged from the building, the invasive lenses turned in her direction. Pulling her hood up over her head, she tossed the maps into the front seat of the Suburban, stalked across the pavement to the Ranger, and hauled her heavy pack from the truck bed.

Every search was different. The required equipment and vehicles varied according to victims, circumstances, weather, and location. Expertise, experience, and personalities changed with personnel—civilian and sworn. As a result, some searches were run with precision and executed without a hitch. Others were bumpy, fraught with fly-by-the-seat-of-your-pants moves that left Gracie feeling frayed and wrung out.

Gracie knew—*knew*—that the search ahead of them was going to fall into the latter category.

She hefted her pack onto one shoulder. "Here I am," she crabbed aloud, "in the biggest media event of my SAR career"—she slammed the tailgate shut and plunked the back window down—"and I'm saddled with the world's biggest weenie."

# CHAPTER

# 10

"**C**ONTROL. Ten Rescue Twenty-two," Gracie said into the radio microphone.

With Cashman behind the wheel, the Suburban lumbered out of the Sheriff's Office parking lot and onto the main boulevard.

"Go ahead, Twenty-two," a female dispatcher answered.

"Departing Timber Creek SO with two SAR members. Heading for two Nora zero five on San Raphael."

"At fifteen forty-three."

Gracie rested the radio microphone on her knee and shrugged out of her parka. She tossed it into the backseat, then settled in for the hour-long ride up to the trailhead.

As the Suburban wove its way through the stop-and-go Boulevard traffic, wonking its siren to move slow-moving drivers out of the way, Gracie fine-tuned her equipment and rearranged the gorp, candy bars, and slap-dash peanut butter sandwich into various pockets for easier access on the trail.

"Damn, I hope we find him." Cashman's voice barged in on Gracie's contented fiddling. "I could get Wanda an autograph. She fuckin' loves Rob Christian." A few seconds of silence, then, "Yeah. I need to get his autograph."

Gracie re-Velcroed her knee-high gaiters and retied them at the top with double bows. "Who is this guy anyway?" she asked. "What movies has he been in?"

Steve rattled off half a dozen film titles only one of which—*Far Horizons*—sounded remotely familiar to Gracie.

"Didn't he punch a reporter or something like that?" she asked, pulling the elastic from her hair and combing through the tangles with her fingers.

"Yeah. Nailed the sucker. Broke his nose. Fuckin' awesome!"

The Suburban turned a sharp corner at the far eastern end of the valley. Incredibly for a holiday weekend, the highway leading up to the summit then down the back side of the mountain was free of traffic. Cashman floored the accelerator and the Suburban crawled forward at the speed of a full-bellied mastodon running uphill.

Gracie French-braided her hair in the back, refastened it, and pulled on her fleece beanie, tucking the braid up underneath. She leaned back in the cushy leather seat. "What's all the hoopla about movie stars anyway?" she asked. "Aren't they all just a bunch of self-important, pampered . . . ?" What was a good alliterative noun? Poodles? "This guy is probably as bad as all the others. Maybe even worse." She sighed. "God, I'm tired. Joshua Bradford really got to me."

Gracie watched the scenery flow past as Cashman launched into a lengthy diatribe of the previous night's recovery, railing about the mistakes everyone else made and why they should have done an infinitely riskier technical ropes litter raise instead of unglamorously hoofing the body out, and why maybe it was time Hunter retired and someone else (namely Cashman) was elected the team's Commander.

A dense forest of yellow pines scrolled by on their right. On their left, rounded hills dotted with piñon pines and manzanita with Joshua trees behind fell away to the desert beyond. In the distance, milk chocolate–colored mountains glowed pink as the sun sank lower in the west.

The Suburban tires squealed as they rounded a tight curve and drifted over the double yellow highway line into the oncoming lane which, thankfully, was unoccupied. Gracie clutched at the armrest with both hands.

Cashman swerved the Suburban back into its own lane and shifted his monologue to the present search. "Maybe we'll make the news," he said with a grin. "That would be fuckin' awesome."

Gracie rolled her eyes at the pines.

The Suburban crested the summit. Across a wide valley on the right loomed the monolith that was Mount San Raphael.

Imposing, forbidding, the mountain's austere beauty beckoned unsuspecting hikers and mountaineers into its ice chutes and rocky canyons, every year claiming lives of men and women alike for its own. An early-season snow had draped a white shroud atop the mountain's barren dome. Behind it, delicately fringed mare's tail cirrus caught the late-afternoon sun to blaze tangerine fire against the turquoise sky.

The Suburban picked up speed on the downhill and sailed around a curve. San Raphael was swept from view.

# CHAPTER

## 11

**D**IANA grabbed the toes of her tennis shoes with both hands and flexed them up and down to get the blood flowing again. The lower half of her body felt like a block of ice from sitting in the same position without moving for so long.

How long had she been there crouching between the two rocks? How long had it been since the devil had passed her by and continued down the trail? She had no concept of the passage of time, only of the paralyzing terror and the violent images that played and replayed in her mind's eye.

She took several long swallows of water, emptying her water bottle.

Tristan's bright blue eyes and his smile with its crooked lower tooth filled her vision. A single sob forced its way past her lips and tears stung her eyes. She rubbed them with her fists and steered her thoughts back to the others at the trail-head. What were they doing now? Had they called the police? Was someone out there looking for her?

"Please God," she whispered. "Please let someone be looking for me. Please let someone come and help me."

She lay back, stretching out full-length on the thick, soft cushion of pine needles, and stared up at the sky. The sun had dropped behind the western peaks, drawing shadow—blue and cold—across the valley. Pink and orange clouds swirled directly overhead. As Diana watched, the last blush of color faded to rust, then charcoal as swiftly and silently as death.

The feeling in her body crept back, a thousand tiny ice needles pricking her feet and moving up her legs.

The chill of early evening deepened. In spite of her heavy coat and hat, she shivered. She needed to move. She needed to try to get back to the trailhead, to the others, to safety.

She gathered up the knit gloves she had torn off earlier and pulled them, dirt-covered and stiff with dried blood, onto her hands.

Then, willing her stiff body to move, she pushed herself to her feet.

# CHAPTER

## 12

"**CONTROL**. Ten Rescue Twenty-two."

"Twenty-two."

"We're turning off Highway 26 onto two Nora zero five."

"At sixteen fifty-two."

The Suburban turned left off the highway and onto the unpaved Forest Service road. For thirty minutes, it climbed up through the San Raphael Wilderness Area toward the Aspen Springs Trailhead, gaining more than three thousand feet in elevation. The SAR vehicle crawled up through steep-walled canyons swathed in darkness, across riffling late-season creeks, slowing almost to a standstill at the hairpin turns, and rounding curves where, inches from the front tire, the mountain dropped precipitously away for a thousand feet.

By the time the Suburban rolled into the trailhead parking lot, the sunset was a memory in swirling pewter clouds against the fading blue sky.

Parked across the entrance of the wide gravel lot was a Sheriff's Department Chevy Tahoe with a deputy sitting inside. Bright yellow Sheriff's Department tape cordoned off the entrance to the trail itself. At the far end of the lot sat a giant black motor home and three cars.

The Tahoe rolled ahead to let the Suburban past, then backed into place. Cashman swung the vehicle wide to park in a space opposite the other vehicles.

As Gracie stepped out onto the gravel, a blast of icy wind almost lifted her off her feet. "Windy," she yelled. She grabbed her parka from the backseat of the Suburban and threw it on. "And cold. Not a good thing for those city people." She flipped up the hood of her parka. "Unless we find 'em tonight," she added to herself, "or they have halfway decent karma, this could turn into another body recovery. Or two. Or three."

In a churning of dust, Ralph circled behind the Suburban in the team's Ford utility truck, pulling a refurbished travel trailer serving as the team's mobile Command Post. With maps, whiteboards, radios, batteries, office supplies, dishes, food, water, blankets, and a combination shower/toilet, it held everything anyone could possibly need to run a search.

Cashman swung open the back door of the Suburban and lifted out his pack. "He hauled ass up here."

"You made great time, Hunter," Gracie called over to where her teammate was already out of the truck and chocking the trailer tires.

"I gotta piss so bad my eyes are yellow," Cashman said and trotted off in the direction of a boulder the size of an elephant sitting at the edge of the parking lot.

"I'm going to talk to the deputy," Gracie yelled to Cashman's back. She yelled the same information to Ralph, who gave her a thumbs-up in acknowledgment.

Leaning into the wind, Gracie fast-walked across to the Tahoe and tapped a finger on the driver's-side glass. The window slid open.

The Deputy inside sure was cute. Gracie wished she could remember his name. "Hey," she said.

"Hey," the cute deputy returned.

"You interview the RP?"

"RPs. As in plural. They're in the motor home," he said indicating the RV with a nod of his head. He handed her a copy of the team's own LPQ—Lost Person Questionnaire. An accurate, complete LPQ provided a Fort Knox of invaluable information: clothing, equipment, experience, mental state, medications. An already completed questionnaire would save them half an hour, maybe an hour, and could literally mean the difference between a successful mission and not, between life and death, between rescue and recovery.

Gracie glanced down at the form. Half the questions remained blank. Only the most basic—contact information and physical descriptions of the multiple missing persons— had been completed in the deputy's neat cursive.

"Sorry," the cute deputy said. "It's all I could get out of them." He followed up with a brief overview of what had happened, which essentially was that fewer people came back than had started out.

"Okay, thanks," Gracie said. "Guess I'll go over and give it a try."

"Good luck," the cute deputy said in a tone that implied Gracie was really going to need it.

The Tahoe window whispered closed.

# CHAPTER

## 13

**T**HE wraith that was Diana crept down the trail.

Overhead the last of daylight's glow outlined the ragged mountain peaks. But the black velvet curtain the approaching night had already laid across the canyon was so opaque, so complete, that Diana could see nothing of her hands stretched out in front of her. The harsh wind moaned up the canyon, rocking and creaking the unseen trees on all sides.

Diana slid her feet along the ground, feeling for the smooth dirt of the trail. She squinted ahead, but saw no sign of anyone, no movement ahead on the trail. She listened, but could hear nothing above the wind.

She froze.

She had caught a hint of something in the air.

What was it?

She closed her eyes and breathed in the frigid night air.

Cigarette smoke.

Her eyes flew open. She half turned, muscles tensed to run. Her breath came in quick shallow puffs through her nose.

She peered down the trail over her shoulder.

Then she saw it—a black shape moving slowly, methodically up the trail. The burning end of a cigarette flared—a red eye winking in the darkness.

Milocek.

Searching for her, for where she had left the trail.

Panic rose as sour vomit in Diana's throat. She took a step backward. Then another. And another. Until she rounded a curve in the mountain.

Then she turned and sprinted on silent feet back up the trail.

GRACIE slammed the door of the Command Post trailer so hard the windows rattled. The clock on the wall shook loose from its nail, zipped past Ralph's right ear, and smashed onto the metal desk an inch from his arm. The single battery flew out of its casing and landed in the wastebasket next to the door.

Without so much as a flinch, Ralph swiveled around in his chair sat and glowered at Gracie.

"Sorry," she said, pulling off her gloves. She flopped into another chair, forgetting about its broken back, and almost tipped over backward. "Dammit!" She flailed with her legs to regain her balance and plant her boots back on the linoleum.

"All right, Kinkaid," Ralph growled. "Spill it."

The use of her last name told Gracie that the reason for her behavior and the near-miss with the clock had better be a good one.

*  *  *

**PAVEMENT QUEEN, GRACIE** thought as she crossed the
parking lot to the sleek black motor home. How did they get
this behemoth all the way here?

She stopped in front of the door at the side of the RV, the
butterflies that always made a cameo appearance whenever
she had to actually socialize with strangers pirouetting in
her stomach.

This was one part of the job she dreaded—talking with
people she didn't know. But who the hell else was going to
interview the RPs? Cashman?

Inside her fleece gloves, her palms were as sweaty as if
she had been clutching a handful of pennies. She pulled the
gloves off, tucked them into a pocket, then wiped her hands
dry on her parka.

Her legs were trembling.

*Dammit, Kinkaid! Get a grip.*

She sucked in a long, heavy breath through her nose, blew
it out through her mouth, and rapped on the door.

Her knuckles had barely left the metal before the door
swung open revealing a woman with shoulder-length blond
hair and water-balloon breasts so enormous they threatened
to burst out of her fuchsia cashmere sweater.

Gracie actually took a step backward. Self-consciousness
flared up and she threw off her hood in an attempt to look
slightly less dorky. "Sheriff's Department. Search and Rescue," she announced, employing her official voice. "I'd like
to ask you some more questions— Crap!" She slammed
her hand on her head to anchor her beanie as a gust of wind
almost lifted it right off.

Gracie was expecting anything from Lauren Bacall to
Betty Boop, but the voice that said, "Come on back," definitely sounded Midwestern.

Without waiting for an answer, the woman climbed up
the stairs, leaving the door open behind her.

Gracie clumped behind her, feeling even more acutely like the Michelin Hippopotamus. She pulled off her beanie and tried in vain to smooth down the wisps of static-cling hair floating around her face.

Polished wood, black leather, and mirrors were all Gracie noticed about the interior of the motor home. The blond woman slid behind a table in the kitchen, which, Gracie noted with dismay, was bigger than her own.

Sitting around the table were another woman and three men, all as physically flawless as air-brushed fashion models, all looking some combination of unhappy, unfriendly, and bored.

The detritus of a high-rent brunch littered the table: half-empty bottles of champagne and vodka along with several containers of what Gracie guessed were various juices, a giant platter holding the remnants of Brie, prosciutto, melon slices and kiwi, and other Epicurean delights that Gracie couldn't identify.

She slid into the only empty seat, trying not to think about her own pathetic dinner of a peanut butter sandwich and a PayDay candy bar. She cleared her throat, introduced herself, and explained that she needed to go over some of the information the deputy had already covered.

"My name's Michael," said an angelic-faced man who looked young enough to be taking Beginning Composition at Hollywood High. "What's your pleasure? Mimosa? Bloody Mary? Something stronger?"

*Love to*, Gracie thought. She declined with a smile and a shake of her head and cleared her throat again. "First off, the faster I can compile this information, the more quickly we can get into the field and begin looking for your friends."

"They're not my friends," said an Asian woman, wearing a mink fur vest that left Gracie feeling slightly nauseated, whose stunning beauty was marred by a perpetual pout.

"Shut up, Monica," grumbled one of the men who Gracie

identified from the LPQ as Jeremy and who she would swear was wearing clear fingernail polish.

"To confirm, there are three people we know to be missing." She glanced down at the LPQ. "Rob Christian, Joseph Van Dijk, and Tristan Chambers."

"That woman is with them, too," said the blond woman whom Gracie identified as Brittany.

"She would be," Monica sneered.

"No, she's not," Michael said, taking a lazy sip of mimosa.

"Who cares if she is?" Jeremy asked.

A man with sculpted muscles and skin the exquisite color of rubbed mahogany introduced himself in a deep voice as Erik. "The woman's name is Diana," he said, sounding utterly embarrassed by the rest of the group. "I don't remember her last name. It's unusual. Eastern European maybe. Anyway, she's an actor."

"Wannabe," Monica added.

"She went back down to the hotel with Cristina and Carlos," Michael said.

Gracie scribbled furiously.

"She hiked on with the others," Erik said. "But Cristina and Carlos drove back down to the hotel."

"No, they didn't."

Erik ignored the interruption. "They were heading back to L.A. for the weekend."

Gracie fastidiously filled in the gaps about the physical descriptions of all six possible MisPers about which there miraculously was some consensus. Everyone agreed that Rob and Joseph wore black North Face down jackets. Tristan wore a bright red down jacket over a neon yellow shirt. That tidbit everyone agreed upon since apparently the colors had been the subject of a lengthy discussion about the current trends in men's fashion. Diana wore a full-length maroon coat, almost to her ankles, and multicolored knit gloves and hat, which Monica described: "It had a pom-pom, for God's sake!" Cristina and Carlos wore matching black leather biker jackets with silver studs and blue jeans.

Brittany raised her hand and ventured, "Tristan's wearing tennis shoes." She dropped her hand. "If that helps any."

"It helps a lot," Gracie said and smiled at her.

"Nikes," Jeremy said.

"They're Reeboks," Monica said, her mouth looking as if she had just sucked on a lemon.

Gracie's attention sharpened. Nikes or Reeboks? She had tracked people wearing both brands in the past. The Nike swoosh or the entire word *Reebok* could often be seen in the dirt as clearly as if it had been made with a rubber stamp. She scribbled both brands with question marks next to where the cute deputy had written "white sneakers." Maybe she would get to do some tracking after all. Tracking was time-consuming, fatiguing, back-breaking, but, in Gracie's opinion, one of the surest, most reliable ways to locate a missing person.

"Rob's are some kind of regular shoes," Erik said. "Or boots."

"Black," Brittany offered, more boldly this time.

A long way to hike in city shoes, Gracie thought.

Nothing about the footwear of the other four was known except that Cristina and Carlos were wearing black boots of some kind.

Gracie felt sweat forming at her temples and unzipped her parka. "Are any of them familiar with the area?"

Erik said, "No," while several heads nodded.

"Any have experience in the outdoors?"

Erik said, "Joseph, I think," while others shrugged their shoulders.

Her question of "Did anyone have a map of the area?" was met with a deafening silence that Gracie translated as "What the hell is a map?"

Fielding bits and pieces of the story thrown at her from

all sides, Gracie was able to fill in some of the gaps of information gained during the briefing.

That morning, a group of the movie's cast and crew had driven from a resort hotel in Timber Creek up to the San Raphael Wilderness Area, setting out from the Aspen Springs Trailhead parking lot around midmorning. They had hiked for only about a mile before stopping for an "awesome" brunch packed by the hotel. Some of the group had been drinking along the way: several bottles of champagne, blackberry brandy, and hot chocolate laced with Yukon Jack Permafrost. After they had eaten, six members of the group wanted to return to the motor home ("Too windy." "Too cold." "My feet hurt." "Too dirty."). Rob Christian had wanted to continue hiking. Others in the group—Tristan Chambers and Joseph Van Dijk, possibly Cristina and Carlos Sanchez, and Diana Nobody-Knew-Her-Last-Name—agreed to accompany him down the trail for another mile or two, then return to the parking lot no later than one P.M.

The little hiking party had never returned.

When Gracie left the motor home, the RPs were arguing about who should have gone on with Rob and whose fault everything was and what they were going to eat for dinner. She had to work to uncross her eyes as she walked back to the Command Post. And the beginning of a stress headache was tightening the back of her skull.


**"LIKE HERDING CATS,"** Gracie said to Ralph as he scanned the LPQ. "Hells bells. They can't even agree on exactly how many people are missing. The only thing they do agree on besides what everyone was wearing was that Rob Christian is among the MisPers along with two other guys: Tristan Chambers and Joseph Van Dijk."

She leaned carefully back in her own chair so she wouldn't look like an abject moron by tipping backward again. "Not much," she said, massaging the back of her neck with her fingers. "But it was all I could get. Any potential tracks in the parking lot have been obliterated."

"Where's Cashman?" Ralph asked.

"Haven't seen him."

"Go find him and let's get you two out on the trail."

As if in response, boots clumped up the rickety trailer stairs outside and Cashman burst into the trailer.

"Don't slam the—" Gracie and Ralph said in unison.

The door slammed. Gracie's eyes slid to the clock still lying on the desk at Ralph's elbow.

"Where have you been, Cashman?" Ralph asked.

"Got some autographs for my wife," Cashman said too loudly for the little trailer.

But only after she had left the motor home, Gracie noted. Where had he been before that? Probably gabbing with the cute deputy.

"Really not the time or place," Ralph said with more restraint than Gracie could have mustered. One reason Ralph was the team's Commander and Gracie never would be.

Cashman dropped into a metal folding chair and the team of three planned the search. Their course of action would be straightforward. For the first portion of the trail, Gracie and Cashman would move fairly quickly, spending little time looking for tracks. Near the trailhead, where the boots and sneakers of countless hikers and casual sightseers had pounded the path smooth, individual prints would be indistinguishable. Farther down, where all but the more serious hikers turned back toward the trailhead was where they would find tracks or portions of tracks. That's where the serious tracking would begin.

Where an offshoot trail rose up to meet the Aspen Springs Trail—the point at which Gracie calculated the group had eaten their lunch, then separated—the steep terrain on both sides prevented anyone from easily leaving the trail. Up to that point, there was essentially one way in and one way out.

"I'll call down to the SO," Ralph said. "Try to get a deputy or two to do a bastard search in town. See if any of the MisPers show up there."

"Make sure they check the hotel first," Gracie said. "According to one of the RPs, Cristina and Carlos may have headed back there."

"I'll get Montoya out there to go back and talk to the RPs. Interview them separately if need be. See if we can sort out some of this cluster."

*Montoya. That's the cute deputy's name.*

"Eight-TAC-One," Ralph said.

Cashman turned the little knob at the top of the HT to the search channel. "Got it."

Ralph picked up his GPS. "Ready for coordinates?"

# CHAPTER

# 15

I⟨T⟩ was fully dark by the time Gracie and Cashman set off hiking at a fast clip up the Aspen Springs Trail with Cashman in the lead. Rounding the first curve of the trail plunged them into perfect darkness. The glare of the Command Post floodlights vanished as if a giant switch had been flipped.

The obsidian sky exploded with stars. High altitude and pristine air rendered them large, brilliant and unwavering. The Milky Way splashed a hazy river of light across the zenith.

The searchers followed the trail as it meandered along the natural contours of the mountain. In, out, and in again. Rising, falling, then rising again. On its deceptively casual way toward the summit of San Raphael at almost twelve thousand feet.

On the steep canyon walls above and below the trail, their headlamps spotlighted curl-leaf mountain mahogany and huge mounds of manzanita with smooth bark as deep and rich in color as venous blood. All around them, the eerie skeletons of dead pine trees loomed out of the darkness, their needles orange in death, weakened by years of overgrowth and drought, and killed by scavenging bark beetles.

Occasionally the searchers stopped to call out the names of the missing persons or blow long earsplitting blasts on their whistles. Mostly they hiked in silence, the only sounds their own rhythmic breathing, the chink of a trekking pole on rock, the crunch of a boot on grit.

And the wind.

When the trail curved inward into the folds of the mountain, they were mercifully out of its brunt. But most of the time, it whipped around them, howling like a being from the netherworld, rocking tree carcasses and creaking dead limbs, occasionally blasting the searchers so hard with dirt and small stones that they turned their backs, or sought shelter in the lee of a giant boulder or behind the barren husk of a tree.

But in spite of the wind, possibly because of it, Gracie drank it all in—the darkness, the peace, the relative solitude, the sharp, cold air—and felt her spirits lifting. She felt the impulse to burst into song and almost laughed outright at the reaction a Puccini aria would elicit from Cashman.

Gracie often returned from searches mentally spent, physically exhausted, but spiritually renewed. This, she was reminded, was one of the reasons she had joined the team in the first place. The natural world at its purest and most elemental always breathed life into her, reviving her like water to a withered plant.

Gracie was working hard and had descended from the high that came with every callout. Still she felt energized, yet relaxed. Her mind clear, alert. She looked up into the night sky and noticed a deep shadow obliterating the stars in the west. "Clouds moving in," she called up to Cashman. "Maybe it won't get so cold tonight."

As Gracie and Cashman traveled, the hard-packed dirt of the trail gradually softened, growing more malleable, yielding tracks and portions of tracks of hikers traveling in both directions.

Crouching low and off to one side, sometimes on hands and knees, face inches from the dirt, Gracie was finally able to identify a series of fresh tracks laid by someone wearing Reeboks, presumably Tristan Chambers. Selecting the clearest, most complete track she could find, Gracie used the tip of one of her trekking poles to draw a circle around the track, then marked it with pink flagging tape. With her mini measuring tape, she measured the track itself and the stride—the distance from the heel of a right footprint to the heel of the next right footprint. She drew a rough sketch of the tread in her little notebook. Then, again with the tip of trekking pole, she marked the prints, first a left, then a right, then another left, following Tristan's and hopefully his two, maybe three, maybe five, hiking companions' progress up the trail.

Theoretically one never tracked alone; rather teams of three tracked with a point person doing the actual tracking with two flankers ahead on either side watching out for hazards. With Timber Creek SAR's shortage of trained personnel, tracking teams usually consisted of two searchers.

So Gracie examined the dirt, focusing on the Reebok tracks, flashlight held low and parallel to the ground to make even the tiniest portion of a track stand out, with Cashman up ahead on the trail, calling back an occasional "Low-hanging branch" or "Watch it, Gracie. Part of the trail's eroded away here."

What she couldn't afford to dwell on while she tracked was that people's lives might very well hinge upon her spotting that single stone that had been trod on and moved a millimeter, the remaining indentation casting a sliver of a shadow in the beam of the flashlight. Or the slightest compression of a leaf or pine needle. Or a miniscule section of tread pressed into the soft dirt.

Up ahead on the trail, Cashman stopped and called back, "Here's where the other trail comes in." Invisible but for the halo cast by his headlamp, Steve turned on his mag flashlight and fastened its beam on a little cairn of stones.

Gracie hurried forward. The beam of her own flashlight brought to life a muddle of prints on a wide trail juncture, along with scattered cigarette butts and a discarded soda can. "This is where they had lunch all right," she said. "Haven't they ever heard of an ashtray? This, hypothetically, is where some of them turned back and the MisPers continued on."

She walked to the far end of the juncture and pointed her flashlight up the main trail. The beam caught footprints flattened in the dirt, making them shine in the darkness. "Good. We've got clear tracks going up the trail," she said. She pointed with her trekking pole. "There'll be fewer tracks from here. Maybe now we'll be able to discern prints separate from the Reeboks." To herself, she added, "That, at least, is the plan."

Cashman stood behind Gracie drinking great gulps of water from his water bottle.

"Want to take a waypoint and call it in while I pee?" She unclipped the straps of her pack and let it slide to the ground.

Steve wiped the back of his mouth with his sleeve and screwed the bottle lid back on. "Sure thing."

When Gracie returned from relieving herself in the privacy of her own boulder, Cashman was still monkeying with his GPS, a handheld receiver using satellite signals to pinpoint their location.

Thankful for the respite, Gracie sat on a rock at the side of the trail. She munched on her PayDay and sipped from her own water bottle until Cashman acquired enough signals for a reading.

"Got 'em," he announced. He lifted the radio mic to his mouth and keyed the transmit button. "Command Post. Ten Rescue Fifty-six."

"Go ahead, Fifty-six," came Ralph's voice, loud and clear. To Gracie, it was comforting to know that he was in the Command Post looking out for them, monitoring where they were. She had been on searches where that wasn't the case and she didn't like it.

"We've gone point nine miles up the trail," Cashman radioed. "We're where the group stopped to have lunch."

"Copy that."

"I have coordinates."

"Stand by one." The radio was silent, then, "Go ahead."

Cashman read the coordinates, then signed off.

Gracie stood up and hefted her pack onto her back, feeling its substantial weight settle onto her already sore hips. "Ready?"

"Ready."

# CHAPTER

## 16

**D**IANA stumbled to a stop in the middle of the trail. Adrenaline spent, energy exhausted, she could go no farther. Heavy sobs wracked her body and tears dripped from her chin onto her coat.

Vaguely aware that if she traveled down the side of the mountain, she might never be able to crawl back up, she left the trail again. In the impenetrable darkness, she crawled blindly up the steep slope on all fours. A hundred feet up, she fell full-length onto the ground.

Pulling her knees to her chest, she reached behind her and scraped armfuls of leaves and pine needles and tree bark over her body like a blanket.

**M**ILOCEK stood in the middle of the trail and rolled his cigarette between his teeth.

He found the fresh digs in the dirt where Diana had left the trail and scrambled up the side of the mountain. He found where she had hidden between two boulders, even where she had relieved herself on the ground, leaving behind a wadded-up piece of blue tissue.

But she was gone. And now it was too dark for him to search for any sign of her without the aid of a flashlight.

He swallowed, but not without effort. His dry throat caught and his tongue stuck to the roof of his mouth. He needed water.

He had drunk all of his water at lunch and finished off the pint of brandy. He had several more gallons of water, but they were stored in the earthquake kit he kept in his car.

Milocek shrugged. He had gone without water before. He could go without it again.

He clambered up on top of a six-foot-high boulder perched on the side of the trail and sat down on his haunches.

There was only one way out. And that way led right past him. When Diana came back, he would be waiting.

The night closed in around him.

Minutes ticked by.

Milocek's head snapped up. He had heard something above the sound of the wind. Back down the trail. The high-pitched blast of a whistle.

He heard it again, closer, more clearly. Then voices—a man and a woman.

Milocek slid down the back of the boulder into the darkness.

## CHAPTER

# 18

GRACIE and Cashman followed the tracks along a narrow portion of the trail where the canyon walls jutted steeply upward on the right and fell away into darkness on the left. According to the altimeter on Gracie's watch, they had climbed to over ninety-five hundred feet in elevation. Snow fields above and below the trail had grown larger and more frequent. Any snow on the trail itself had been trampled into a muddy slush.

By then, Gracie had been able to positively identify additional print patterns mixed in with the Reeboks. One had a smooth sole with a distinctive pointed toe that could very well be from Rob Christian's city shoes. Another, a honeycomb pattern, was small enough to belong to a woman. Other prints were the lug sole typical of a hiking boot.

"What the—?" Gracie stopped abruptly and squatted at the side of the trail. "Cashman, hold up a sec," she yelled up to her teammate who was hiking out of sight ahead of her.

"What?" came Steve's voice out of the darkness ahead.

"I've got a whole mishmash of tracks going in both directions."

She heard a crunching of boots and Cashman appeared next to her. "What's up?"

Gracie trained her flashlight beam on the ground and pointed. "Look. Here's a honeycomb. And here's a lug sole. They're heading back to the trailhead. But not the Reeboks. Or the smooth sole." She studied the ground. "I don't get it. What were they doing?"

The lack of any response from Cashman told Gracie he wasn't the least bit interested. She knew from past searches that her teammate was focused on one thing—finding Rob Christian and Rob Christian only.

"Call Ralph, will you?" she asked. "Tell him what we have." To herself, she mumbled, "What the hell? If they were heading back, why didn't we see them?"

As Cashman held his GPS up to get a reading, Gracie measured the prints and scribbled the measurements into her little notebook.

"Command Post," Cashman said into the radio. "Ten Rescue Fifty-six."

But instead of Ralph's gravelly drawl in return, the radio emitted a loud, obnoxious wonk indicating they were out of range of a repeater to relay their radio signal back to the Command Post.

Cashman said he would see if he could get better reception and trotted back down the trail.

"Dammit," Gracie whispered. "Sloppy work, Kinkaid." She had been careless, concentrating only on one set of tracks—the most easily identifiable, the Reeboks. She had missed where the other tracks had begun heading in the other direction. It didn't matter that she was doing the job of at least one full tracking team, possibly two. She should have noticed the tracks before. They might have to backtrack and see if she could figure it all out.

"Dammit!" she said again and staggered to her feet. Her

legs and sacrum felt stiff from tracking with a full pack on and the wind had left her eyes gritty and dry. With the tip of her trekking pole, she drew large circles in the dirt around the clearest, most complete tracks, then tied a long length of pink flagging tape to a nearby branch.

She heard Cashman try the radio again. Another wonk. Cashman jogged back up to her.

"We need to think this through, Cashman. We now have four sets of tracks going in one direction and two sets going in the other. I have to think about what to do."

"I know what I'm doin'," Cashman said. "I'm going up the trail." He stepped past her and continued up the trail.

"Wait," Gracie said. "Cashman! Wait a minute!"

Cashman stopped ahead on the trail, but didn't look back.

She stood for several seconds, muttering curses about Cashman, about the tracks, about her life in general. What the hell was she going to do? Let him go off on his own? "All right, dammit," she called up to her teammate. "I'm coming." She followed Cashman up the trail.

Gracie loved the challenge of the wilderness, treasuring it for its deadliness, not in spite of it. Most people wandering its trails seemed to underestimate the risk, treating the outdoors too casually, overestimating their own importance, assuming nothing would happen to them. And, if it did, help was just a cell phone call away.

Every once in a while, the nature gods would sit up and take notice. Fed up with the arrogance of humankind, they would take someone out.

Gracie skidded to a stop. "Dammit."

"*Now* what?" Cashman called back to her.

"Now there are only two sets of tracks altogether. Only the smooth sole. Going in both directions. And the honeycomb. But in only one direction. What do you see up there?"

With flashlight trained to the ground, Cashman disappeared around a bend in the trail. Half a minute later, he reappeared. "Looks like a couple of 'em went to take a whiz or a crap or something."

"What happened to the other tracks?" Gracie asked. She turned and backtracked down the trail to the last Reebok print she had marked—a right. Logically the next track should be a left. She examined the ground.

The Reeboks had vanished.

"Where'd they go?" Gracie turned 360 degrees, shining her flashlight beam along the ground in a wide swath until, finally, she spotted an indentation from a boot heel where someone had stepped onto a wide, foot-high berm of dirt and stones, and out onto an expansive promontory of boulders.

"There!" Her sweeping light illuminated a chaos of footprints in the soft dirt. "They must have stopped and taken a break here or something."

Gracie trained her light on the ground. "What's that?" She stepped over the berm and crouched down. She picked away several stones and branches strewn on the ground, and brushed away the top layer of dirt with her hand, revealing a large dark stain standing out against the drier, buff-colored dirt. Her stomach muscles tightened. "Cashman, does this look like blood to you?"

Steve moved to stand next to her. "Yeah, that's blood," he said, his tone matter-of-fact. "Some hunter probably field-dressed a deer he bagged out of season. Covered his tracks so he wouldn't get busted for poaching."

Cashman moved to the far end of the outcropping and looked down over the edge, his headlamp emitting only a meager radius of light into the void. "Think they went down?"

Gracie stared at the stain, focused on the fact that there were probably no deer at that altitude that time of year, if ever.

"Wanna search down below?" Cashman asked.

"I don't think this is deer blood. I wonder if there was

some kind of accident. Maybe with our missing hikers. This is getting way too complicated. We need to call this in."

"Roger, Roger," Cashman said with a shrug. But when he keyed the microphone, the radio wonked. "Dead spot," he said. He paced back down the trail a short distance and tried again.

From where she was, Gracie heard the wonk of the radio. "Nothing," Cashman called back up to her.

"Why go down if someone was hurt?" Gracie asked herself. "It doesn't make any sense."

Cashman reappeared beside her. "Wanna walk farther back to see if you can get a signal?" he asked. "I can search on down the hill."

Gracie pushed herself to her feet. "Not a good idea to separate," she said. Which Cashman knew full well. "Never leave your partner" was one of the most fundamental tenets of search and rescue. "Never go off on your own."

"How 'bout we at least find where they went down?" Cashman suggested.

Gracie dragged her attention away from the stain. With flashlights and headlamps trained on the dirt, she and Cashman scoured the area until they found where someone had descended into the canyon—a furrow of churned earth and leaves leading down one side of the outcropping.

"Let's follow it down," Cashman prodded.

Gracie stood her ground, chewing the inside of her cheek. Leaving the trail to go down into the canyon was tricky business—bushwhacking off-trail, off-radio, in the dark, on a steep, rocky slope leading to who knew where. She had been there and done that. It totally sucked.

*Don't get dead* flickered through her mind. *Don't take unnecessary risks. Don't do anything stupid. Don't become a victim yourself.* "I think we need to backtrack down the trail to find a signal," she said. "We need to let Ralph know what we're doing. About the tracks. And about the blood."

"Fuck the blood!" Cashman yelled. "And fuck Hunter!"

Gracie took a step backward. "Cashman!"

Steve backed off immediately, softening his tone. "Sorry, Gracie. But if somebody's hurt down there, a half hour could mean we find a DB instead of a person. You can stay here. Or go try and radio. I'm goin' down."

Gracie stared at her teammate. This was a side of Cashman she had never seen before. She had never even heard him raise his voice, much less yell at anyone, least of all her.

"Not a good idea, Steve," she said. "Ralph needs to call in more teams."

"I'll mark where I went down." He hauled out a long strand of neon green flagging tape and tied multiple strands around the branches of a manzanita bush growing out of the dirt next to the trail.

"Cashman, are you hearing me?" Gracie asked, struggling to keep the irritation out of her voice. "This is not a good idea. We need to radio in."

"I'm Team Leader," he said without looking at her. He drew out his GPS and held it aloft to collect the satellite signal. "I'm goin' down. You can come with me. You can stay here. Whatever you want."

"What the hell!" Gracie stormed several paces up the trail, then stopped, breathing slowly, deeply, trying to squelch her anger.

The risk in altering their course without notifying the Command Post was monumental. Once they left the formal, maintained trail, they would be flying blind, off the radar. If anything bad happened, they would be on their own. Gracie alone with Steve Cashman.

What was she going to do? Let Cashman go down into the canyon by himself? Hike all the way back to the Command Post alone?

Cashman was right about time being critical. She would never forgive herself if someone died because she had a thing about sticking to the rules.

She turned and stomped back down to the outcropping.

"Dammit, Cashman, you win. But I don't like it. One. Bit. Don't ever do this again." Gracie hauled out her own GPS and took a waypoint.

With a voice in Gracie's head shouting a fortissimo, "I've got a bad feeling about this," she and Cashman plunged down off the side of the trail and into darkness.

# CHAPTER

## 19

**M**ILOCEK ground his back teeth together. Frustration burned in his chest. The arrival of Search and Rescue presented yet another complication.

He had crept up behind the searchers, tailing them as they followed the tracks to the rock promontory. Motionless and invisible back down the trail, he listened as they discussed the stain in the dirt and argued about what to do.

Milocek's hand moved to the knife at his waist. He itched to pull it out.

There had been a time when he would have taken on two adversaries at once. But years of fast food and living the anonymous civilian life in America had made him soft, flabby, had reduced his stamina and dulled his reflexes. He would have to wait for the right moment and take them one at a time.

His hand dropped from the knife.

He watched the rescuers leave the trail to follow the path down into the canyon.

The tracks the woman searcher had found confirmed

what logic had already told him—that Diana was hiding still farther up the trail.

Milocek considered his dilemma. Should he go after Diana? Or should he follow the searchers who might lead him to Rob?

The razor-edged knife blade sliced easily through the green plastic ribbon the searcher had tied to the branches of a bush next to the trail. Milocek gathered up the multiple strands and stuffed them into his jacket pocket.

# CHAPTER
# 20

RALPH sat at the green metal desk in the Command Post. The HT lay inches from his left elbow, the volume turned up all the way so he wouldn't miss the tiniest hint of a transmission.

The wind outside buffeted the rickety trailer, sucking heat out through invisible cracks and seams and forcing Ralph to wear his Gore-Tex parka, wool hat, and fingerless wool gloves to stay warm.

Half an hour earlier, David Montoya, the deputy on-scene, had knocked on the trailer door to notify Ralph that Carlos Sanchez had been reached on his cell phone. He and his wife, Cristina, had in fact checked out of the hotel in town and were driving on the 10 Freeway to their home in Santa Monica.

Montoya had also handed Ralph a piece of paper on which he had scribbled basic information obtained from a check of license plates of the vehicles in the trailhead lot.

The chair creaked as Ralph leaned back to study the information. The motor home and one of the cars, a Cadil-

lac Escalade, had been rented the week before by the production company. A second car, a 2008 Toyota Corolla
belonged to one of the MisPers: Joseph Van Dijk of River-
side. The third, a late model Ford Mustang convertible,
belonged to one of the RPs: Michael Benjamin of Brent-
wood. Nothing much pertinent to the search.

Ralph didn't like searching without reliable physical
descriptions of the missing persons. In a few minutes, he
decided, he would walk over to the Tahoe and talk to Montoya again to see what the deputy could do about obtaining
more information on each of the MisPers. It might take a
little time, but what else did the man have to do while sitting
in his unit all night long?

Ralph switched his thoughts to the Sanchez couple. The
fact that they had driven down the hill was significant to
the search in that it definitively narrowed the number of
MisPers from six to four.

He needed to notify his search team.

Ralph lifted the HT to his mouth. "Tracking One. Command Post."

No response.

"Tracking One. Command Post."

Still no response.

They're in a dead spot, Ralph thought. He would have to
wait until they called in.

Gracie and Cashman had radioed in the coordinates of
their location at regular intervals since they had left the
Command Post. It had been almost ninety minutes since
their last transmission.

In the rugged terrain, with no repeater high or close
enough to catch the team's signal and rebroadcast it back to
the CP, long radio silences were to be expected. There wasn't
a damned thing Ralph could do about it except assume his
team would radio in when they were able.

Ralph pulled a crumpled pack of Marlboro Lights from
his parka and drew out one of four remaining cigarettes. He

had started smoking again when Eleanor had been diagnosed with late-stage breast cancer. Throughout the long ordeal, he had managed to keep it below half a pack a day. Now, six years after her death, he was finally trying to quit.

He stuck the unlit cigarette in the fold of his wool hat and turned his attention back to the search.

Ralph had meticulously recorded each new set of coordinates called in from the field on the laminated USGS topo map of the wilderness area spread out on the little desk. With a black transparency marker, he had drawn an X on the map at the location pinpointed by each set of coordinates, then highlighted the team's progress in yellow.

Ralph looked at the last black X, the point where the meandering yellow line ended. Where the hell were Gracie and Cashman? They could be just about anywhere within sixty thousand acres of precipitous canyons and jagged mountain peaks.

Ralph scowled down at the map. He hated being out of contact with his search team, Gracie in particular. There were too many variables. Too many things could go horribly wrong.

"Come on, Cashman," he said. "Call the hell in."

# CHAPTER

# 21

**G**RACIE and Cashman dropped down from the trail, following the obvious signs that someone had descended there. Fallen leaves had been churned up, their dark wet underbellies gleaming in the light of the headlamps. Newly scuffed and overturned dirt showed darker brown against the dryer top layer.

Negotiating their way into the depths of the canyon proved even rougher and more hazardous than Gracie had feared. The mountainside was steep, plunging down for more than a quarter mile. Headlamps illuminated only puny circles of dim light ahead of them. Loose stones, sticks, and leaves melted away underfoot. Soft soil released its hold on seemingly well-anchored branches. Gracie's anger at Cashman dissolved as she concentrated on keeping her feet from flying out from under her.

The searchers slithered down the incline, heavy packs propelling them forward. The inclination was to hurry, allowing gravity to do most of the work. But gravity was a wolf in sheep's clothing, urging them to go faster. Traveling fast on a search wasn't always better. Sometimes it was stu-pid. And dangerous. A misstep invited a turned ankle or torn ligament or becoming part of the scrabble of pebbles and stones trickling down before them.

And in this case, if they hurried too much, they might bypass any deviation from the main track, or overlook some sign or key piece of evidence along the way.

So Gracie maintained a slow, deliberate rate of descent, cautiously picking her way down, bracing herself with her trekking pole on the downhill slope, placing each boot securely on stable ground before lifting the other. "Slow down, Cashman," she called down to her teammate who was barely visible below her. "I can't see squat."

Cashman hadn't heard her. At least he hadn't altered his pace.

On searches Cashman always traveled too fast, hiking far ahead of the others, ignoring field protocol that dictated the team travel at the pace of its slowest member. When someone—not always Gracie—reminded Steve of that fact, he invariably stepped to the back of the line, deferring the lead to another—the implication being slower, therefore weaker—member. Someone else should set the pace, he would say. He always went too fast.

"Cashman!" Gracie yelled. "Slow down!"

He definitely heard her that time for he stopped and waited for her to catch up. "Maybe you should go first," he said as Gracie stepped down past him. "I always go too fast."

The farther they descended into the canyon, the rockier and less stable the ground became with more fallen logs blocking their path. The trail grew less obvious, harder to follow. Individual footprints were nonexistent.

Because they were out of the worst of the wind, Gracie was beginning to overheat. Not a good thing. As long as they kept moving, she was fine. But as soon as they stopped, if she didn't dry off the sweat forming on her body and pack the warm layers back on, evaporation and conduction would sap every last bit of heat from her body and hypothermia would swoop in. *Stay dry or die* was one of those slogans actually based on fact.

"I have to stop and ventilate," she called up to Cashman. She slid to a stop, propping herself on the uphill side of a ponderosa pine trunk. "I'm starting to sweat." Avoiding the sap caked on the tree's giant plates of bark, she unzipped her fleece top as far as it would go and the side zippers of her pants from the waistband to below her knees even though they would flap about ridiculously like cowboy chaps. "Nobody said this was going to be a fashion show," she announced to the tree.

Cashman slid to a stop beside her. He uncapped his water bottle and gulped down the remaining liquid, which reminded Gracie that she too needed to keep hydrating. Altitude plus exertion equaled dehydration. She took a long draw from her water bottle.

Gracie's shoulders and hips ached from the heavy pack. It didn't bode well if the search lasted well into the night which it very possibly might.

"Whistle," Cashman said.

Gracie plugged her ears as he blew three blasts on his plastic whistle.

The sound ricocheted around them and faded away to nothing.

The searchers listened, not breathing, but heard only the wind whispering through the surrounding bushes and trees, drowning out even the natural murmurings of the night.

Gracie formed a megaphone around her mouth with her hands. "Rob!" she yelled. "Cristina! Joseph!"

"Carlos!" Cashman yelled. "What's the other one's name?"

"Diana."

"Diana! Rob!"

Gracie stopped. What was that? Had she heard something? She cupped her hands behind her ears, silent, straining to hear something.

Nothing.

"Let's go," she said, stepping out from behind the tree and continuing down the incline.

"Rock!" Cashman's yell split the darkness above her head.

Instinctively Gracie hunkered down as a waterfall of stones and rocks rattled and bounced around her, one basketball-sized shooting past only inches from her head.

Cashman called down from above, "Sorry about that, Chief!"

Gracie scrambled to her feet. As calmly as she could, she said, "I'd like to remind you of the most basic of SAR principles that says 'Don't kill your teammate.'"

"Shhh! I heard something." The excitement in Cashman's voice was unmistakable.

The two leaned forward to discern any sound that might be remotely human.

Gracie opened her mouth to say that she didn't hear anything when Cashman yelled, "Down there!" so loudly it almost made her lose her balance.

He pointed down and off to their right.

*He has the ears of a jack rabbit*, Gracie thought. Then she heard it—a faint voice. "Down here!"

Together Gracie and Cashman raced down into the canyon, caution abandoned, surfing the dirt, loose rocks, leaves, pine needles, adrenaline coursing, recklessly ignoring any danger.

"Careful, careful," Gracie warned herself as much as Cashman. "It's not going to do anyone any good if one of us gets hurt."

As soon as she said it, Gracie's boot slipped. She was sliding, gaining momentum, heavy pack driving her forward like a giant hand giving her a nudge. Frantically she grabbed on to a passing branch. Her body swung in a wide arc and she landed flat on her stomach with an "oof," banging her knee on something hard. *Another bruise tomorrow* was the only thing her brain registered.

"You okay?" Cashman called back without stopping.

"Terrific," Gracie answered, spitting dirt and tiny stones out of her mouth.

She rolled over to squat on the hillside. "Rob Christian!" she yelled. "Tristan Chambers!"

Again she heard the voice, louder this time. "I'm here!"

"Oh, screw it," Gracie said and slid the last couple hundred feet on her backside. Not pretty, but effective. She reached the bottom at the same time as Cashman.

"Where are you?" Gracie yelled as she struggled to her feet.

Cashman zoomed past her.

"Across the brook," came the voice, unmistakably British. "Up."

With Gracie on Cashman's heels, the searchers picked their way across the wide, shallow creek that had carved out the canyon, stepping cautiously from rock to rock to rock, then scrambled up the six-foot-high embankment on the other side.

Two flashlight beams skimmed the hillside. Two pairs of eyes peered in the crisscrossing circles of light to spy anything resembling a human being.

"There!" Gracie focused her light on where, twenty feet above them, a single man sat on the ground with his back to a tree, one leg outstretched, arms hugged to his chest.

"It's Rob," Cashman said with undisguised excitement.

Side by side, Gracie and Cashman climbed up the remaining distance to where the man sat. "Rob Christian?" Gracie asked.

The man's teeth chattered so violently he could barely speak the single word. "Yes."

Fighting not to sound as winded as she was, Gracie said, "Sheriff's Department. Search and Rescue." She unclipped the chest and waist buckles of her pack and let it slide off one shoulder to the ground. "I'm Grace Kinkaid," she said, unfastening her helmet and tossing it on the ground next to the pack. She pulled her beanie from her pocket and stretched it on, then knelt on the ground in front of the actor.

"How do you do?" was what Gracie supposed the Englishman tried to say, but his words were so slurred they were practically unintelligible. Amazing, Gracie thought. *The guy's half-dead and he still remembers his manners.*

"How you doin'?" Cashman asked, thrusting his hand over Gracie's shoulder and into the actor's face. "Steve Cashman."

With more aplomb than Gracie could imagine, Rob Christian accepted the outstretched hand in his own. "How do you do?" he mumbled again between clattering teeth.

"Cashman, why don't you heat up some water so we can give Mr. Christian something hot to drink?"

"Sure thing," he answered. "Goody. I can try out my new stove."

Gracie turned her attention back to the actor. "We've been looking for you," she said, extracting a pair of latex gloves from her chest pack.

"My wife's a big fan," Cashman said from behind Gracie. "I'd love to get an autograph."

"Glad you found me," the man slurred. "I'd already made my peace with God."

*I bet you had,* Gracie thought. She stretched on the gloves while identifying herself as an EMT and doing a lightning visual assessment of the man sitting before her.

Beneath the caked-on layer of dirt and dried blood, Rob's face was pale. The eyes that followed her every move were shadowed and dull. Several abrasions on his face, neck, and hands had bled and dried. A two-inch laceration on his eyebrow still oozed blood, black and shiny in the dim light. Sea anemones of white down waved from tears here and there in his black down jacket, and a bloody and scratched kneecap showed through a rip in his black jeans which, upon closer scrutiny, Gracie determined were wet.

Uncontrollable shivering, slurred speech, and poor coordination were classic hypothermia symptoms, most likely the result of spending a good ten or so hours out in the elements, and being wet to boot. But, Gracie considered, some of it could also be manifestations of brain trauma. There was no way to tell which the symptoms represented. The best she could do at the moment was warm the man up, give him some water to drink, treat the superficial injuries, and see which symptoms, if any, remained.

"Drink this." Gracie unscrewed the cap from her spare water bottle and handed it to Rob. "It's only warm, but it's important to get fluids on board as quickly as possible."

"Thank you." He reached for the bottle, but fumbled, almost dropping it. "C-c-can't . . . quite . . ." Gracie steadied the bottle as the man gripped it with both hands and took a long, slow drink.

"Loved *Best Enemies*," Cashman said.

Gracie hauled her sleeping bag from her pack and shook it out from its stuff sack. "Is anyone else here with you? Tristan Chambers?"

"Who?"

She settled the sleeping bag around Rob's shoulders. "Tristan Chambers."

"T-Tristan?" He swiped a hand across his forehead, then drew it back, staring at the dark blood on his fingertips as if not quite comprehending what it was.

"Or Joseph Van Dijk? Or a woman named Diana? Cristina? Carlos?"

"N-n-no. Why?"

"We thought maybe they were with you." Gracie yanked off her glove and grabbed his wrist. His pulse was strong and regular, a positive sign.

She pulled a granola bar from her parka pocket, tore it open, and handed it to him. "Eat this."

Rob took the bar with slow, uncoordinated movements.

"Do you know what happened to you?" Gracie asked, watching as he aimed the granola bar at his mouth and missed. He tried again more deliberately and took a bite.

"Had a b-b-bit of a t-t-tumble." Rob said, chewing slowly. "I c-c-can't . . . don't remember."

"You don't remember falling?"

"No."

"Looks like you hit your head."

"Stings like a son of a b-b-bitch." He touched the cut on his eyebrow again.

"Don't touch the lac—the cut," Gracie said.

He dropped his hand.

"Do you know if you lost consciousness?" she asked.

"I . . . I must have done."

"Any idea for how long? Keep eating."

"No." With a surer aim to the mouth, he took another bite.

"Any vomiting?"

"A bit. When I first t-tried to s-stand up."

"Can you tell me what day it is?" she asked. Hell, she didn't even know the answer to that one. Oh, yeah. Thursday. Thanksgiving Day. How could she have forgotten?

Rob angled his wrist toward the light of her headlamp and looked at his watch—gold and, from all appearances, very expensive.

A smile nudged Gracie's mouth. "Without looking at your watch."

"Friday, maybe. Or Saturday?"

"Where besides your head does it hurt?"

"P-pretty much everywhere."

"Any place worse than others?"

"My ankle. I'm pretty sure I sprained it. C-can't put any weight on it. Don't think it's b-broken though."

A bad sprain might be better than a break in the long run, but could be initially more painful.

Behind her, Cashman rummaged noisily through his pack. Over her shoulder, Gracie could see his Cheshire cat grin with the word *hero* practically scrawled across his forehead. She dreaded the prospect of having to listen to him crow about this very moment.

But the thought of Cashman's future braggadocio did nothing to dampen Gracie's own spirits. She felt positively giddy herself. There was nothing more satisfying than finding a missing person still breathing. She had had a number of searches go the other way. Bringing them home alive was definitely better. She reminded herself not to get too far ahead of herself. Three other people—maybe five—were still missing.

The initial medical assessment convinced Gracie that none of Rob's injuries were life threatening. Getting him dry and warm emerged as the number one priority.

"Excuse me," she said, reaching out to finger the black sweater Rob wore beneath his jacket, trying not to notice the dark chest hair peeking out from the V-neck. "What's your sweater made of?"

"Why?"

"I need to know whether we need you to take it off. What's it made of?"

"Cashmere."

Naturally. "One hundred percent?"

He looked at her as if he couldn't figure out why now was the right time for a conversation about men's fashion, but answered, "Yes," anyway.

"Is it dry?"

"Pretty much."

"But your pants are wet." A confirmation.

He nodded. "Fell in the water down below. Mostly it's the bottom half of me that got wet."

"Mr. Christian . . ." Gracie began.

"Rob. Call me Rob," he said, which Gracie took as a good sign that there was a trace of irritation in his voice and that he enunciated the words without stuttering.

"Fair enough, Rob," she said. "Before I treat your injuries, we've got to get you into some dry clothes."

"I've got extra fleece," Cashman announced in a loud voice.

From the looks of it, Rob Christian outweighed Steve by a good twenty, twenty-five pounds. But, as long as the actor could squeeze into the clothes, they would serve their function.

"I hate to take off your shoe? Boot? Shoe?" She inspected his foot more closely, taking in the black leather over-the-ankle boot. Apparently butt-ugly roach killers had come back into style.

"Boot," Rob said.

"Okay, boot. But at this point I think it's more important to get you dry and warm. You have gloves. Are they dry?"

"One is."

"Do you have a hat?"

"I did have."

"That's all right. We have gloves and a hat for you to wear." Gracie stood up and turned toward Cashman, who, to his enormous credit, already had water heating. "Steve, you want to help Mr., um, Rob out of his hypothermia pants while I make up some soup?"

"Sure thing."

She turned back toward the actor. "Steve will help you change out of those wet pants. We have some dry ones for you to put on."

"Terrific." He sounded as if he really meant it.

"How does some chicken noodle soup sound?"

"Brilliant."

"Cashman." Gracie tossed him the plastic vacuum-packed bundle of spare clothes from her own pack, which Steve caught with an exaggerated flourish. "There are fleece socks and a hat in there. And another Polartec shirt. If it fits, have him put it under his sweater. And here's a pair of down booties. See if they fit."

Cashman helped Rob to his feet as Gracie dug into her pack for the Tupperware container that held her food stash. Unsnapping the lid, she picked out a well-worn but intact packet of dehydrated soup, ripped the package open and poured the contents into the steaming water.

As she stirred the broth, she glanced over her shoulder and did a classic double take.

In the light of Steve's headlamp, Rob Christian stood in all his glory, stark raving naked from the waist down. With a hand on Steve's shoulder to steady himself, he was hopping on one foot, fighting to put his injured foot into the leg of a pair of fleece pants.

"Holy . . ." Gracie whispered to herself, turning back to hunch over her stove. "Steve, you might want to have Rob sit down," she said, hardly able to suppress a giggle. "It might be easier that way." *Yikes, is he white! My butt's not even close to being that white and it hasn't seen the sun in ten years.*

**R**OB Christian sat inside Gracie's half-zipped sleeping bag on a twelve-inch-square pad of closed-cell foam insulation. His injured leg stuck out the side, propped up on her pack. She had pulled one of her down booties—which had proven to be too small—over his toes to keep them warm. He was fully clothed in dry fleece and socks, a pair of Cashman's gloves, and Gracie's hat with the earflaps pulled over his ears. He cradled a steaming cup of chicken noodle soup in his gloved hands.

Rob had stopped shivering and had regained complete coordination of his limbs. His speech was fully coherent. Gracie eyed the man surreptitiously and was pleased that in spite of the dirt and dried blood on his face, he appeared to have stepped a couple of paces back from death's door. There was no doubt that he had been close. As cold as it was, and being as wet, hypothermic and injured as he was, the august Englishman may very well not have lasted the night. She found it mind-boggling that people all over the world would have mourned the loss.

But even with the actor sitting surreally before her, a gnawing feeling remained in her gut. Where were the others? Had she screwed up big-time and misread the tracks? Had she missed something in their hurry down into the canyon? Would someone die because of her mistake? And how did the blood on the outcropping figure into the story, if at all?

Gracie questioned Rob further about his hiking partners as she wiped grime and blood from his face and neck, daubed antibiotic cream on the worst of the abrasions, and irrigated and butterfly bandaged the cut on his eyebrow. But whether from the bump on his head or because he simply didn't know, Rob produced little useful information. No, he didn't remember why he had left the trail. And, no, he couldn't remember separating from the others or know where they might be at this moment. The last thing he could remember clearly was eating lunch with the entire group.

"Excuse us a moment," Gracie said to Rob. She pushed herself to her feet and drew Cashman a couple of yards down the hill out of hearing distance of the actor.

She put her mouth inches from Cashman's ear and breathed, "Really bad idea to separate, but someone needs to radio in to the CP. Let Ralph know where we are. That we've found Rob and—"

"I'll go."

"Okay, good. I'd like to keep an eye on Rob. Tell Ralph we're bivying for the night. Ask him to page out more teams to look for the other MisPers." She left unspoken that finding the other missing persons alive was becoming less and less likely with every passing minute.

Cashman plunked his helmet back on his head and fastened the strap beneath his chin. "I'll keep an eye peeled for 'em."

"Give Ralph as much info as you can so he can plan for the next Ops Period. If it's still too windy in the morning for an air evac, we'll need a litter team for the carry-out."

Cashman swung up his pack and threaded his arms into the straps.

"But *ask* him, Steve. He's IC."

"Yeah, yeah."

"I'll build a shelter while you're gone."

"Not for me." He fastened the waistband on his pack. "I've got my bivy."

"Okay." Gracie thought for a moment, then said, "Cashman?"

"Yeah."

"Be careful."

"I always am," he said with a grin, then jogged off down the hill at a pace Gracie knew was for Rob's benefit and which would be hard to maintain on the uphill side of the canyon. Still, she had to hand it to Cashman. It looked good.

Gracie trudged up the hill to sit on the ground a couple of feet away from Rob. "Steve's going back up to the trail to call in to the Command Post. We're too low in the canyon here for radio reception. We're going to bivouac here for the night. Bring you out in the morning."

"We're spending the night out here?"

Gracie didn't begrudge the man the merest hint of a whine in his voice. Even she thought sleeping outside in any temperature less than forty degrees sucked. And she wasn't a city boy, injured and exhausted and mildly hypothermic.

"I'm sorry," she said with genuine sympathy. In her best caretaker-to-patient voice, she added, "I'm going to do my best to make sure you're as warm and comfortable as possible. But I don't think you're able to hike out on your own."

"What about a helicopter? Can't they fly in and fetch us out?"

"Did you finish the soup?"

As he dutifully scraped at the bottom of the cup with her Lexan spoon, Gracie answered his question. "Sheriff's Department helicopters don't fly in the mountains at night. And it's very windy up top. It's too dangerous."

Rob handed her the empty cup.

"We'll most likely airlift you out at first light," Gracie said. "Don't worry about being too cold. I'm going to build us a shelter for the night."

"You are? *You* are?"

Gracie narrowed her eyes at him. Just how much of a male chauvinist was this guy anyway? "You're injured," she said, keeping her voice neutral.

"I'm laid up like a . . ." Rob blustered. "You shouldn't have to . . . I feel like an effing child!" He threw his hands up in exasperation, then reacted to the movement with a wince. He leaned forward and cupped his hand to the bandaged cut on his eyebrow.

*Ah*, Gracie thought. *Male pride.* She slid over to kneel on the ground in front of Rob and smiled up at him. "This is what I'm trained for," she said. "First, though, I'd like to take a look at your ankle. May I?"

He blew out a long breath. "By all means."

A wave of unreality washed over her as she plucked off the down bootie and eased the sock from his foot. A lump the size and color of a plum protruded from his porcelain ankle just below the bone. "Tell me where it hurts," she said and palpated his foot with her fingertips.

"Bugger!" Rob yelled. He jerked his foot out of her hands and fell back onto his elbows.

Gracie sat back on her heels and looked at him. "I'm sorry," she said, keeping her voice calm. "But I have to see how badly your foot is injured."

She lifted his foot again, resting it in her lap, and started feeling around the ankle again.

"Bloody hell, woman!" Rob yelled again and yanked his foot away from her so hard she tipped over sideways.

*This guy is starting to get on my nerves.*

Gracie shoved herself upright and grabbed up her first-aid kit. "I don't think your ankle is broken," she said. "But I don't have X-ray eyes and an X ray is the only way to conclusively determine whether you have a bad sprain or a fracture. Both are incredibly painful."

"No bloody shit," Rob said.

"First I'm going to put a wet bandana on it. It'll be cold, but it'll help with the swelling and hopefully it won't be quite as sore tomorrow. Then later I'll wrap it tight with an elastic bandage to ease the pain some and make it more stable."

Down at the creek Gracie soaked her cotton bandana in the icy water, then kneeling in front of Rob again, draped the folded cloth on the injured ankle.

Rob yelped and fell back again, which made him groan again with pain.

"I am sorry," Gracie said. "This is going to hurt a lot right now, but, please, trust me that it will make it feel better tomorrow."

When Gracie placed the cold bandana around his ankle, Rob said, "Effing hell!" through clenched teeth, but kept his foot still. "So, what should I call you?" he asked. "Florence?"

Gracie couldn't tell if what she heard in his voice was disdain or amusement or something else. "As in Nightingale?" she returned as she tied off the bandana. With Rob's eyes burning the top of her head, she concentrated on not dropping his foot as she lifted it up to place it gingerly on her pack.

"Quick, aren't you?" he asked, then groaned as she tugged the down bootie over his toes.

"Sorry again."

From her first-aid kit, she pulled a plastic film canister. "My mini-pharmacy," she announced holding it up. She flipped off the lid and poured a multicolored pile of pills into her hand. "You name it. I carry it. If it's legal, that is."

She extracted two white caplets and dropped them into Rob's open hand. "Acetaminophen. Tylenol. They'll take the edge off the pain." She funneled the rest of the pills back into the canister. "I'm not supposed to dispense medication, but I won't tell if you won't."

"Thank you," Rob said so quietly Gracie hardly heard him. She handed him the water bottle. "You're welcome."

As he tossed the pills into his mouth and tipped back the bottle to drain the rest of the water, Gracie grabbed the seconds to study the man before her.

So far, she decided, Rob Christian wasn't all that bad. She'd had better patients. She'd definitely had worse. Preconceived ideas of how an über-wealthy, high-maintenance megastar would act had prepared her not to like him. But he wasn't acting out nearly as badly as she had anticipated he would.

At the moment he didn't even look much like a mega-star. In fact, in the unforgiving light of Gracie's LED headlamp, Rob Christian looked like a thoroughly grimy half-drowned pack rat in need of a long, hot soak and a tall brewsky.

# 23

**G**RACIE left Rob looking like a little boy with wide eyes, as if the slightest breeze would knock him over. She zigzagged back and forth up the hillside behind him in search of a suitable place to build an emergency shelter.

In less than five minutes she had located what she needed at the base of a jumble of elephantine granite boulders, some twenty feet tall. A large flat rock shelf jutted out for several feet, then angled back to the ground, providing a level nook protected naturally on two sides. Construct the third side of the triangle, close off the ends and, voila, a serviceable shelter for Rob.

The smaller the space, the warmer. Gracie thought she remembered from the Lost Person Questionnaire that Rob was six feet two inches tall. The only time she had actually seen him standing up was when Cashman was helping him into the fleece pants and then she wasn't exactly paying attention to his height. The shelter, once completed, needed to be about four feet wide, tall enough to sit up in, and long enough for Rob to stretch out comfortably. She would add an extra couple of feet for gear.

Way too early to wrap her mind around the fact that she might be sharing the teeny space along with him.

Gracie doffed her pack and knelt beneath the ledge. Using her hands, she scraped and shoveled together a thick nest from the duff that had accumulated for years. Dust from decomposing twigs, leaves, pinecones and needles, and other earthy matter billowed up around her, filling her nostrils and making her hack and cough. She forged ahead, holding her breath while she dug, stopping every few seconds to take in deep gulps of air over her shoulder.

She pulled a large sheet of orange plastic from a small zippered compartment in her pack. Anchoring the length to the rock shelf with a line of rocks, she stretched the plastic down at an angle and secured it at the ground with more rocks and dirt. She closed up the far end of the shelter with pine branches scrounged from around the area sprinkled with more duff to fill in any cracks. The other smaller end would serve as the doorway and be closed in with her pack and more branches once he . . . they . . . he was inside.

Gracie crawled into the shelter and laid out her insulated sleeping pad on top of the thick layer of duff, ready for her sleeping bag on top. From her pack, she produced a small yellow flashlight that pulled out into a lantern and hung it from the strap at the apex of the shelter so that when turned on, it produced an incongruous amount of light, warm and welcoming.

Gracie sat back on her heels and surveyed her handiwork from the doorway. *Not bad, Kinkaid. Those countless pain-in-the-neck trainings really do come in handy.*

Her shoulders slumped at the unwelcome thought that it wouldn't be good enough for a movie star used to five-star hotels and room service and the fawning, obsequious masses. "Well, it'll have to be," she grumped.

"Shelter's ready," Gracie called as she half-slid down the

hillside to where Rob sat. She caught sight of his face and stopped dead.

Rob sat immobile, face oyster white, eyes shadowed in their sockets and staring off into space.

"Rob?"

He turned his head slowly and looked up at her.

"What's going on?"

"Something happened."

Gracie sat down next to him. "What happened?"

"There was a fight."

"A fight? When?"

"More than a fight."

"When was this?"

"Up there. On the trail. I can't quite . . . Someone . . ." He massaged his forehead with his fingertips. "I remember . . . trying to get away."

"To get away from someone? From who? Do you remember?"

"It's all a fog. I remember a lot of . . ." He stopped, frowning.

"A lot of what?"

He looked straight into Gracie's eyes. "Blood."

Goose bumps walked ghostly fingers up Gracie's arms and made all the hair stand on end. "Blood."

He nodded. "I remember a woman screaming," he said, his eyes never leaving Gracie's. "I think I saw someone die. And I think someone tried to kill me."

# CHAPTER
# 24

"POST." The single word blared throughout the little Command Post trailer.

Ralph snatched up the HT. "Tracking One."

With the poor reception, Cashman's radio transmission had gone digital, his voice sounding like a robot with a screw loose. As a result, Ralph was able to catch only part of a series of numbers followed by intermittent intelligible words. He scribbled down what he could decipher: "Rob," then "ankle," followed by "for the night."

"Tracking One," Ralph said into the radio. "You're Ten-One." Unreadable. "Ten-Nine." Repeat.

Again the digital voice with only two clear words: "Other MisPers."

The radio was silent.

"Tracking One. Ten-One. Ten-Nine."

No response.

Ralph studied the words and numbers he had scrawled on the log. Not much. But for now apparently, it was all he was going to get.

# CHAPTER

# 25

**W**HERE *the hell is Cashman?*

It was after two o'clock in the morning. He had been gone for more than three hours.

Up the slope behind Gracie, Rob lay within the shelter, warm and, she assumed, sleeping.

As she waited for Cashman to return, she had wrapped herself in an emergency space blanket the thickness of a sheet of cheap paper and sat down with her back to a pine tree, knees pulled in to her chest. "I wish I had a rad-i-o," she whispered, tapping a syncopated rhythm with her feet. "Next time I'll keep the rad-i-o. Next time I'll bring my own."

Not that a radio would have been of the least bit use to her at the moment, but it was like a hard and heavy security blanket, offering succor even in times of canyons and dead spots and things that go bump in the night.

Gracie leaned back against the uncomfortable knobbly bark of the pine. She had turned off her headlamp, telling herself it was to save batteries and allow her eyes to grow accustomed to the dark, and not that sitting with her head-lamp turned on allowed anyone creeping about in the darkness to see her without being seen.

While she waited, she examined more fully what Rob had told her about seeing someone die and that someone had tried to kill him. Head injury often manifested itself in confusion of facts. But the combination of his story with the presence of blood on the outcropping was too serious to be ignored.

If a murder or accidental killing had occurred and Rob had been attacked, who had done it and where was that person now?

Could the group have met someone else on the trail? Gracie had read about hikers who had been murdered—gruesome, horrific murders. What if there was a psycho killer wandering around the wilderness area?

She looked around, eyes wide. She held her breath to listen, but the heavy *thud thud thud* of her heart overrode all other sound.

*Quit scaring yourself, dope. Take a deep breath.* She inhaled deeply, filling her lungs to capacity, then slowly blew it out.

The probability that someone was out there attacking innocent hikers was so remote as to be ludicrous. And besides, there had been no new tracks up on the trail. The only other option was that it was one of the hiking group itself. Who was the killer, Mr. X? Tristan? Tristan the Psycho Killer? She snorted out loud.

Had Tristan killed Joseph and then tried to kill Rob? Could Carlos have done it? Or Joseph?

And what about Cristina? Or Diana? Gracie had almost dismissed both women as the attacker out of hand. But since not considering either one simply because they were women seemed way too much like reverse sexism, she reconsidered both women as the potential killer.

From the description Gracie had received of Diana, she

knew the woman was only about five feet tall and weighed
less than a hundred pounds. Cristina was a string bean, taller
than Gracie by three inches, but weighing twenty pounds
less. Unless either woman was a black-belt in karate, chances
were pretty slim she had taken out Carlos, Tristan and/or
Joseph and then had tried to kill Rob.

Except if she—Ms. X—had a weapon of some kind—a
gun, even a knife. Any garden-variety kitchen knife was
a potential weapon. And guns were as easy to get in L.A
as . . . guns. A gun or knife would certainly tip the scales
in a woman's favor—or anyone's for that matter. If Rob had
no weapon with which to defend himself, he might have
had no choice but to run. And very possibly the only direction for him to run had been down.

Was the killing an accident? Or was it intentional?

Gracie decided there were too many possibilities of who
had done what to whom, accidentally or purposely, and
turned to what she should be thinking about, which was
where Mr. or Ms. X and the others might be.

Maybe she had missed something on the way down from
the trail. She had been so busy trying to keep from falling
on her face that she hadn't really been keeping much of any
eye out for clues or evidence of any kind. Maybe Mr. X was
hiding from them when they had come by. Maybe that
was why they hadn't found him.

What if Mr. X came down into the canyon looking for
Rob? What if he had seen her and Steve hiking the trail and
had been tracking the trackers? What if, at this very minute,
he was watching her, waiting for his chance to pounce?

Suddenly every sound of the night was a foot stepping
on a stick, every whisper of wind the brushing of fabric
against a branch, every shadow a man leering out from
behind a tree. Or bush. Or boulder.

Gracie wasn't law enforcement and so carried no firearm.
Ice axe. Crampons. Trekking poles. Any potential substantial weapon was strapped to her pack currently posing as

the shelter door. Gracie pulled up her jacket, ripped open the sheath attached to her belt and pulled out a four-inch hunting knife. Not that she had the slightest clue of what to do with a knife in a fight. And even if she did know, the thought of sticking it into someone's flesh made her skin crawl. Pretty much useless then, she decided, not quite sure whether she was referring to the knife or herself.

*I wish Ralphie were here*, she thought and immediately felt better, the thought of him acting as a balm on her frazzled psyche. "The ballast in my stupid-ass, rudderless life," she said out loud.

Gracie crashed back to earth, belatedly and with no small amount of guilt thinking of Cashman. He was out there somewhere actively looking for the MisPers. Maybe that was why he was late. Maybe Mr. X got him. Maybe at this very moment he was lying on his back with his throat cut, sightless eyes staring up at the—

*Quit! It!*

Cashman would be very hard to take out, Gracie assured herself. Plus the chances were slim that Mr. X would attack someone wearing Sheriff's Department patches on his neon orange parka and helmet.

A branch breaking on the hillside below sounded like a rifle shot in the dark. Adrenaline sizzled like a jolt of electricity all the way to Gracie's fingertips.

Someone was stealthily climbing up from the creek.

Gracie froze, her breathing shallow. She prayed that Rob would make no sound inside the shelter. The hand that gripped the knife's handle was slippery with sweat inside its glove.

Leaves rustled. A footstep. Then another. Closer.

She held her breath.

"Gracie?"

"Of course it's Cashman," she mumbled in disgust. "I have to quit reading those true-crime books."

"I'm here, Steve," she called in a stage whisper. She slid

the knife back into its sheath before Cashman could see it and wonder what she was doing. She would never live it down if he discovered she had thought he was Tristan, the Psycho Killer.

She switched on her headlamp so he could locate her. "Why aren't you using your headlamp?"

"Could see without it," he said in a perfunctory voice.

Hard to argue with that. Fear melted into irritation. "What took you so long?"

Ignoring Gracie's tone, Cashman dropped his pack onto the ground and plopped down next to her. "Didn't find nothin'. No other tracks. Reception pretty much sucked. Still windier'n hell up there. I radioed that we found Rob and are bivying for the night and I'll call in again in the a.m. Not sure it went through."

"Did you ask him to page out more teams?"

"Tried. Don't think he could hear me anyway. Where is he?" Gracie assumed he was talking about Rob since he glanced around, eyes homing in on the orange plastic. "Up there?"

Disturbed by the possibility that Ralph might not have received the request for additional teams, Gracie answered absently, "Yeah. Good enough for one night."

"Hell, yeah! Can't expect a Holiday Inn out here." Cashman pulled out a water bottle and tipped it back, gulping loudly.

"Rob told me why he left the trail," Gracie said.

He wiped his sleeve across his mouth. "Yeah?"

Gracie related what the actor had told her, along with her theory that while his story might be injury-induced, it, along with the blood on the outcropping, might be more than a coincidence, and that they needed to be careful. There might be someone out there looking for Rob and intending him, and by default the two of them, harm.

Cashman recapped his water bottle. "Don't buy it. He probably fell, got conked on the head and is seein' things."

He pushed himself to his feet and grabbed up his pack by a strap. "Too many slasher movies or whatever."

Leaving Gracie openmouthed, he stepped a half-dozen steps away to a relatively flat spot and pulled the bivy sack from his pack.

# CHAPTER

# 26

**M**ILOCEK sprang from the shadows at a crouched run. In seconds he covered the fifty feet from the edge of the trailhead parking lot to his car, an inconspicuous white Toyota Corolla specifically purchased to blend in among the countless other little white cars in Southern California.

The motor home and cars were parked in a line at one end of the parking lot. At the opposite end, a marked Sheriff's Department unit blocked the entrance. On his right sat a Suburban and white utility truck hooked up to a small travel trailer. Lettering and seals identified both vehicles as Search and Rescue. Generator-powered spotlights lit up that half of the parking lot like the Las Vegas Raceway. A yellow glow from inside the little trailer itself suggested someone inside.

Back at the outcropping Milocek had decided that inaction was his best course of action. If he stayed where he was, he could watch for Diana and the two searchers at once. He had been prepared to wait as long as it took.

But his body had finally betrayed him. His throat was so

parched he couldn't swallow, and his last urine output had been sparse, what little there was a dark, opaque yellow. He could feel his body growing weaker.

He needed water.

Without it, all other actions, all other decisions, were meaningless.

He had trotted down the trail the entire way to the trailhead.

Now Milocek squatted in the shadows next to his car. Lying inside on the passenger seat was a half-carton of cigarettes, a handful of Slim Jims, and a roll of peppermint Life Savers. The earthquake kit in the hatchback contained a blanket, several cans and packets of food, a penlight, and, most important, two gallon jugs of water.

He opened the driver's-side door. The interior light flared on. Sliding into the seat, he pulled the door toward him until he heard the soft click of the latch. The light blinked off.

# 27

**S**HIT. Hell. Dammit. Shit.

Gracie had been standing outside the makeshift shelter for fourteen minutes and twenty-seven seconds. The space blanket was doing almost nothing to keep her warm. Her teeth were clacking together at woodpecker speed and she was growing colder by the second.

The prospect of crawling into the tiny shelter and spending the night with Rob Christian—the very thought of which would make the average woman swoon—had rendered Gracie immobile with . . . She couldn't quite identify the emotion. Fear? Shell shock? What she finally settled on, much to her disgust, was teenage angst.

Five of the fourteen minutes she had spent chiding herself for not bringing a bivy sack—not even owning a bivy sack anymore, because someone on some search somewhere had borrowed hers and never returned it—and she had spent all of this year's SAR budget money on other necessities like her high-tech sleeping bag and titanium ice axe.

Yet unless she wanted to sit up all night propped against

a tree, freezing her rear end off, or bury herself in pine needles or burrow beneath some giant fallen log to stay warm, she was going to have to crawl inside the shelter to warm up.

She didn't move.

Against her will, her thoughts flitted back to Mr. X. To Tristan the Psycho Killer. Maybe he really had killed someone and tried to kill Rob. Maybe right now he was out there in the woods. Maybe he had slunk up behind her when she was dithering about whether to crawl into the shelter. Maybe at this very moment he was leering out at her from behind a tree.

Gracie dropped to her knees, hauled the pack aside, and wriggled into the shelter.

"Sorry to barge in on you like this," she whispered in case Rob was awake. "It's friggin' freezing out there."

Of course Rob was awake. With her every move, the space blanket crinkled as loudly as a candy wrapper in church.

Gracie replaced the pack in front of the doorway and lay down on her back, half of her body on the two-inch thick sleeping pad, the other half off.

"Well, this is about as comfortable as standing on my head in a rainstorm," she muttered.

"Do you want to share this sleeping bag thing?" Rob's voice sounded only inches from her ear, which, in actuality, he was.

"I'll be fine. Believe it or not, it's quite a bit warmer in here. And this is a warm parka. Thanks anyway."

But within minutes, she could feel the cold from the ground seeping in through her pants. Another few minutes and she was shivering audibly again.

"If somehow we could unzip this bag," Rob said, "then we could put it—"

"I'm fine."

"You're not fine. You're shivering. And I'm feeling a bit of a dick hogging—"

"Give it a rest! I'm fine!"

"Damn, woman. Are you always this bloody cheerful?"

"Quit calling me that!" she practically yelled back at him. "I am most decidedly not your *woman*. The name is Gracie. Grace. In fact, to you, it's Ms. Kinkaid."

It was quiet in the little shelter.

When Rob spoke again, his voice was calm and steady. "You're absolutely right, Ms. Kinkaid."

Was that a smile she heard in his voice?

She heaved a sigh. "Sorry. I get cranky when I—" *What? Am forced to sleep two inches away from a hunky movie star?* "I get cranky when I have to . . . overnight in the winter, I get cranky," she finished quickly and pulled the gap in the space blanket closed.

*Well, that was brilliant. If we had ham, we could have ham and eggs . . . if we had eggs.*

Boredom was the bane of a one-person Command Post. Ralph had learned from countless interminable nights running searches in the Command Post trailer that keeping his mind occupied between radio transmissions was the key to staying alert and awake.

As a result, he busied himself with minutiae, filling out ICS forms and organizing the Command Post trailer. For an hour, he segmented the map, making assignments for the relief teams due to arrive at 0700. He passed some of the time rereading the vehicle registration information Deputy Montoya had provided. Some of the RPs were still in the RV across the parking lot. Still drinking. Still bickering. Some had driven back down to the hotel in town.

Ralph's eyes burned from the wind stirring up something outside and his nerves jumped from the steady infusion of too-strong coffee. He flexed his right leg, trying to relieve the pain and stiffness in the joint. He had aggravated the old injury on a recent training. Plus, a drop in barometric pressure always made it ache more than usual.

As far as he knew, his search team was bedded down for the night. There was nothing else for him to do at the moment except monitor the radio and wait out the rest of the shift.

Still it rankled that he didn't know exactly where his search team was, especially Gracie.

He had been aware for several years that he was protective of Gracie. He wasn't sure why since she was tough, and more highly trained and experienced than the majority of the men on the team. Had he revealed his protectiveness to Gracie or anyone else on the team by an outstretched hand to help her across a wide gap between rocks, or an offer to carry a portion of her gear when she was tired, she would have been indignant, even outraged.

She worked hard to maintain the level of "one of the boys," more than pulling her own weight, expecting no special favors. In return, she expected only the same respect afforded her teammates possessing the Y chromosome.

Yet there was a vulnerability about her, a frailty hovering below the surface, carefully guarded, about which she had never spoken to him.

And why should she? Everyone had their secrets. Hell, Ralph certainly did.

He glanced at his watch. 0158. A little more than five hours until he needed to leave.

He drew the crumpled cigarette from the fold of his hat, spending an inordinate amount of time straightening it out.

Both Department and team rules prohibited smoking inside any Department building or vehicle. When he was alone in the Command Post was the only time Ralph could smoke uninterrupted and in peace during a search. So he did.

He mussed around in a side drawer of the desk, found the box of Strike Anywhere Matches he kept stashed there, and lit the cigarette. Cracking open the window nearest him, he blew a pencil of smoke in its general direction.

He balanced the cigarette on the edge of the desk and

stood up, arching his back and cracking his knuckles over his head. Ignoring the acid corroding his stomach, he poured himself another cup of stale coffee. He was going to regret it tomorrow. Hell, he already regretted it.

It was going to be a long goddam night.

# CHAPTER

# 29

THE neon green numbers of Gracie's watch read 3:11. She had slept all of four minutes. Now she was wide awake and shivering with her teeth clacking so loudly she was sure they could be heard all the way to Anaheim.

Get the blood moving. Do some isometrics.

Trying not to crackle the space blanket too loudly and awaken the man lying six inches away from her, she clenched every muscle in her body. Held it for two seconds. Three. Four. Five. Then released for two seconds. Three. Four. Five. Then clenched again. A little better. She could feel the warmth creeping through her body.

Rob's voice came sleepy and soft. "You still cold?"

"I'm f-f-fine. Sorry t-to wake you."

The unzipping of the sleeping bag within the confines of the shelter sounded as loud as a fire engine siren. "Get in the bag then. There's room enough."

"I'll b-be all right."

"You're freezing to death!" Nothing sleepy about the voice now.

"I just have to make it 'til it gets light."

"Quit being so pigheaded and get in the bag here."

"Fine then!"

"Fine!"

Gracie sat up and, with a maximum of rustling and wiggling, shed her parka and boots. "I'm not getting naked or anything, so don't get your hopes up."

"Pity," came the voice out of the darkness.

She patted her hand over to where she felt him holding the sleeping bag open, scooted over and slid her legs into the luxurious warmth. She lay down on her side, ramrod straight, as far away from Rob as she possibly could and still zip up the bag, which was only about a centimeter.

It had been a while, years, since Gracie had lain next to a man. She had forgotten how big they could be. Rob had looked large. She knew in reality he was only five or six inches taller than she was. But lying full-length beside the man made Gracie feel like Jill and the Beanstalk next to the giant.

"I have to put my arm—" Rob began.

"Fine."

The two lay together as cozy as newborn chicks in a nest.

Gracie detected a hint of cologne. Or maybe it was aftershave. Couldn't quite identify the scent. It had been a while. Nice though.

*Quit it!*

She realized that her body was as taut as a climbing rope under load. *I'll never sleep. And I can't move. At least I'm warm.*

She exhaled slowly, trying to release the tension in her body.

Rob moved his leg.

"I don't care if you are hurt," she hissed. "You try anything and I'll punch your lights out."

"Petrified." He sighed, his breath tickling the back of her neck.

Gracie was toasty within two minutes, and, in spite of the fact that a killer might be lurking out there in the darkness, she was dead to the world within three.

# CHAPTER

# 30

**MILOCEK** squatted on the trail across from the rock out-cropping.

He knew daylight was coming by an almost impercep-tible lifting of the darkness that half an hour before had been absolute. It was more humid than the previous day, the damp chill burrowing through his multiple layers of clothing, the moisture drawing out the rich, full scents of the surrounding evergreens and shrubs.

For more than five hours, Milocek had waited in the dark, listening, smoking, sucking on peppermint Life Savers, even dozing. But he heard and saw no one.

The water had rejuvenated him. And, as far as he could discern, the time spent traveling to his car had cost him nothing. And he had gained valuable information. No alarms had yet been raised. No manhunt begun. No dogs barking. No glaring searchlights.

He pushed himself to his feet and stretched his arms above his head to keep the blood flowing to his fingers and toes. As a young man, he could remain motionless for hours, then rise to strike, unaffected by the immobility.

But in that regard, time had also taken its toll. A single hour was the longest he could last without moving.

His dry lips pulled back into a smirk. Still, he thought, not bad for an old man.

Milocek squatted back down and waited for the darkness to lift.

# CHAPTER
# 31

**G**RACIE snapped fully awake with the comprehension that she was lying on her back with her cheek molded up against Rob's scratchy, but deliciously warm neck. His arm was draped around her as naturally and comfortably as if they were longtime lovers.

Crap.

Gracie wormed away to scrutinize the man with whom she had just spent the night.

If Rob had awakened at that moment, he would have caught Gracie with her mouth hanging open like a large-mouthed bass. Even in the dim early-morning light within the orange plastic shelter, and beneath twenty-four-hours' worth of beard and a disguise of grime and scratches, Rob Christian was the most beautiful man she had ever seen.

In Gracie's opinion, God's biggest mistake was bestowing upon men eyelashes for which any red-blooded female would commit first-degree murder. Rob's were so dark and thick and long, Elizabeth Taylor would have been snap-pea green with envy. Dark, heavy eyebrows slashed a straight, thick line across his forehead, then tapered downward at the temples. Straight nose sloped off at the tip. Lips curved upward at the corners like a cupid's bow. Hair, which apparently had been dyed from blond to black for the movie, curled out from beneath her own forest-green fleece cap. The dirt-smudged hand that was visible looked strong, but expertly manicured and smooth, as if it hadn't done anything more taxing lately than lift a glass of Beaujolais.

She wondered what color his eyes were. The night before it had been too dark to tell. Somewhere in a pocket of her parka was her notebook with notes of Rob's physical description. And it was on the LPQ. That's the kind of thing she should remember. Maybe she could—

What the *hell* was she doing?

He was a screen idol. He was supposed to be good looking. Plus he was nothing but a big baby. From the *city*. And he called her *woman*. What was that all about? Anyway, she was the rescuer. He was the victim. She was supposed to remain detached. Professional. Aloof.

Holding her breath, Gracie plucked at his sleeve with two fingers and moved his hand off her body.

That task accomplished, her breathing resumed. Her next thoughts were that she was warm, but stiff and sore from the previous evening's foray into the canyon and sleeping on the ground in one position, followed by the realization that her bladder was fair to bursting.

Gracie lay contemplating the unpleasant proposition of leaving the warmth of the sleeping bag and, she was loathe to admit, the British Adonis who slept beside her and going outside into the chill of early morning.

*Hmm, let's see. Snuggling up to a hunky warm body? Or exposing my bare butt to the cold? Tough choice.*

She stayed where she was, listening to Rob's steady breathing and reveling in the warmth until she decided she'd better not stall any longer or by the time she actually exited the shelter it would be too late.

It took what seemed like infinity to unzip the sleeping bag one tooth at a time. Then millimeter by millimeter she wiggled her way out of the warm cocoon, no mean feat since every joint in her body felt as creaky as the tin man's in need of a couple of good squirts of oil.

She crawled to the entrance, silently lifted her pack aside, and poked her head outside the shelter.

Oh. Shit.

An opaque veil of cloud enshrouded the entire mountainside, so thick that particles of moisture hung visibly in the air. Gracie could see nothing of the surrounding trees, boulders, or mountains. She could barely even see Cashman, still sleeping in his bivy sack a few yards away.

She inhaled deeply, filling her lungs and senses with the heady scent of wet evergreen, then exhaled a long, slow breath of white vapor.

A moan floated up behind her.

Gracie looked back over her shoulder at Rob, who was sitting up and scratching his cheek. Not a vision. Not a demigod. Just a normal man doing what men do when they wake up stiff and sore the morning after a nasty fall and a night sleeping on the hard ground.

Gracie sat back on her heels so he wouldn't be overwhelmed by her Gore-Tex-covered bottom staring him in the face. "How are you feeling?" she asked.

In a voice slurred with sleep, Rob answered, "Like I've been rode hard and put up wet."

"I'm not touching that one with a ten-foot avalanche probe," Gracie said and was thoroughly charmed to see, even in the dim light, a blush creep up his cheeks.

"Line from one of my movies," he said. "Bit of a habit, I'm afraid."

"Ah," she said.

"Actually I'm feeling better than I would have expected," he added. "Still have a bugger of a headache though."

"How's the ankle?"

"Throbs a bit. Tolerable if I don't move it."

With an understandable amount of groaning punctuated with "sodding this" and "bleeding that," he crawled over and plopped on his stomach beside Gracie to look outside.

"We're in a bloody fog!"

"Actually it's cloud," she said, noting his eyes were large and bright and a dark brown so piercing and intense she felt as if they wouldn't simply look at her, but see right through into her soul.

She scootched herself back inside the shelter to pull on her parka and boots.

## CHAPTER

# 32

"**D**AMMIT!" Ralph checked his watch, then the Command Post clock, confirming it was 0627.

His search team hadn't called in. He would expect this of Cashman, blundering baboon that he was. But Gracie was as reliable as Old Faithful.

Ralph could count on one hand the number of people currently on Timber Creek's SAR team whom he considered truly competent. Grace Kinkaid was one of those people.

Steve Cashman was another story. The man was a screw-up with something to prove. That made him unpredictable. And dangerous.

Anything could happen with Cashman, and Ralph didn't like it that Gracie was alone in the field with him and out of radio communication for so long.

The inside of Ralph's eyelids felt like 40-grit sandpaper. The year-old chocolate-chip granola bar he had washed down with cold, bitter coffee still sat in his stomach as a lead brick in an acid bath. His patience had drained away along with the hours of the cold, solitary night and now stood at low tide. At the same time, his anxiety for Gracie had increased until now it felt like a pair of fists slowly twisting his gut. His surly mood had intensified when it had grown light enough for him to realize the entire mountain was enshrouded in cloud so thick he couldn't see the motor home parked across the parking lot.

The weather translated to no aviation. Any injury to the MisPers would necessitate a litter carry-out. Relief personnel due at 0700 would arrive chomping at the bit to be deployed into the field.

Except Ralph had no idea where to send them.

"Come on, Cashman!" He glared at the radio as if it were an animate object intentionally withholding information. "Why the hell haven't you radioed in?"

I took several seconds for Diana to realize that her eyes were open and that the reason she wasn't seeing anything was because there was nothing to see. No trees towering overhead. No green, rounded bushes. No gargantuan boulders. Only an impenetrable wall of cloud.

There was no sound but that of her own breathing.

It was as if, sometime during the interminable night, she had been entombed in a shifting white sepulcher.

Her hips and shoulders felt bruised from lying on the hard ground. She had slept only in fits and starts and was exhausted to the marrow.

Her water bottle was empty. She hadn't eaten since lunch the day before, yet the thought of food nauseated her.

She considered trying to walk out again, but the thought of Milocek out there looking for her pinned her to the ground.

She would stay where she was, encapsulated within the cloud.

Eventually someone would come for her. Surely help would come.

# CHAPTER

# 34

To answer the call of nature, Gracie clambered over rocks and tree trunks to a reasonable distance between her and the shelter.

Baring her backside to the elements in below-freezing temperatures didn't bother her. It was simply what one had to do if the urge was great enough. It was, however, a major pain to get up in the middle of the night and put on one's boots to walk what hygiene, courtesy, and modesty, in that order, determined was a reasonable distance from the sleeping area to tend to normal body functions. Peeing in a strong wind or driving rain was the worst. Gracie envied the physical strength that most men seemed to take for granted, but peeing outside in inclement weather was the only time Gracie truly regretted not being male.

Back at the bivouac, with Cashman still snoring inside his bivy sack, Gracie crouched a few feet from the shelter and fired up her little Dragonfly stove to brew up a nice cup o' tea for the British gentleman who, judging from the noises emanating from within the orange plastic, was due to make an appearance at any moment.

Moving around had worked the stiffness out of her joints, and, in spite of minimal sleep, Gracie felt well rested. While the threat from ghoulies and ghosties hadn't totally vanished with the night, it had dissipated, pushing into the realm of the improbable that someone had been killed the day before, that Rob had been attacked, and that someone was actually out there intending them all harm. By the light of day, muted as it was, everything she had thought and felt the night before all seemed so melodramatic.

Gracie sat on the square of insulated foam, waiting for the water in her canteen cup to heat and anticipating with dread her next encounter with the Englishman.

Seized with a surge of self-consciousness, she yanked off her gloves and beanie and combed through her unruly hair with her fingers.

Her hair had always been thick and wavy and, as a result, totally unmanageable. It made women with thin, limp hair jealous and men want to run their fingers through it. But, ever since she could remember she had thought it a royal pain. She kept it long not because of its attraction to men, but in spite of it. By braiding her hair or clipping it up, it actually took her less time than with short hair to look halfway decent in general and not have "helmet head" after a search.

Gracie had only half completed a rough French braid when Rob appeared in the shelter doorway, looking around him, hands tucked under his armpits for warmth. "It's cold."

"It is that," she said, tying off the braid with the elastic, although, in her estimation, the temperature wasn't much lower than about forty-five degrees.

"May I?" He gestured to her trekking poles still clipped to the outside of her pack.

"Be my guest. You sure you want to be up and about?" she asked, eyes riveted on the little bubbles drifting up through the heated water to the surface. "I'd be happy to bring you a hot cup of tea. Water's almost hot."

"I have to piss like a racehorse." When she looked over at him, he reddened. "Sorry."

Gracie shrugged. "That's a good thing. Means you're not dehydrated anymore."

"I don't usually swear around women," he said, fiddling with one of the trekking poles. "Somehow with you, though, it feels like one of the boys."

"Ouch."

"Hang on. That's not what I meant. How does this thing work?"

"Untwist it, pull it out to length, then twist it back to tighten it. There are two joints."

With more dexterity than Gracie had the first time she messed with the poles, Rob set the pole to maximum length.

"This strong enough to hold me?" he asked.

"It's titanium."

He shot her a look that said that wasn't much of an answer, then used both hands on the pole to pull himself upright.

Gracie noticed that as Rob stood up, he was careful not to let even the big toe of his injured foot brush the ground. They were definitely not hiking out. "Would you like some privacy?" she asked.

"Stay put," Rob said and hobbled around the side of the shelter, leaning heavily on the pole.

As Rob stood with his back to her and watered a large manzanita, Gracie openly admired his wide shoulders and narrow hips. On the previous night, she had seen in the blinding snapshot of his nakedness—which she knew would be forever embedded in her brain—that his long-limbed body was well-muscled without an ounce of fat. She wondered what he did to get a body like that. And what movies he had been in. For the first time in her life, she wished she had read some of those vacuous celebrity magazines in her dentist's lobby. But who knew?

Rob turned around and limped toward her. Gracie noticed that, even injured, he moved with the fluidity of a big cat. A tiger. No, a panther. She swatted at her face to drive the thoughts away.

After some gentlemanly resistance, Rob accepted the proffered insulated pad. With much maneuvering to protect his ankle, he sat down on the ground not far from Gracie.

Even in the stark light of day, such as it was, the overall grime and the deep shadows beneath Rob's eyes did nothing to diminish his excruciating good looks. If anything, the cold air rendered him even more handsome, giving his cheeks a ruddiness that, much to her chagrin, Gracie was finding enormously appealing.

She tractor-pulled herself back to reality. She dipped and redipped the two-year-old tea bag, concentrating on the burnt sienna tannin swirling into the steaming water, hyper-aware of the man sitting silently a few feet away.

As if of their own volition, her eyes lifted and met Rob's.

The actor sat with head tilted slightly, a quizzical look on his face, eyes focused directly on her, intent, studying.

Gracie's hands trembled. Instantly she felt clumsy, awkward, every movement clunky, unnatural. In a flash, her nose was longer than Pinocchio's. Her breasts were the size of hen's eggs. Her bottom was a beach ball stuffed down the back of her pants. She found herself desperately wishing that, instead of all those new Search and Rescue toys, she had spent some of her carefully hoarded money on getting her teeth whitened or a decent haircut instead of hacking at it herself.

Defiance muscled the discomfiture aside and she lifted her chin. "What are you looking at?"

"You," he said. His voice was calm, unaffected by the intimated challenge. "I'm not looking really. Rather . . . observing."

The defiance dissolved as quickly as snowflakes in the sun. "I wish you wouldn't," Gracie said, dropping her eyes again.

"Why not? I thought women liked being looked at."

"I don't." To cover up the abruptness of her remark and bridge the resulting silence, she announced, "Tea's ready," as gaily as if they were sitting in some snug little kitchen in the Cotswolds. She poured the tea into his cup and handed it to him, concentrating on holding the cup steady. "It's really hot. You might want to let it cool a bit."

Gracie moved over to a flat-topped boulder a safe distance away from Rob to enjoy her own spot of tea. As she blew on the hot liquid, she tried to imagine objectively what someone—what Rob—was seeing when he looked at her. Five-foot-eight. Reasonably slender, although not by fashion-runway standards. Any flagrant lumps and bulges blessedly disguised beneath layers of fleece and Gore-Tex. Dark auburn hair sloppily braided and topped off by the highly attractive fleece beanie with the flaps pulled down over her ears. Hazel eyes. A little mascara probably wouldn't have hurt, but who the hell wore makeup on a search?

Imagining what Rob saw was easy. Knowing what he thought about it was an entirely different matter. Surely nothing noteworthy when compared to leading ladies of Hollywood or London. Her entire summation of her positive physical attributes had taken no more than ten seconds. She concluded that no way, even on a good day, could she measure up, much less after twelve hours in the field, including a night in a cramped makeshift shelter.

"Not only are you not in the playing field, sweet pea," she whispered to herself, "you can't even see the parking lot." Her eyes flicked over to Rob, then back to the tea. "So what do people call you?" she asked. "What should I call you? Mr. Christian? Fletcher?" She faked a silent laugh. "I crack myself up."

When he didn't respond, she said, "That was supposed to be a joke. You know, a joke? Not that it even resembled one."

She didn't dare look at him. She knew he was still watching her.

When he did finally answer, his voice was mild. "I asked you to call me Rob."

"Yah. Right." Her cheeks felt hot, which meant they and her entire neck was bright red. "How could I have forgotten that?" Her voice trailed off.

"What do people call you?" Rob asked.

"Grace. My friends call me Gracie."

"That's a beautiful name. Grace."

Gracie snorted.

"Why the snort?"

"One of the reasons my parents named me that was they were hoping I would turn into a clone of my sister. Life is full of disappointments."

"Why do you say that?"

"Instead of gorgeous, smart, law degree, they got a tomboy with zero brakes for the brain-speech connection. When I was little, my mother washed my mouth out with soap so many times I became quite the connoisseur of brands."

Rob's mouth twitched.

"I always preferred the taste of Ivory to Dial." He chuckled. "So what did you do to warrant such extreme retribution?"

She mentally sifted back through the myriad examples. "One of the most memorable occasions was when I was ten, I told my squirrelly faced teacher to kiss my ass."

Rob's face lit up like sunshine on aspen leaves, eyes bright, teeth white and perfect. He threw back his head and laughed out loud.

It was the first time Gracie had really seen him smile, much less laugh.

So this is what all the fuss was about.

Rob took a sip of tea. His face scrunched up as if he had bitten into a sour pickle. He spat out the mouthful and dumped the entire cup onto the ground.

Gracie sat up with indignation. "Hey!"

"What the hell was that?"

"It's tea."

"That's supposed to be tea?"

"What the hell! This isn't some Notting Hill café, you know. If you don't want to drink it, then . . . too bad. It's all you're going to get."

"Right then," Rob said. Lips pursed, he looked around while nodding his head several times.

"The British and their friggin' tea," Gracie grumped under her breath.

Rob held his cup out toward Gracie. "Got any more of that delicious concoction? That . . . tea?"

She stood up, snatched the cup from him, refilled it with the steaming liquid, and handed it back to him.

He looked at the cup in his hand. "Don't suppose you've got any milk around here."

Gracie glowered at him.

"Didn't think so." He blew on the tea, then took a sip, this time swallowing it with visible effort. "The purtier the gal, the worse coffee she makes," he muttered with an exaggerated drawl, then aloud he said, "Thank you for the tea. It's excellent. Nectar of the gods."

"Oh, shut up," Gracie said.

"I don't give a fat rat's ass about your protocol," a man's voice yelled from directly outside the Command Post trailer. "I want more manpower out there and I want it now."

Through the CP's paper-thin walls, Ralph could hear the angry voice as clearly as if the man were standing right next to him. He leaned over in his chair to peek out through a slit in the yellow gingham window curtains.

At the foot of the trailer steps, two men stood face-to-face only two feet apart: Sergeant Ron Gardner and Miles Kleinman.

Gardner had arrived on-scene a few minutes earlier and received a lightning briefing of the search from Ralph. He had dropped off the printed results of the various searches Deputy Montoya had run on the MisPers the night before, information that Ralph was studying when Miles Kleinman had blown into the parking lot in a canary yellow Corvette and introduced himself as one of the movie's executive producers. The man was dressed for an Antarctic expedition in knee-length parka with fur-lined hood and Sorel boots. A young woman whom Ralph assumed was a production assistant of some kind stood several feet back from the pair, looking bleary eyed and hugging a manila envelope to her chest.

Ralph noted that Kleinman appeared not the least bit cowed by Gardner, who stood a full twelve inches taller and outweighed him by at least seventy-five pounds. It amused him that the Sergeant for once was having to take the shit while someone else dished it out. "Herr Kleinman," Ralph said to himself, "you've got balls."

"We believe our search team located Mr. Christian last night," Gardner said. "They overnighted in the field and are bringing him out this morning."

"A team?" Kleinman interjected. "How many men on a team?"

"Two," Gardner answered.

"Two! What the—!"

"Mr. Christian is with one of our most experienced members. Grace Kinkaid is—"

"He's with a goddammed woman out there?"

Gardner took a step closer and looked down on the man. "Mr. Kleinman, Ms. Kinkaid is one of the most competent members on this team. Or anywhere. If anyone can keep your man safe, she can."

The muscles around Ralph's mouth twitched. If only Gracie could hear this. Gardner was actually defending her.

Kleinman waved a ski-gloved finger inches from Gardner's nose. "I want more manpower out there. I want him brought in and I want him brought in now. I don't give a good goddam what it costs!" He spun around and stalked across the parking lot.

The assistant timidly stretched out the manila envelope toward Gardner, who snatched it out of her hands. She hurried across the parking lot in Kleinman's wake. Gardner turned toward the Command Post.

"Here it comes," Ralph said to himself as he let the curtain drift back into place. He was already standing when the trailer door banged open and Gardner climbed in, dwarfing the tiny trailer. He smacked the manila envelope on the metal desk. "Personnel records," he said. "Have they radioed in yet?"

"Negative," he said. "I'm expecting them to call in at any minute."

"Goddammit! What the hell are they doing out there?" An artery pulsed visibly at the man's temple. "Call V Forces and get more teams up here."

"Teams should be rolling on-scene anytime now."

"I want a county-wide page out," Gardner said. "Saturate the field. I want teams crawling over every inch of this goddam mountain until this guy walks through the front door of the SO."

Ralph felt his blood pressure inching higher. He despised the "do something even if it's wrong," mentality, especially when it needlessly endangered lives. The worthless expenditure of manpower and money was for two things only: public relations and Gardner covering his own ass.

Gardner grabbed the door handle in his ham-hock fist. "And close down this rattletrap. It's an embarrassment to the Department. V Forces will bring a real Command Post up to Sandy Flats."

He pulled the door open, and said in a parting shot over his shoulder, "How the hell did we end up with a screw-up like Kinkaid in the field on this one?" In a perfect imitation of Cashman, he left, slamming the door behind him.

Ralph checked the clock still swaying on its nail. 0655.

As soon as the replacement Incident Commander arrived and Ralph briefed him on the operation, he would have to leave. He was tempted to cancel the appointment and work another shift. He hated leaving the CP with teams in the field. He simply didn't trust anyone else to look out for them, especially with the search ballooning into a full-fledged county-wide operation.

But he had no choice. His prescription had run out and his cardiologist wouldn't renew it without an office visit. He would have just enough time to drive home, shower and shave, then drive down the hill. Barring an unforeseen delay, he should be able to return to the Command Post by mid- to late-afternoon.

He lifted the radio to his mouth. "Control. Command Post."

# CHAPTER
# 36

**G**RACIE knelt on the ground, wiping both of her metal cups clean of the tea. "So have you been able to remember anything else of what happened up on the trail?" she asked Rob, who sat leaning up against a boulder, eyes following Gracie's every move in a way she was getting used to, but still found intensely perturbing. "Or how you became separated from everyone else? Or where they might be now?"

"I've tried," Rob answered. "Believe me. But I can't remember a thing. Makes me wonder whether I didn't dream it. The bit about the blood. And the person lying on the ground. Hallucination or something."

"Sometimes happens with head injuries," Gracie said, choosing not to mention the fact that she had seen the blood with her own eyes.

"Don't mention it to anyone, please. Publicity and all that."

"Not a word."

Rob lifted his eyes skyward. "So what does this mean? This fog or whatever it is?"

"Cloud."

"Cloud then."

"First off," Gracie said, setting the cups aside and sitting cross-legged on the ground, "it means no aviation. No helicopter evacuation. At least not until the sky clears. And it looks like your ankle is bad enough that we're not hiking out. They'll most likely send in a relief team and litter you out . . . carry you out on a litter, a stretcher."

"Humiliating. How long will that take—the relief team?"

"Hard to say. A team should have already been called in. They have to hike in, package you—"

"Package me?"

"Secure you in the litter. Then carry you out. Best guesstimate? They should have you back to the CP by midafternoon. Maybe. Hard to say exactly when."

"Late afternoon! Bloody-blast-it-all-to-hell!"

Gracie leaned back on her heels and watched Rob warily. She relaxed again when the explosion tapered off to a muttered string of obscenities. Rob pulled off his cap, scratched his head, which made his hair stand up in little spikes, then pulled the cap back on. He looked up at Gracie, saw the look on her face and said, "Sorry. Sorry." He blew out a breath. "It's just that I *have* to get out of here. I'm supposed to fly out of LAX this evening. My sister's getting married. I'm giving the bride away."

"You may not make your plane."

"It's my own damned fault," he said with vehemence. "Where is this . . . Command Post, did you call it?"

"Trailhead parking lot."

"And who will be there?"

"You mean aside from all the reporters that are probably camped out there by now?"

"The media is there? Effing hell! Just shoot me now." He pressed the heel of his hand to his forehead.

Gracie made the effortless leap into caregiver mode and noted that beneath the pink cheeks Rob's pallor resembled homemade flour paste. "Take it easy," she said. "Try not to get yourself worked up. It's possible they're not allowed up there, in which case they're all still back at the SO—the Sheriff's Office—in town."

Rob looked not at all placated.

Gracie could empathize somewhat with the man's distress. She despised the media, the constitutional right to free speech and the public's right to know notwithstanding. Whenever reporters appeared at a search, they were an unwanted distraction. The vans. The cameras. The lights. The incessant prying and prodding. And even when they were spoon-fed details from a search, nine times out of ten they got it wrong.

She shuddered at the thought of them focusing their microscopes on her and her life. She couldn't begin to imagine what it was like for any kind of celebrity, and decided that in that area Rob most decidedly received her sympathy vote.

"How far are we, right now, from the . . . Command Post?" Rob asked suddenly.

Gracie mentally calculated the distance. "Four miles. Maybe five. I'd have to check the map for an exact distance."

"Five? That's all? I can walk five miles." He grabbed the trekking pole. "I'm walking out."

"Hmm," Gracie said, watching him carefully. "I don't think you'll be able to with that ankle."

"Well, I have to try, don't I?" He pulled himself to stand on one foot, then swayed, almost falling.

"Whoa!" Gracie jumped up to catch him in case he toppled over. "You better sit down before you fall down."

Rob obediently sat down, looking more ashen still.

"We're going try to get you out of here as quickly as we can. I promise." She pushed her sleeves back to check her watch: 7:08. They should have called in to the Command Post an hour ago.

She looked around for the radio, then remembered that

Cashman had it, probably inside his sleeping bag to keep it dry and the batteries warm. Her eyes wandered over to where her teammate lay a few feet away, silent and unmoving, encased within his army-green bivy sack.

He looks like a big fat zucchini, Gracie thought and fought off the urge to prod him with her toe.

She stood up abruptly, hands on her hips.

"What's going on?" Rob asked.

"We need to call in," she answered distractedly. "Steve has the radio." She stepped down to where the man lay. "Cashman. Wake up."

Not a twitch from the bivy sack.

She leaned directly over him. "Cashman. Get up."

Still no response.

"Cashman," she yelled in a shrill voice reminiscent of her ninth-grade algebra teacher. "Eeesh." She tried again in a normal tone. "Cashman, you have the radio and we're late checking in with the CP. Cashman!"

With an enthusiasm too fully charged for him to have just awakened, Cashman unzipped his bivy and popped out his head. Ignoring Gracie completely, his eyes sought out the actor on the hillside above him. "'Morning, Rob."

Rob lifted a hand and smiled. "Good morning."

*How long have you been awake?*

Cashman sat up and kicked out of his sleeping bag. He produced his hiking boots from inside the bivy and pulled them on. "You survived the night," he said to Rob, then guffawed loudly at what he obviously thought was a great joke.

"Thanks to Gracie," came Rob's casual reply.

When Gracie looked over at the actor, he winked at her.

Gracie felt her cheeks flame. "We need to radio the CP, Steve," she croaked. "Rob's stable enough. I can take my turn and hike up to radio in."

# 37

**G**RACIE collapsed full-length onto the ground next to where Cashman was crouched sipping coffee. "Nothing," she said, panting. "No reception."

Since they hadn't been able to raise the CP from anywhere near where they had left the trail, she and Cashman had studied the topo map and decided to take a calculated gamble in order to save time. Instead of climbing all the way back up to the trail, Gracie would climb the shorter, presumably faster, distance up the mountain directly behind them to try to acquire a radio signal.

Before she set out, she and Rob had set a world's record for fastest breakfast consumed mainly because throughout, Cashman stood over Rob bragging about how he never got cold and that he could hike faster and farther than anyone else on the team. Rob gulped down his instant apple-and-cinnamon oatmeal, then politely announced, "I'm knackered. I think I'll lie down for a bit," and withdrew into the shelter.

Equipping herself for expeditious travel, Gracie left her SAR pack behind, taking only her chest pack with the HT

fastened to one strap and her GPS to the other, a minimal
amount of survival gear, a full water bottle and a single
trekking pole. She headed straight up from the shelter and
was instantly swallowed up by beckoning wisps of cloud.

With visibility at ten feet, sometimes less, Gracie climbed
the mountain blind.

She tested for radio reception at regular intervals. The
telltale wonk of the radio grew more obnoxious with every
failed attempt.

She scrambled up the incline, hauling herself up by a
branch to gain ten feet, clawing at the earth with both hands
to scramble up fifty, then a hundred, two hundred, only to
find the way completely blocked by boulder piles or fallen
trees materializing out of the mist. Each time she fought
back her mounting frustration, sliding back down far enough
to circumvent the obstacle, then clambering back up to
regain the distance lost and plod on. Each breath seared her
lungs. Leg muscles quivered. Hair clung like damp yarn to
her forehead and neck.

She stopped and pulled out her GPS to reassure herself
once again that it was tracking her route so when she
descended in the cloud, she could retrace her steps and find
her way back to the bivouac.

She pulled the map from her pocket and pinpointed her
location, confirming what the altimeter on her watch told
her—she had climbed more than twelve hundred vertical
feet and now stood higher than the trail across the yawning
canyon, invisible in the pearl gray sea of cloud.

She turned on the radio. Still no signal. And the battery
was almost dead. She turned it off again.

She studied the op art of contour lines on the map. In the
area above where she stood, the lines grew more densely
packed together, indicating the mountain grew steeper and
even more treacherous farther up.

As a last resort, she pulled out her cell phone and turned
it on. No little bars indicated reception, but no message

announced "No signal" either. She pressed 911 and waited. Nothing. She moved ten feet in every direction, each time with the same discouraging result. No signal.

"Shit! *Shit!*"

They had made the wrong call. She should have climbed back up to the trail again and hiked to where they knew there was reception. The fact that hindsight was always twenty-twenty provided her not one ounce of comfort.

She glanced again at her watch. It had taken her an hour to climb up from the bivouac. It would take at least half that to descend. The miscall would cost them more than ninety minutes.

Ralph would be apoplectic that she hadn't radioed in. The brunt of his wrath would fall on her shoulders—that was a given. She wasn't the designated team leader, but seniority and experience made it her responsibility. Making the wrong decision and not calling in on time was egregious. Even worse, relief teams might already be out looking for the other MisPers. Her miscalculation could cost someone his or her life.

"Sorry, Ralphie," she said, unable to shake the feeling that she had let him down personally. "Well, absolutely nothing to be accomplished by sitting here sniveling . . . um, blubbering . . . uh, wringing your hands . . ." Since she couldn't think of a single other synonymic phrase with which to waste a little more time, she stashed the phone and map back into her pocket and started back down the mountain.


**CASHMAN LEANED BACK** on an elbow and crossed one well-muscled leg over the other. "So the CP still doesn't know where we are."

Gracie pressed her forehead to her knees. "I should have gone up to the trail."

"So if any relief teams are out there—"

"They're searching blind."

"They could search for hours before they found us. Fuckin' *if* they found us."

"Gee, thanks, Cashman," she said. "Push the knife in a little deeper." She stared at the ground, biting her lip. "Let's think this through. Rob can't hike out. Aviation can't fly in. We go much longer without contacting the CP and the search for the MisPers will shift to a search for us, and I really don't want that to happen. Plus, the longer relief teams are out there looking for us, the higher the risk to them."

"I'll hike up to the trail again," Cashman offered. "Call in. Lead the relief team in."

As much as Gracie loathed the idea, that was exactly what they were going to have to do.

Gracie hated breaking the rules. She was secretly proud of her reputation on the team for adhering to regulations and procedures, or, as she liked to put it, for "dotting her t's and crossing her eyes." But when emergencies or situational anomalies occurred, flexibility was an asset. Rules needed to be broken or at least bent a little in order to problem solve. If they had to separate again, then so be it.

Cashman pushed a little harder. "I'm the faster hiker. I can get help here quicker."

Before Gracie could respond, he jumped up and flicked away the dregs of his coffee. He hauled his sleeping bag out of the bivy sack and began mashing it into its own little stuff sack.

"Don't hike all the way back to the CP," Gracie said as she watched him pull the drawstrings tight. "Just hike as far as it takes to get a signal."

Cashman stuffed his bivy into its sausage-shaped sack.

"Cashman? Are you hearing what I'm saying?"

"Yeah, yeah."

For some reason, Gracie didn't believe him. "Just call in the coordinates."

"Gotcha."

Gracie watched Cashman pack together the rest of his gear. She hadn't liked it last night when he had taken the radio with him. She definitely didn't like it now.

The specter of an unknown attacker out there somewhere reemerged. Gossamer fingers of unease tickled the back of her neck. "I've got a bad feeling about this, Cashman," she said.

"It'll be fine," Steve replied so flippantly Gracie knew he was blowing her off.

Her mind reached back to an avalanche class she had taken the winter before last where her male instructor had emphatically drilled into their brains that proportionately far more men died in avalanches than women, mainly because women tended to listen to those still, small internal voices when they whispered, "Are you out of your fucking mind?!"

Gracie pushed herself to her feet. "Maybe we're rushing this a bit," she said. "Let's think this through some more. What are our other options?"

"There aren't no other options," Cashman said. "You'll be okay 'til I get back."

Ignoring the condescension, she asked, "Will you leave me your sleeping bag?"

Cashman's face told her that was the last thing in the entire world he wanted to do.

"Never mind," she said. "Bad idea. How about your sleeping pad at least?"

No answer.

"C'mon, Cashman. It's only for a couple of hours. You won't need it. We'll be stationary. You'll be moving." She felt like she was asking a ten-year-old if she could ride his new shiny red Schwinn. "You'll get it back. Cross my heart and hope to die."

Cashman thought for a moment, then made a big show of unclipping the roll of closed-cell foam from his pack and tossing it at her feet. The sleeping bag landed next to the foam. "Rob can use this, too," he said, the implication obvious. He clipped the top of the pack closed and threw it onto his back, cinching up all the belts. With no further word, he turned away from her and started down the hill.

"Cashman," Gracie called.

He paused and looked over his shoulder.

"Keep an eye out for any sign of the others," she said in a low voice. "And don't take any chances, okay?"

He gave her a thumbs-up.

With no small amount of trepidation, Gracie watched her teammate disappear into the cloud.

# CHAPTER

## 38

**M**ILOCEK squatted next to the trail.

When daylight had finally crept across the valley, he found he could see nothing outside a ten-foot radius. An oppressive, suffocating white wall of cloud curled and writhed around him like a living being in agony.

But as the day progressed, the cloud had gradually lifted, allowing occasional glimpses of the granite walls cutting steeply upward behind him and, in front, falling away in a precipitous quarter mile of jagged boulders, evergreens and manzanita.

Diana was somewhere up the trail. Rob and the searchers were somewhere down below him in the canyon. Sooner or later one or all of them would appear. His patience would pay off. He was certain of it.

Milocek froze.

Dried leaves crackling. Footfalls on rocky ground. Someone was climbing up to the trail from down in canyon.

Without a sound, Milocek jumped to the ground and

crouched behind the boulder. With a single eye he peered out from behind the rock and watched as the male searcher climbed up over the edge and stepped out onto the trail.

GRACIE sat cross-legged at the shelter entrance staring out at the pea soup that was the world outside through a small gap between the orange plastic and her pack.

Behind her, Rob lay inside Cashman's sleeping bag, which Gracie had magnanimously offered him since the thought of climbing inside her teammate's bag gave her the willies. Rob didn't seem to care one way or the other as long as the bag was warm. Gracie had turned off the lantern flashlight to save batteries and to make it easier for Rob to get as much sleep as possible. Although she couldn't see clearly into the murk at the back of the shelter, she was fairly certain from the actor's measured breathing that he was sleeping.

As Gracie waited for Cashman to return with the relief team, she blew bubbles with her gum and brooded over what might have happened with Rob and the other missing persons. There were a few things she knew definitively. There was blood—a lot of it—up on the outcropping. Fact. Rob had become separated from the others, who were still miss-

ing. Fact. He had somehow injured himself, sustaining a
head injury of undetermined severity, which might or might
not manifest itself in delusion. Fact. There was a lot happening up there on the trail with footprints leading in both
directions at various points along the trail. Fact.

Gracie blew a large bubble, popping it quietly so as to
not disturb Rob.

She had been able to identify only four distinct sets of
prints. The Reeboks, the honeycomb, and the flat sole were
unique enough that probably only one person had laid each
of them. Hiking or work boots with a lug sole were common
enough that several different people could have laid them,
but possibly only one person.

She dug inside a side pocket of her parka and pulled out
her little notebook. She paged back until she found where
she had cursorily scribbled the track measurements. The
smaller prints with the honeycomb pattern measured three
and a half inches wide by ten inches long, small enough to
indicate a woman had laid them—Diana or Cristina,
although they were probably too small for the string bean,
Cristina. The lug-sole pattern going both ways was four and
a half by thirteen inches, almost an inch and half longer
than Gracie's ladies size 9 hiking boots. That was probably
too big for Cristina. Unless Cristina's feet were the size of
Hippolyta, Queen of the Amazons, those tracks had definitely been laid by a man. Rob's boot had the smooth sole.
If Tristan was wearing Reeboks, that left Carlos or Joseph
wearing the lug-sole boot.

At least two people had left the outcropping and hiked
back down the trail. Two people, one with the flat soles,
presumably Rob's, and one with the honeycomb pattern,
very possibly Diana's, had continued up the trail past the
rock promontory. But only Rob had come back. Why? Why
separate? And why would Diana or whoever it was go that
way in the first place? There was nothing out there but acres

and acres of wilderness area. The Aspen Springs Trail eventually split—one fork leading up to the summit of San Raphael, the other meandering for almost fifteen miles down the mountain all the way to the desert floor. No matter which way she had gone, the odds of her being found alive were pretty close to nonexistent.

But where had the rest of the group gone? Had they descended into the canyon as Rob had? Gracie was confident the churned earth she and Cashman had followed had been caused by only one person, two at the most. Certainly not by three and definitely not five.

Dead end.

She turned her attention back to the two sets of tracks returning to the trailhead.

If someone had been injured severely enough to produce as much blood as there was on the outcropping, then two people—a man and a woman—might have headed back to the trailhead to call for help. Since Gracie had noticed no blood on the trail itself, it was a safe assumption that neither person traveling down the trail had been seriously wounded. But that didn't answer what had happened to the injured person. Or the two people hiking back.

No one from the second, smaller hiking party had returned to the trailhead before she and Cashman had set out from the CP and they had met no one along the trail.

She and Cashman had blown their whistles while walking along the majority of the trail. No one had responded to the whistles.

So where had they gone?

Another dead end.

Gracie stretched, taking great satisfaction when she felt her back snap, crackle, and pop. She knew she hadn't taken her analysis of what had happened far enough. If she gave it enough time and thought, she might be able to figure it all out. But her neck and shoulders had tightened up from sitting in the same hunched position for so long. If a crime had occurred, she decided, there were detectives to deal with it. From now on, her main focus would be to keep Rob Christian warm and safe until the cavalry arrived.

Then get the hell out of there. Fast.

# CHAPTER

# 40

UPON gaining the trail, Cashman had paused momentarily to allow his breathing to slow enough so he wouldn't sound winded over the radio. But when he had turned on the HT and pressed the Transmit button, he received only the loud wonk. Another effort fifty yards down the trail produced the same result. He stashed the radio inside his jacket intending to try again farther on.

Now Cashman hiked down the trail, maintaining a fast, steady pace. One misstep could mean death. Or worse. But the searcher's mind wasn't focused on where to place his feet, nor the trail itself, nor even on gaining a radio signal to call in. It had leapfrogged ahead to the Command Post, where reporters and TV cameras most likely waited.

*This is the big time*, Cashman thought. Rob Christian is big news. Exhilaration snared his breath inside his rib cage. If, instead of radioing in, he hiked all the way back to the CP, he maybe could make tonight's L.A. news. Maybe even national news. Maybe even international!

He increased his pace to a trot, then almost immediately

skidded to a stop as he remembered that up ahead a bootleg trail fell off from the main trail, zigzagging down into the canyon and up the other side, cutting off the long, time-consuming switchback that constituted the final approach to the trailhead and the parking lot. The offshoot trail didn't show on the map because the National Forest Service prohibited leaving the marked trail in a wilderness area. But years of hiking in the mountains had taught Cashman most of the shortcuts.

His hands shook as he pulled his map from his parka and unfolded it. He located his position. *Fuckin' A!* he thought. *I can cut off more than a mile!*

Because the bootleg trail wasn't maintained, it was riskier than the main trail—steeper, rockier, more unstable footing. But the danger didn't faze him. He had hiked thousands of miles in his lifetime. He was at his peak physically, nimble and foot-sure. "Piece o' cake!"

*This is really it,* he thought as he refolded the map. *This is my chance to make the big time. This'll prove to Wanda I'm not such a fuckup after all.*

Images flashed in his mind's eye. Wanda and the girls smiling up at him as a medal was pinned on his chest. Rob shaking his hand. His own picture plastered on national television.

His breath caught in his chest at his next thought. The team might even make him Commander.

Cashman stuffed the map into his jacket pocket and turned back toward the trail, a wide grin on his face.

*Wouldn't that just fry Hunter's ass! Arrogant sonofa-bitch.* "This is gonna be great!" he crowed to the heavens.

Cashman heard a footstep on the dirt behind him. He was turning, a questions on his lips, when a heavy blow from behind knocked his head back and pitched him headlong over the side.

His body slammed into the side of the mountain. A shock wave of pain shot through him. He tumbled and cartwheeled, picking up speed, out of control, bouncing off tree trunks and sharp rocks, arms and legs flailing.

He heard his thigh bone break with a loud *crack!*

The last thought that flashed through Steve Cashman's mind was *I'm going to die*.

Then the missile that was his body hurtled over the edge of a precipice, free-falling two hundred feet to smash onto the jagged tumble of rocks and brush below.

# CHAPTER
## 41

"THAT dumbass piece of crap peckerhead! That's exactly what he did!"

Gracie still sat cross-legged at the entrance of the shelter staring out through the peep-hole. Her legs and back were stiff and her butt was numb from sitting so long in the same position.

Rob lay behind her, still sleeping.

Or he had been until her outburst.

His voice floated up out of the depths. "Precisely what dumbass piece of crap peckerhead did precisely what?"

"Nobody important," Gracie said over her shoulder. "Sorry if I woke you."

"I wasn't asleep."

Rob was lying, she knew. But she had lied, too. The dumbass piece of crap peckerhead wasn't nobody. And he wasn't unimportant. The dumbass piece of crap peckerhead was Cashman. He had been gone for more than three hours.

*What's taking him so long?*

As the morning had lazed toward afternoon with no reappearance by her teammate, Gracie's nerves had stretched tighter and tighter. By her reckoning, it shouldn't have taken Steve more than ninety minutes, two hours at the most, to climb out of the canyon, hike up the trail the distance it took to locate a clear radio signal, relay to the Command Post the coordinates of their location, receive the well-deserved accolades upon finding Rob Christian, and hike back to the bivouac to wait for the relief rescue team to show up.

Cashman was more than an hour late.

Had something bad happened to him? Had he injured himself somehow? Gracie had considered the different possibilities until it hit her in a blinding flash of the obvious. Nothing bad had happened to him. He hadn't injured himself in some way. He had hiked all the way back to the CP right into the waiting arms of the media.

As soon as she thought of it, Gracie knew without a doubt that this was exactly what he had done.

"When I see you again, Cashman" she whispered, "I'm gonna wring your neck like a Thanksgiving turkey."

Her normally low blood pressure shot upward toward the national average as she envisioned him lounging in the Command Post's blissful warmth and comfort, sipping hot chocolate and reveling in the congratulatory handshakes and slaps on the back, never ever thinking of giving Ralph or Gracie their due as fellow team members.

Not that she sought out the limelight. And recognition for superior service was appropriate. It just goaded the hell out of her when someone else grabbed it for his or her own instead of acknowledging the team as a comprehensive unit. They were, after all, the Timber Creek Search and Rescue Team, emphasis on *Team*. Gracie and every man on the team took the hit for every member's screw-up. It was only right and fair that each team member should also bask in the glow of a successful mission.

For the umpteenth time Gracie glanced at her watch. She calculated that if Cashman had hiked all the way back to the Command Post, considering the snail's pace that circumstances were evaluated, assignments were doled out, and a relief team actually hit the trail, the earliest anyone would arrive at the bivouac would be another half an hour.

With that realization, Gracie arched her back again and relaxed the rubber band of her nerves with a little deep-breathing session.

The clamor inside her head diminished and she became aware of the silence behind her. She had jolted Rob awake with her outburst, then retreated back into her own thoughts.

She swiveled her body around so that she faced the man. "Are you awake?"

"Yah."

He didn't sound very convincing. She forged ahead anyway. "Can we talk again about what might have happened up there on the trail?"

Rob propped himself up on one elbow and ran a hand down his face. "Sorry?"

"You don't remember if there was a fight of some kind? Or if someone actually tried to kill you?"

Rob yawned. "Well, we—"

"Wasn't there alcohol or something for lunch? How much did you have to drink?"

"What are you asking?" Rob sounded fully awake now. He sat up the rest of the way, eyes dark and focused on Gracie. "I wasn't pissed, if that's what you're implying."

"Pissed?"

"Pissed. Arseholed. Drunk. I wasn't drunk." The anger in his voice was unmistakable. "I had one glass of champagne. Less than one."

"Your friends said you didn't have any."

"Did they?" he asked, taken aback for a moment. "Publicity damage control, most likely. I was barely merry when we set off hiking again. I was stone-cold sober farther up the trail."

"I thought you said you don't remember what happened."

"I don't remember exactly what happened later." Rob's voice was so low and quiet it reminded Gracie of a German shepherd's silent growl, more ominous and threatening than before. "I do remember having almost nothing to drink at lunch." He jabbed his hands around in his jacket pockets, finally producing a sandwich bag filled with something Gracie couldn't identify, a packet of rolling papers, and a small gold lighter. He began to construct what looked like a giant joint.

"What . . . What is that?" Gracie sputtered. "What are you doing?"

Rob looked up at her with eyes that still sparked, back down at the makings in his hands, then back up at her again. "Rolling a fag," he said. He expertly licked the paper and sealed it.

Her mind groped for the British to American English translation. A fag. A *fag*. Oh, a cigarette. Words galloped out of her mouth before she could rein them in. "You're not smoking that in here."

"Why not?"

"You are not lighting up within a hundred yards of this sleeping bag. This is an eight-hundred-fill down minus-twenty-degree bag with dual draft tubes, welded baffle construction, and laminated, double external zipper flaps."

"What the—"

"It's the highest-tech sleeping bag money can buy," Gracie cut in. "Or at least that I could afford. I sold my little sister into slavery for that bag and don't want it peppered with little ash holes." She heard what she had just said and fought the smile that tugged at her mouth. "Besides those things will kill you."

"What are you, my mum?"

"And *another* besides, I don't want to be breathing in your secondhand smoke. You are not smoking in here."

"Bloody hell, woman!"

The two glared at each other until Rob stuffed the cigarette makings back into his pocket. "Puffed up like a green bronc on a cold morning," he mumbled.

"What does that mean?"

"Nothing. It means bloody nothing." He unzipped his sleeping bag. "I'm going outside."

ROB sat on a boulder outside the shelter, smoking in silence.

Gracie stood leaning against another boulder about twenty feet away, feeling remorseful.

The fact that Rob was a celebrity meant nothing to her. What did matter was that he wasn't deserving of the accusations she had made, or the manner in which she had made them. Common courtesy alone dictated she apologize. Not to mention that they were stuck armpit-to-armpit in a tiny shelter for an indeterminate amount of time.

Crap.

Gracie pushed herself off the rock. With feet that felt like wet cement, she crossed over to where Rob sat and slid onto the rock next to him.

His eyes glided over to her, then away. Out in the chilled air, he was back to looking rosy-cheeked again.

And gorgeous. Crap.

Rob took another drag off the cigarette.

The fine smell of cloves filled Gracie's nostrils. "I'd like to apologize," she said.

Rob blew out the smoke.

"I was out of line," Gracie said, fiddling with the zipper pull of her jacket. "About the drinking and all that."

Still nothing.

"I could have been more diplomatic. It's just that . . . It's just I hate, no, loathe being stuck . . ." When Rob was still silent, she leaned over to look in his face. "Hellooooo?"

Rob looked back at her. "What?"

"Did you hear what I said?"

"Yes."

Her exhaled breath exploded into the moist air. "Well?"

"Well what?"

"I'm apologizing and you're being a shit."

"How am I being a shit?"

"Because I said I wanted to apologize, which, by the way, is really hard for me because it means I was wrong and I hate being wrong and I'm trying to apologize and you're ignoring me."

"I'm not ignoring you. I'm waiting."

"For what?"

"For you to apologize," Rob said. "You said you wanted to apologize. So apologize. Saying you want to and actually doing it are two entirely different things."

Gracie detected the hint of a smile on his lips. He covered it up by taking another drag from the cigarette. "It's true," he said shrugging, blowing out the smoke.

"I'm sorry! Okay? Satisfied?"

"Apology accepted," he said.

With approval, Gracie watched Rob flick the glowing end of his cigarette onto the rock, shred the unburned contents into the air, and stash what little paper was left into this pocket.

After several seconds of silence, she said, "I'm trying to figure out what happened to you. And the others. Can you tell me exactly what you remember from the time you left the trail? Whatever you haven't already told me?"

Rob pushed himself farther back on the boulder so his injured foot stuck out in front of him. He described how, after the lunch, the next thing he remembered—with any clarity he emphasized—was lying on his side on the steep incline, not knowing for how long he had been unconscious, where he was or why he was there, and with his head and ankle hurting "like bloody hell." Disoriented, he had yelled for a bit. When no one came, he tried to climb back up the hill, but it was so steep and the ground so soft he kept sliding back down. "A bit tough with a dodgy ankle. And I felt like shit." He tried his cell phone. No reception. By that time he was shivering and couldn't stop. He hobbled and slid the rest of the way down to the creek, then stumbled and fell in the water trying to cross to the other side where, for some reason, he thought it might be warmer.

Gracie absorbed what he told her, then asked, "What can you tell me about Tristan? I have a physical description, but what about his character? What kind of person is he?"

"Tristan? He's an actor. Don't really know him that well. Nice enough. Talks a blue streak."

Gracie prodded him along with, "Anything else?"

"I don't know what it is you're looking for."

"Anything that might help me figure out where he could be. Anything to establish his habits. Thinking patterns. That kind of thing."

"What I told you is all I know."

"What can you tell me about Joseph?"

"Joseph?" Rob shrugged. "My manager hired him. He's a personal coach. Hand-to-hand combat. Excellent at what he does. Otherwise don't know him very well either. Only up here for a few days. He doesn't say much. Keeps to himself."

"That it?"

"Yeah. That's about it."

"What about Diana?"

"Actor. Minor role." He shrugged and looked over at her. "Sorry. I'm not being much help."

"What about the couple? Cristina and Carlos Sanchez?"

"Leather'n'Studs?" At Gracie's look, he grinned. "I heard someone call them that once. That's all I know."

"There was some disagreement as to whether they had been hiking with your group or not."

"That one I do remember. They were not."

Gracie sat up straight. "They weren't?"

"When the others left to go back to the motor home, they stayed behind at the lunch spot. They were making noise about driving back down to the city. They were still sitting there when we left to hike on a bit."

"Really." Here finally was relevant information. Carlos and Cristina not among the MisPers reduced the number of still missing from five to three: Tristan, Joseph, and Diana.

Gracie processed the information.

Three missing hikers. Rob's memories of someone dying. A woman screaming. The bloodstain. Rob's injuries. The tracks.

Tristan was wearing tennis shoes, probably Reeboks. The prints leading back down the trail were honeycomb pattern and lug sole, those of Diana and the only person left: Joseph. But then the honeycomb had also continued on past the promontory.

Rob pushed himself off the rock. "I'm going back in."

Gracie watched as Rob hopped on one foot back to the little shelter, dropped to his knees and crawled into the shelter.

For several minutes, Gracie stood motionless outside the shelter, staring into the mist, thinking about the tracks and the implications, thinking about Tristan, and Diana, and Joseph, and the fact that Cashman hadn't returned.

She unsnapped the keep on her hunting knife and crawled into the little shelter.

# 43

"**MONKEYS** fucking a football," Ralph growled as he strode down the gravel berm at the edge of the highway. Taking a last drag off his half-smoked cigarette, he broke his own rule by flicking it, still lit, onto the asphalt. It rolled away in a flurry of sparks.

The vans, cars, lights, cables, and satellite dishes of the media, interspersed with reporters and technicians, choked the shoulder on one side of the highway. Looky-loos and groupies lined the opposite shoulder, forcing Ralph to park almost a quarter mile back from the Sandy Flats Visitor's Center, adding compounded interest to his already foul mood.

A canopy of low clouds hovered over the tall pines lining both sides of the highway, wispy tendrils clutching at the top branches.

Ralph shivered and zipped his parka the rest of the way up. It was damp and cold. And getting colder. He had checked the thermometer inside the truck as he shoved it into park on the berm. Forty degrees at this altitude would translate to much colder on San Raphael.

He hadn't been able to shake the sense of foreboding he'd had ever since he learned the search was still ongoing. During the drive back up to Timber Creek from the desert, Ralph had tried both Gracie's cell and home phones, but hadn't been able to reach her. A call to Dispatch told him that not only was the search still in progress, but also none of the MisPers had been brought out of the field. No further details were available. Not wanting to take the time to drive into town to pick up a SAR unit at the SO, he had driven his own truck down to the staging area. Monitoring the search channel on the mobile radio along the way told him the Command Post had been moved from the Aspen Springs Trailhead parking lot down to Sandy Flats.

Ralph scrunched closer to the visitor's center. Clogging the pavement were Search and Rescue vehicles of all makes and models interspersed with searchers, men and women alike, in variations of orange shirts and jackets with shoulder patches and helmet labels identifying individual teams.

The presence of so many SAR personnel confirmed Ralph's fear that the search had ballooned far beyond what was needed. And what was prudent.

A large-scale search was difficult to run, requiring a skill level Ralph knew the current Incident Commander, Nelson Black, didn't possess. Allow a search to grow out of control and it became unwieldy, a mythical beastie with multiple heads and appendages and a will of its own. That's when mistakes were made. That's when accidents happened. That's when searchers got themselves lost. Or injured. Or killed.

He was certain that on the previous night Gracie and Cashman had located at least one of the MisPers. Now it appeared, almost eighteen hours later, none of the MisPers were out of the field. He needed to talk to Gracie and find out what the hell had happened.

The Sandy Flats Visitor's Center itself was a large stone chalet-style building with a low, sloping, green metal roof. Parked on one side of the building was the Volunteer Forces mobile Command Post—a giant motor home, white and emblazoned on both sides with the Department's chevron seal.

Ralph walked past a Sheriff's Department Tahoe blocking the entrance to the parking lot to all except SAR vehicles, wove his way through the groupings of searchers, and walked up to the sign-in table set up in front of the Command Post motor home. Behind it sat a woman with Brillopad hair frizzing out from beneath a Day-Glo orange knit hat. A space heater blew hot air at her feet.

As Ralph scribbled his name on the sign-in sheet, he asked at what time Grace Kinkaid and Steve Cashman of Timber Creek SAR had signed out that morning. He waited patiently as the woman leafed back through the pages of sign-in sheets.

"Should be the first names on the list," Ralph offered, hoping the woman would take the hint and speed up the process. "Timber Creek. Kinkaid. Ten Rescue Twenty-two. Cashman. Ten Rescue Fifty-six."

"Sorry," the woman said finally, looking back up at Ralph. "Don't see those names on the list."

"I was in the Command Post when they signed in last night," Ralph said, feeling the knot in his gut tighten. "Their names are there. I just need to confirm what time they left the field."

Once more, moving at glacial speed, the woman paged back through the pile of sign-in sheets. Once more she looked back up at Ralph. "Sorry."

Unable to keep the irritation out of his voice, Ralph asked, "Can you tell me who's the first name on your list?"

Flipping to the bottom page, the woman said, "Nels Black."

"Time?"

The woman lowered her face to the page. "We need more light out here."

Ralph methodically sucked air in through his nostrils to slow the beating of his heart. "How many teams are in the field? Can you tell me that?"

The woman's clipped tone told Ralph that he had lost a friend. "There are six teams in the field. Mr. Black signed in at seven twenty-five this morning."

"You're certain that's the very first sign-in sheet you have?"

"That's the first sign-in sheet I have," the woman answered, beady eyes blazing back at Ralph.

*Goddammit!* Ralph spun around and stalked toward the Command Post motor home.

They had lost track of two searchers in the field. A monumental screw-up. Not to mention a black eye for the Department. Personnel would have to be pulled from the search and redeployed to search for the missing SAR members. And on top of everything else—according to the weather on the radio, it was pouring rain in L.A. The massive fast-moving front was heading in their direction, bringing with it snow. Lots of it.

# CHAPTER

# 44

**W**HERE the hell was the relief team?

Gracie sat with her nose inches from the peephole, chomping furiously on a stale, tasteless piece of bubble gum. She was running low on gum and reduced to rationing the pieces, stretching out how long each one lasted.

She calculated how long it should have taken Cashman to hike back to the Command Post, muster a rescue team, and hike back to the bivouac. She got the same answer as the previous three times. They should have been here by now. All of which made her wonder again if Cashman hadn't reached the Command Post at all.

An ogre of a thought reared its ugly head—somewhere along the trail Cashman had met up with the killer, possibly Joseph, a man who taught hand-to-hand combat. She mouthed a quiet, "Shit."

"What's wrong?" Rob's groggy voice filtered up from the depths of the shelter where he lay, no doubt trying to sleep.

"Nothing," she replied without turning.

"That 'shit' didn't sound like nothing."

"Didn't mean for you to hear that."

"You're worried," Rob said, a statement, not a question.

Gracie swung her feet around so that she faced him. "I'm . . ." She stopped. Up a creek without a paddle? Over a cliff without a rope? Scared shitless? ". . . Concerned."

Rob sat up and leaned over to turn on the little lantern, filling the tiny space with its warm glow. "They should have been here to pick us up by now, shouldn't they?"

"Yes."

"And you're feeling responsible for me, aren't you?"

"That's because I am."

"What do you think has happened?"

Gracie mulled over exactly how much to tell him. Usually unofficial protocol dictated telling a rescued party as little as possible. She wasn't sure why, but she thought it had to do with lessening the chances of anyone noticing if somebody on the team screwed up. Regardless, she didn't want to stir things up with Rob by sharing with him that she knew about the blood on the outcropping and her fear that something bad had happened to Cashman. There were any number of reasons why Steve or a relief team had failed to show up. Everything besides the blood and the tracks on the trail was pure speculation on her part, probably the result of an overactive imagination because of her latest book kick—true crime. Rob needed to be resting and recovering from his injuries, not stressing over what had occurred up on the rock outcropping. Gracie was doing enough stressing for the both of them.

"There are a number of possible scenarios," she finally answered. "It might not be logistically feasible. There might not be enough personnel available to send in. Cloud cover could be so bad, they're holding or pulling teams in from the field. Cashman hurt himself somehow along the way and can't relay where we are from where he is."

"Is that possible?"

She nodded. "Just not probable. Cashman's an animal. It would take a lot to take him out of service."

"Makes me wonder if what I remembered is really the truth," he said. "That someone was killed. Maybe something has happened to your friend, too." His eyes flew up to meet Gracie's. "Bugger it! I'm sorry. I didn't mean to frighten you. I mean—"

"You didn't frighten me," Gracie lied. "I don't think anything bad happened to Cashman. Much more likely that he screwed up somehow. He suffers from a terminal case of cranial-rectal inversion syndrome."

Rob stared at her blankly for the split second it took him to work it out, then he chuckled. "I'll have to remember that one. I know quite a few people suffering from that very same malady."

Gracie turned back and sank into silence, thinking dark, foreboding thoughts about cats and mice.

"Tell me about this search and rescue work," Rob said, startling her.

Willingly Gracie turned her thoughts away from the terrifying to the ordinary and spun around to face the actor again, noting with no small amount of surprise how quickly she had become comfortable around him.

"Let's see," she said, trying to collect her thoughts. "We work under the Sheriff's Department. Our county is the largest in the country. Two hundred seventy miles long. It takes over four hours just to drive from one end to the other on the highway."

"That's bigger than some European countries," Rob said, looking impressed.

"Our little team is one out of maybe ten in the county. We're on call twenty-four/seven. We respond to everything from lost kids and hikers and mountain bikers to cars over the side of the highway and airplane crashes."

"So this is your job?"

"Nope. We're all volunteers."

"You're a volunteer?"

"At your service."

Rob shook his head. "I can't believe you risk your life for blokes like me. For free. Out of the goodness of your heart."

Gracie could feel the warmth of a blush rising and wished fervently that she didn't possess whatever complexion or genetic makeup was required for her face to turn into a pomegranate at the slightest provocation. "I never think about it as risking my life," she said. "And out of the goodness of my heart is way too lofty. I have a low boredom threshold and get to feed my adrenaline habit. Simple as that."

Seconds dragged by until Rob asked, "If this is a volunteer thing, what do you do in real life?"

Shit. Even though the question was predictable, Gracie hadn't anticipated it. What was she going to say? That she didn't have some important, worthy job, but spent her time jumping from one low-paying gig with no real responsibility to another? That she wasn't nearly as strong and confident as she tried to project? That the person to whom he was entrusting his life was a burnout and a fraud?

What her face registered, Gracie had no idea, but it prompted Rob to ask what was wrong.

"I'm hungry," she responded, which was only half true.

The distraction worked, however, because Rob didn't press the issue, instead saying with enthusiasm, "Me, too."

"Then let's see what we have to eat." Gracie tipped her pack away from the shelter door and pulled the drawstring loose. She had won a reprieve, but only a temporary one. Sooner or later, she was going to have to come up with some kind of nebulous answer for what she did for a living. Failing that, she could always take the fall-back position and lie.

Rob watched as Gracie emptied every pouch and pocket of her pack and parka, laying the items on the sleeping bag behind her. "I can't believe you fit all that in there," he said. "You're like Mary Poppins pulling things out of her satchel."

"I like to be prepared. I have backups for my backups. It's called redundancy." *Or anal retentiveness*, she thought and almost told herself out loud to shut up.

He picked up a mesh bag filled with various odds and ends and scrutinized its contents. "What's the mirror for? Doing your makeup?"

She retrieved the bag. "Signaling, dolt."

Gracie replaced the pack in front of the entrance and turned back to paw through the pile of detritus. "What all have we got? One package of dehydrated chicken noodle soup. One hot chocolate. One freeze-dried coffee. Another instant apple-and-cinnamon oatmeal." With two fingers, she picked up a sandwich bag so old the once-clear plastic was milky white. "Gorp." At Rob's look, she said, "Peanuts, M&M's, and raisins."

"Mmmm," was his unenthusiastic response.

"A bag of stale Skittles. Two peanut butter granola bars. Half a peanut butter sandwich smashed flatter'n a pancake. Two tea bags."

"Yippee ki yay," Rob said.

Ignoring him, Gracie said, "And most important, my bubble gum. What little I have left. I'm an addict."

"I hadn't noticed."

"Are all actors such smartasses or did I just get lucky?"

"You got lucky."

Gracie picked up a large brown plastic package. "This would be our lunch."

When Rob eyed the package dubiously, Gracie explained, "MRE. U.S. Army–issued meal ready to eat. Or meal rarely edible as some people call them. Or meal rejected by everyone."

"Lovely."

"Or as those politically incorrect are inclined to say: meal rejected by Ethiopians.'"

Rob laughed.

She tore off the top of the MRE and poured the contents

out onto the sleeping bag. They both stared down at the pile of cardboard boxes that was to be their meal.

"So this is it," Rob said.

"Pretty grim, eh? Especially if we're stuck out here longer than a day."

Rob's eyes whipped up to meet hers. "Do you think we might?"

She shook her head. "If it clears soon, we'll be out of here tonight."

"And if it doesn't?"

"Let's jump off that cliff when the time comes."

**D**ESPAIR penetrated every cell of Diana's being.

She sat perched on the side of the hill, arms wrapped around her legs, knees hugged in to her chest, unable to stop shivering.

No one had come for her. No Canadian Mountie. No white knight. As the hours had whittled away the day, hope for rescue faded like green grass after a hard frost.

She was alone.

Why hadn't anyone come looking for her?

At one time she thought she heard the high-pitched sound of a whistle. With soaring spirits, she slid down to the trail and waited, not daring to call out in case Milocek was somewhere nearby. When she heard nothing further, she crawled back up the incline to her hiding place.

*This isn't happening to me*, she thought. *It feels like a dream. Not reality at all.*

She wished she would just wake up and be in her cozy little apartment on Courtney in sunny, warm L.A.

She considered lying back down and submitting to the

overwhelming desire to close her eyes, to sleep, to be at peace.

But she was certain if she did, she would never wake up.

There was no one else on whom she could depend. If she wanted to live, she needed to save herself. If she wanted to live, she needed to move.

She wished she had paid more attention to the discussions about the trail itself. She knew she had passed a smaller trail splitting off to the left, but she didn't know where it led. And the portion of the trail she was on kept climbing up and up to what she presumed was the top of the mountain. She didn't have the will or the strength to keep climbing. Back down the trail was the only sure way out, back the way she had come, back where she had seen Milocek before.

She had two choices. Try to walk out where death was a possibility. Or stay where she was where death was certain.

She groaned as she straightened her legs. With arms that felt as if they had been injected with lead, she swept the dirt off her coat and picked off the pine needles one by one.

Then, holding on to the branch of a nearby bush, she hauled herself to her feet.

"**A**REN'T you married?" Gracie asked.

She and Rob had partaken of rice pilaf topped with beef mushroom sauce, which Rob dubbed "not bad" and Gracie "vile," but choked it down anyway. They were now spreading jalapeño cheese on surprisingly crispy crackers.

At her question Rob's face had gone slack, wiped clean of any emotion. Gracie had struck a fresh nerve. Time to backpedal. "Don't answer that," she said through a mouthful of crackers and cheese. "None of my business."

"I left her six months ago," Rob said casually, but not quite enough to hide the strong emotion held in check by a well-honed reserve. "I'm amazed you didn't read about it in the tabloids."

"I'm not much for supermarket reading," Gracie said. "Why did you leave her?"

"She didn't love me."

Gracie winced. "Sorry." She knew how that felt.

Rob nodded, eyes focused on the uneaten cracker in his

hand. "Loved the attention though. And the money. And the fame."

"Ouch" was the most erudite thing Gracie could think of to say. "Don't I remember hearing something about you punching out a reporter?" she asked to move on to a different subject.

"Now that particular story was spot-on." Rob took a bite of cracker and washed it down with a swig of water.

"And . . ."

"And I found out my wife was shagging a friend of mine. A week later my mum died of a heart attack. After the funeral—we're still at the church—some punk reporter sticks a camera in my face and asks me how I feel about my wife shagging my friend."

"Guess he found out, didn't he?"

"I'm not proud of what I did. I lost control."

"Gee, I wonder why."

"What about you?" he asked and stuffed the rest of the cracker into his mouth.

Gracie straightened her back. "What about me?"

"Married?"

"No." She tore open a package of oatmeal cookies and handed him one, hoping to distract him with more food.

He persisted. "Never?"

"Engaged."

"Care to elaborate?"

"No."

"We'll talk about that later."

"*You* will maybe."

"So no boyfriend even?"

Gracie's thoughts flickered in Ralph's direction. "No," she answered finally.

"Girlfriend?"

A look provided him the answer to that one.

"Dog?" he pushed. "Cat?"

"No."

"Turtle? Plants?"

"Had a cactus once. It died."

"So you live alone?"

Gracie squirmed and rubbed her palms on her pants. "Holy . . . It happens, ya know. People do actually live alone. You just said you did."

"I do, but I don't like it. I want someone to share my life with. Someone to do the dishes with. Someone to take care of when she's sick."

"Some people enjoy living alone."

"Or so they tell themselves."

She shot him her frostiest ice-queen look. "I like my privacy."

Rob touched her arm. "Sorry. That was too personal. I, of all people, should be sensitive to prying questions." But his eyes were twinkling. "I'm trying to figure out what kind of person does what you do. Risk your life for total strangers. You never told me what you do for a living."

Gracie cleared her throat. "At the moment I'm unemployed. I'd rather not talk about it."

Rob seemed unfazed. "What do you do for fun then?"

"This is it. This is my fun."

"What else besides this?"

"I read books. Do puzzles: Jigsaw. Crosswords. Boring old-lady crud. That's all I'm saying. Hells bells. Now I know what it's like to be on the receiving end of a bona fide grilling." When Rob still looked at her expectantly, she said, "I like movies, okay? But I hardly ever go. I might have seen one of yours once though. The swashbuckling one."

"*Far Horizons*. Did you like it?"

"Don't really remember. I was smashed when I went in." She stopped, mortified by that inadvertent window into her life. "Weren't you in a Western, too?" she asked.

He nodded. "Did you see it?"

"Nope." She stopped, feeling as if she were living one of her recurring bad dreams where she walked out on stage in front of a packed house on opening night only to discover that not only did she not know her lines, she hadn't even read the play.

"Keep talking," Rob said.

"No."

"Why not?"

"I don't like talking about myself. I loathe being the center of attention. I hate having my picture taken or seeing myself on TV. H-A-T-E it. Cashman loves it. That's why he's on the team. But that's not why I am."

"Why are you then?"

"I love it. I love being outdoors. I love that it's contributing positively to a crummy world. I love its immediacy. I do it because when I'm on a search—" She clapped her mouth shut.

"When I'm on a search . . ." he prompted.

"That's all I'm going to say." She almost said that on a search was the only time she felt at ease and in control of her life, but stopped because she didn't want him prying into that area of her life so closed off and private that even she didn't like venturing there. "Your turn," she said. "What do you do for fun?"

"Fair enough." Rob gathered the remnants of the meal together and began stuffing them back into the plastic MRE package. "Rugby," he said. "Football. Well, soccer to you Yanks. I'm a bit of a fanatic actually."

"Go on."

"Like to sail. Fencing. Learned it for *Far Horizons*. Martial arts to keep in shape."

"Go on."

"Theater."

"What do you read?"

"American westerns. Old ones. Louis L'Amour. Zane Grey. "

"Who woulda thunk? What else?"

"That's it."

"You're not getting off that easily. Tell me something hardly anyone knows."

"That's a hard one. Oh, I know. I played the clarinet once."

"The clarinet?"

"I sucked at it." He smiled.

"Pun intended, I suppose."

"Kept squeaking the effing thing. Drove everyone daft. Turns out I'm tone deaf."

Gracie giggled. "Really?"

"Can't carry a tune in a laundry basket. Mum enrolled me in acting class instead."

"And the rest is history," Gracie said.

His eyes crinkled in a hint of a smile. He cocked his head and looked at Gracie in a way that made her wriggle uncomfortably.

"What?" she demanded.

"Everyone seems to want a part of me. I can't trust anyone. Outside of my family that is."

"I can understand that."

"But you . . ."

Gracie felt another blush rising. "I have to go pee."

She reached over to grab her boot, but Rob put a hand on her arm. "Wait. I'm trying to figure something out."

Gracie sat back.

"We've known each other for less than twenty-four hours. I'm telling you things . . . I'm trusting you with things I've never told my best mate."

"Tricked ya. When we get out of here, I'm gonna sell this story to the tabloids."

He smiled at her. "You're a bloody brat, you know that?"

"Can't make headlines with old news," Gracie said and grabbed up her boot.

# CHAPTER
# 47

**I**N a waking nightmare, Diana shuffled down the trail. She could see nothing but her hands with splayed fingers stretched out in front of her, the trail beneath her feet and the cloud drifting around her on all sides.

Moving had warmed her up somewhat, but her hands and feet felt as if they had been carved from blocks of ice, and her eyes and nose ran with the cold.

She slid her foot along the dirt, kicked a buried tree root and lost her balance. She fell hard onto her already bruised and scabbed knees, but the pain hardly registered.

She pushed herself back to her feet and stepped over the tree root.

**R**ALPH'S blood pressure inched upward toward meltdown. He stood inside the massive Sheriff's Department motor home facing a six-foot-square wall map of the San Raphael Wilderness Area. Highlighted and crosshatched segments represented the areas already or currently being searched. Instead of the map, Ralph saw only Gracie smiling, Gracie braiding her hair in the back, Gracie standing with her hands on her hips, one long leg cocked out to the side.

Ralph was able to tune out the organized chaos of a large-incident Command Post: radio traffic, multiple simultaneous discussions. But he wasn't able to not listen to Incident Commander Nelson Black, who stood ten feet away, berating a young man who didn't look sixteen, much less twenty-one, and whose name tape read P. Richmond. It was P. Richmond's assignment to monitor the CP radio and log into a notebook every transmission among the search teams in the field and between the teams and the Command Post.

"Haven't you ever worked in a Command Post before?"

Black demanded, leaning over Richmond. "You have to log *every* transmission."

Nelson Black was small-framed, pale, and freckled. Ralph thought him arrogant inversely proportionate to his capabilities and knowledge. He was compensating for his shortcomings, physical or otherwise, real or imagined, Ralph supposed, and recalled with an inward chuckle Gracie's dubbing Black "the only man I've ever known with penis envy."

Ralph had climbed up into the Command Post in an attempt to ascertain the current status of the search. A terse overview from Black confirmed Ralph's suspicions that his own briefing that morning had been ignored, the established plan of operation discarded. Black had come in with his own agenda, already knowing how he was going to run the search regardless of what had already transpired in the field.

When Ralph had confronted him with the fact that a sign-in sheet and other Command Post paperwork had been misplaced and that two searchers from Timber Creek had been in the field for almost twenty-four hours and of whom the CP had lost track, Black became defensive and hostile. Apparently it never occurred to him, or at least he would never admit, that by expanding the search for political reasons, he had lost track of the very team that may have found at least one of the missing persons, probably Rob Christian.

Even though Black was Incident Commander and therefore in charge of the entire search operation, and the person to whom Ralph had personally handed the clipboard containing the original CP forms, the buck stopped with the elderly Citizen Volunteer who manned the sign-in table and who had since been humiliated publicly and summarily relieved of her duties.

To top everything off, all but two teams of ground pounders had been pulled in from the field due to the heavy cloud cover—a judgment call Ralph might not have made, but one he wasn't willing to second guess.

Before Ralph had the chance to suggest reassigning one or two search teams to the missing SAR personnel, Black had walked over to vent his anger on the unfortunate P. Richmond. Now, as precious minutes were lost, Ralph waited, taking in slow deep breaths to soften the pounding of blood in his ears.

"Command Post. Ground Six." The voice of a female searcher over the radio interrupted Black mid-reprimand.

Richmond picked up the radio and responded in a querulous voice, "Go ahead, Ground Six."

A pause from the radio, then, "Uh . . ." Another pause.

"You stupid . . ." Black said to the invisible searcher in the field. "Everyone with a radio can hear what an incompetent you are."

"Go ahead, Ground Six," Richmond repeated.

"We . . . We've located a four-sixteen."

Ralph's head snapped up. Tentacles of cold flashed down to his fingertips.

Four-sixteen. Dead body.

"Quiet!" Black shouted.

All conversation stopped.

"Ground Six. Ten-Nine," Richmond said.

Radio silence.

"Ground Six. Ten-Nine."

Several more seconds of silence, then, "We've located what we believe is a four-sixteen. Down in the canyon. Off the Aspen Springs Trail." Another pause. "We . . . We think it might be SAR. We can see an orange parka and helmet."

# CHAPTER

# 49

"I need to get out of here," Rob said. "I can't sit here and wait any longer."

He had returned to a prone position and, even though she was tired of sitting, Gracie was back at her post in front of the entrance. "I hear you on that one," she said over her shoulder.

"Can you make me some kind of a brace or a splint or something?" Rob asked. "I'm walking out."

With his pronouncement, Gracie swung around to face Rob, who was already carefully extracting his foot from beneath the sleeping bag. "No, wait," she said. "You can't. Your ankle. And you probably have a concussion."

"My sister's getting married the day after tomorrow," Rob said. "I've got to try to get there, don't I?"

Grace watched Rob pull on his jacket.

Rob was willing to try to hike out. If, for too much longer, Gracie was forced to passively sit and wait—immobile, inactive, not knowing what was happening with the search, with Cashman, with the relief team, whether there was a homicidal maniac out there looking for Rob, for her—she was going to go loony tunes. Or have a heart attack. Or a brain aneurysm. Or all three.

So what was the big, fat problem with what he was proposing?

The big, fat problem was that moving could be considered negligent on her part. Cashman had hopefully delivered the coordinates of their position to the Command Post, which hopefully in turn had passed them on to a relief team. It would be bad, bad, bad if Cashman or a relief team showed up at the location designated by the coordinates and found Gracie and Rob gone. Not to mention that Joseph, or whoever the killer was—if there even was a killer—might be creeping around somewhere up on the trail.

The irresistible urge to pack up and be moving engulfed her. "Okay," she said. "We'll try and hike out." She leaned back for her pack. "I'll splint your ankle."

Gracie untwisted one of her trekking poles and laid a section on either side of Rob's injured foot. "I'm leaving a portion of pole sticking out at the bottom," she told him as she bound the poles tightly to his leg with duct tape from her pack. "That way, hopefully, your foot won't touch the ground." She tested the splint to make sure it was secure and didn't wobble around. "How's that?"

"Brilliant!" Rob's entire visage and demeanor had changed with Gracie's decision to try to hike out. His eyes sparkled and he couldn't keep the excitement out of his voice or the grin off his face.

She looked up into his face. "It may not work."

"Worth a gamble," he said.

Together Gracie and Rob dismantled the little shelter. Rob shook out the plastic, refolded it, and crammed it into her pack. She stuffed the little sack containing her sleeping bag into the lower compartment of her pack, and fastened Cashman's sleeping pad, along with her own, to the outside. Rob kept Cashman's sleeping bag wrapped around his shoulders. When Gracie told him he looked like a Cheyenne Indian wearing a buffalo robe his face lit up with a delighted grin.

Gracie used up the rest of her flagging tape to tie a voluminous hot pink flower on a branch overhanging the creek, worrying the entire time whether she was telling the wrong person exactly where they were going. A five-foot-long arrow she constructed out of stones pointed to a plastic sandwich bag anchored with a rock. A note inside the bag gave the date and time and said that she and Rob were walking back up to the trail and which compass bearing they would be following.

Gracie hefted her pack onto her back and sagged beneath the weight. She humped the pack higher onto her shoulders and clipped closed the fastenings at the waist and across her chest. Then she handed Rob the remaining trekking pole and followed him down to the creek.

# CHAPTER
## 50

**D**IANA stopped in the middle of the trail. She listened, but heard nothing above her own breathing. She peered ahead, but saw nothing but the veil of white cloud.

She wasn't certain how far down the trail she had traveled. She had been moving for half an hour. Maybe more. She sensed that she had passed the rock outcropping, but couldn't be sure.

She slid her feet along the trail.

"*Zdravo*, Diana," came a soft voice out of the cloud. Hello, Diana.

Diana screamed and turned to run, but hands grabbed her arms in a vise grip, anchoring her where she was. Her knees gave way beneath her, but the hands kept her upright.

With tears streaming down her face, she looked up.

Milocek smiled back at her, a death mask.

The Surgeon had come.

## CHAPTER

# 51

ROB wasn't going to make it to the trailhead. In fact, after only a half an hour of climbing, Gracie knew he wasn't even going to make it a quarter of the way up the side of the canyon to the trail. He was limping so badly even with the splint and both trekking poles that he was spending more time stationary than moving. His pallor had returned to pasty gray.

"Stop," she said. "This isn't going to work."

Rather than arguing as Gracie expected, Rob sank to the ground without a word and rested his forehead on his knee. His chest heaved with exertion.

"I'm sorry, Rob," Gracie said.

Without raising his head, he lifted a hand in response.

"I'm so sorry."

**R**ADOVAN Milocek gritted his teeth. With the back of his hand, he swiped away the thin line of sweat that had slid down his temple to burn one eye.

He was naked except for the knit hat he had removed from Tristan's body. The damp cold raised goose bumps on the exposed flesh and made him shiver. But he ignored the cold, knowing it was only temporary and that the work ahead would warm him sufficiently.

With the effort of sawing through tendons and ligaments, his skin gleamed with a fine sheen of sweat. Pine needles dug into his knees as he knelt on the ground. His wet hands, stiff with cold, slipped on the short stub of branch as he scraped a shallow furrow into the dirt.

The larger parts he would bury first with a layer of earthy matter, then with stones and rocks he collected from around the site. Other, smaller parts he would scatter around, not bothering to cover them up. There was no need to invest the time or energy. Animals and the elements would do the work for him.

# CHAPTER

## 53

GRACIE lay stiff as a snowboard, arms folded across her chest, feet jiggling inside the sleeping bag.

Refusing Rob's offer of help, she had constructed another shelter alongside the massive trunk of a fallen tree, longer and wider than the first one, but with less headroom. Again she had anchored the plastic with rocks and tree limbs.

Deciding that once his being reported missing hit the newsstands in England, his sister had probably postponed her wedding anyway, Rob visibly relaxed. After a half-hour nap, he had roused himself and was sitting up inside his sleeping bag, drinking a cup of a watered-down hot chocolate and reading Gracie's laminated survival cards by the combined light of the lantern flashlight and a stubby candle stuck with melted wax to a flat rock.

Gracie's stomach churned like Mount Etna about to erupt. As the afternoon dragged on, anxiety at the delay in the arrival of the relief team and the real possibility that something horrible had happened to Cashman took its toll on her overstretched nerves. Not to mention that a killer might be lurking about in the canyon looking for them. And she had only one piece of bubble gum left. "There's not a damn thing you can do about any of it," she muttered, "so focus on something else. What's another word for *restless*?"

"Royal pain?" Rob said without looking up. "No, wait. Did you say something?"

"This immobility is *killing* me," Gracie said. "I feel like in one day we've devolved from bipeds to amoebae!"

Rob squinted over at her. "What *is* your problem?"

"I can't stand this waiting. I can't stand lying here doing nothing. I need to be doing something."

"Teach me something about survival then."

Gracie ignored his suggestion. Her eyes roved the interior of the tiny shelter, the bark of the fall log, the slanting ceiling, the backpack propped in the doorway, eventually settling on her own hands. She spread her fingers wide in front of her face. Dirt embedded under short, ragged nails. Torn cuticles. Dried blood on skinned knuckles. "Yow," she whispered. "These hands are either a manicurist's wildest fantasy or her worst nightmare."

"Hmm?"

"I need a bath."

"A *what*?"

"I can feel every teeny particle of dirt on my body. One whiff of my armpits would make a New York City garbage collector weep. I need a bath."

"But I'm kind of enjoying that rotting cantaloupe smell," Rob said so quietly Gracie wasn't sure she heard him correctly.

She rolled over to face him. "What?"

"I was *joking*. You know, a joke?" He smiled down at the cards and continued reading.

Gracie propped her head up with her hand and studied Rob.

Abrasion scabs and dirt smudges still showed beneath the thirty-six-hour beard stubble. His hair curled out from beneath the fleece hat like a Chia Pet. He looked adorable.

Somehow, Gracie observed, the grubbier Rob became, the more attractive he became, the more male, if that was in any way possible with someone who had Testosterone Machine practically tattooed on his forehead. She marveled that someone that good looking and famous and rich could be such a regular guy. She had never met anyone as famous as Rob, but she had known a number of good-looking wealthy men in her past life. The vast majority of them were Absolute Shits.

Yep, she decided, Rob Christian was just a regular guy. More than that, he was kind of . . . She searched for the right word. Nice.

Tears blurred Gracie's vision. She wiped her eyes with her sleeve before Rob noticed. The last few days had taken a toll on her physically and emotionally, strip-mining away the protective outer layers like geological strata, allowing horrible, unspeakable things to rise up to hover beneath the surface, things like emotions. "Okay," she said, "what do you want to know about survival?"

"Oh, good." He straightened. "So tell me, oh, guru of all that is the outdoors, what is it like to freeze to death?"

"I don't think this is a good time to talk about that," Gracie said. She sat up and crawled over to her pack. "Why don't I beat your arse in a nice game of poker instead? Somewhere around here I have the world's tiniest deck of cards."

"Don't blow me off. Please." His voice was low. "I'm not asking out of morbid curiosity. I'm looking for information. The unknown sucks. Knowledge, even if it's bad, affords equilibrium."

*Succinctly put*, Gracie thought, and filed the phrasing into a mental manila folder for future reference. She sat back and pulled her sleeping bag up around her shoulders. "Let's see. Freezing to death. Not really such a bad way to go."

Rob's eyebrows merged into a frown. "I'll keep that in mind."

"Not that dying is a pleasant proposition. But some ways of biting the dust are more preferable than others."

"Enlighten me."

"The team's had lots of discussions about this at the bar during our after-meeting meetings. The consensus is that dying in one's sleep is, of course, hands-down the preferred method. Stabbing, bludgeoning, and being killed by a wild animal are horribly violent and painful. Suffocation and drowning are claustrophobic and torturous."

"Do tell," Rob said.

"Burning to death is the worst. Beheading is quick, but the anticipation sucks."

Rob chuckled, bobbling his cup. "I almost spilled my cocoa. Or whatever this foul, barely potable concoction is I'm being forced to drink."

"Bite me," Gracie said.

"I'm getting used to it, you know. The insipid flavor is growing on me." He had a Puckish gleam in his eyes. "Kind of like a fungus."

"Har-dee-har," Gracie said. "May I please continue my pontification?"

"By all means."

"Strangulation is probably the best violent death if there is such a thing. You lose consciousness quickly and have no idea what happens after that. That's it. That's all I can remember."

"So . . . freezing to death is a good thing?"

"Not so bad. Relatively speaking of course. Aside from the initial shivering and extremity pain, the mind and body gradually shut down and you just ease on down the road. So relax."

"Doesn't any of this search and rescue stuff . . ." He gestured with his hand as he searched for the right word. ". . . Scare you?"

"*Scare* me?" Gracie thought for a moment. "This is what we train for. Most of the time you don't think about what you're doing, whether it's dangerous or whatever. You just . . . do it. So scare me? Not really." She added under her breath, "It's the normal, everyday crap I can't handle."

"What was that last part?"

"Nothing."

Rob smiled down at the cards.

Gracie lay back down again, closed her eyes, and tried to take her own advice and relax. She concentrated on clenching every single muscle in her body all at once, then releasing them. Clench. Release. Clench. Release. Tension drifted away.

She was almost asleep when Rob said, "What would I do if I got caught in an avalanche?"

"I'm taking those cards away from you."

"Come on. I want to see how much you know."

It took several seconds for Gracie to wake back up sufficiently to put her train of thought on the same track as Rob's. "The textbook answer is that as soon as you get swept up in an avalanche, make swimming motions through the snow and try to stay as close to the surface as you can. And keep your mouth shut."

"Why's that?"

Since it was apparent that napping wasn't in her near future, Gracie turned over again and propped her head up on a hand. "So when you stop, you don't end up with a big plug of snow in your mouth."

"Bugger."

"If they don't get squished to death by the slide itself, a lot of people suffocate. When the avalanche stops, the snow sets up like cement, like a really cold body cast. If you're still conscious when the slide is stopping, you cup your hands in front of your face like this . . ." Gracie covered her nose and mouth with her hands. ". . . So you have an air pocket. Then maybe, *maybe* you can keep yourself from suffocating to death."

"Bugger," Rob said again. "How would you know which way is up?"

"Drool. Whichever way the spit slides is down. If they haven't found you within about thirty minutes, you're probably dead."

When Rob looked thoughtful, she added, "The best way to survive an avalanche is to not get caught in the first place."

"And how would one accomplish that? It doesn't talk about that on the cards."

"Glaring omission," Gracie said. "A lot of factors create prime avalanche conditions. Recent heavy snow. How steep the slope. Moisture content. Aspect—what direction it's facing. Signs an avalanche has passed that way before."

"What signs?"

"No trees. Only young trees. No branches on the uphill side. Or if you're walking across a snow field—which, by the way, I would not advise. But say you are . . . If, when you take a step, the snow sends out cracks? Or if you hear a loud kind of a crack? Or a weird echoey *whoomph* sound?"

"Not a good thing," Rob said.

"Definitely not. If you hear that sound, you better hightail it outta there or you can kiss your ass good-bye."

She looked up to find Rob staring at her. "Quit looking at me like that," she demanded. "It's *really* starting to get on my nerves."

He grinned. "You have so much knowledge about things I don't. In fact, I never knew enough about them to know I didn't know anything about them."

"Huh?"

"I'm an actor. From the city."

"Ya think?"

"My life is movies. Make-believe."

"Ya think?"

"Will you shut up and let me express this without any editorial comments? This is some kind of epiphany for me."

"I'll be good."

"I won't hold my breath," he said, winking at her, which,

much to her surprise, made her stomach do a backflip. "Movie's aren't the real world."

Gracie stifled the urge to say "Ya think?" again.

"But this." He threw out his arms. "This is the real world. What we're doing here is the real world. And it's fantastic. You are the real world and you're fantastic."

"And you're whacked."

# CHAPTER

# 54

**M**ILOCEK examined the ground where he presumed Rob had landed when he jumped from the outcropping.

He had cleaned and dried himself off with water and his cloth handkerchief and pulled his clothes back on, all the while reformulating his plan. There was no longer any need to wait, to remain inactive, passive. He was on the offensive.

Dodging search teams along the trail had cost him precious time, and the day had slipped into afternoon. By the time he made it back to the outcropping, he had only two or three good hours of daylight left.

A few feet away from the base of the promontory, he found Rob's blue knapsack lying on the ground. Reserving a thorough search of the contents for later, he threaded his arms through the straps and shrugged the pack onto his back. Then he followed the path down the side of the canyon.

For several hundred feet the trail was clearly visible and easily followed. But as Milocek descended, the trail grew more and more diffuse until eventually he lost it altogether.

Like a bloodhound that has lost its scent, he scoured the

ground with his eyes. Bent low to the ground, he made long, slow horizontal sweeps back and forth and back and forth across the incline, dredging for any sign of human passage. Frustration grew inside him like volcanic pressure pushing up the earth's crust. His nostrils flared with each heavy breath. Thick, stubby fingers clenched into tight fists, unclenched, and clenched again.

Halfway down the incline, he stopped to straighten and stretch his aching back.

The cigarette stopped midway to his mouth. The faint, but distinct sound of human voices wafted up from the canyon.

Milocek flicked away the cigarette and plunged the rest of the way down to the bottom of the canyon.

A few feet from the embankment that dropped down to the water, he stopped and stood without moving for more than thirty minutes.

He heard nothing above the rippling of creek water.

A furnace of rage seered his chest. His head swiveled from side to side like an angry bull. Every nerve reached out as if with internal radar, every ounce of energy focused toward the detection of the tiniest movement, the merest whisper of sound that might lead him in the right direction.

Milocek took one final drag of his cigarette and flung it down to smolder on the damp ground.

He turned abruptly and climbed back up the side of the canyon.

GRACIE crouched on the ground several feet up the hill from the creek embankment, eyes fixed on the partially smoked Camel nonfilter lying at her feet. Three cigarette butts lay nearby.

As the afternoon crawled toward evening without the appearance of Cashman or a relief team, Gracie had been forced to accept that she no longer controlled the situation, or the search, and conceded that she and Rob would be spending a second night in the field. Rob accepted the news with equanimity and lay down again for another nap.

Gracie had lain dozing for a few minutes, then while Rob still slept, she crept out of the shelter. As a surprise for Rob, she fashioned little pillows for them both by stuffing pine needles into bread bags kept in her pack.

Then she hiked down to the creek to replenish their water supply. After refilling and adding iodine purifying tablets to both her water bottles and the hydration bladder from her pack, she climbed up the embankment and stopped at the top to readjust her pack. As she loosened the straps, something white standing out against the dark brown of the earth thirty feet away caught her eye.

Crouching on the ground, she drew off her glove and pinched the burned end of the cigarette between her fingers.

Still warm.

Not very long ago, while she and Rob were in the shelter, possibly even while she was hiking down to the creek, someone had stood in the same place long enough to smoke four cigarettes.

Gracie pushed herself to her feet, the hair rising on her scalp. She turned in a slow circle. The heavy cloud had lifted somewhat, not sufficiently for her to see all the way up the canyon, but enough to take stock of the area. There was no further sign of a human being, no movement, no unnatural color. She heard nothing but the rippling water of the creek below.

She studied the ground again and found where someone had stood for some length of time, but no definitive footprints led in any direction. The muted light was the worst possible for tracking.

Gracie slid back down the embankment, stepped stone by stone across the creek and scrambled up the other side. She followed the creek up for a short distance to where the pink flower of flagging tape still hung from a branch. She slit the ribbon with her knife and gathered up the strands, stuffing them into a pocket of her parka. The sandwich bag containing the note she tucked into the same pocket. One by one, she picked up the stones of the giant arrow and placed them at random around the site. Then she crossed over to the other side of the creek and crept up the side of the canyon.

When Gracie walked up to the shelter, Rob was leaning against the fallen log, arms folded across his chest. The frown on his face molded his eyebrows into a single dark line. He looked so much like an angry housewife waiting for an errant husband that Gracie almost smiled at him.

"Where the hell—?" he asked in a sharp voice.

Gracie silenced him by placing a single finger on his mouth.

With her mouth two inches from Rob's ear, she described to him what she had found.

Rob whispered back that as far as he knew, only one of their hiking party smoked unfiltered cigarettes.

Joseph.

As night settled like an icy cloak at the bottom of the canyon, Gracie and Rob demobilized the second shelter and moved deeper into the wilderness. A half mile down, they located a triangle of bare ground, suitably level and surrounded by giant boulders. Evergreen boughs placed over the top effectively masked the beacon of orange plastic and added extra insulation. Unless one stood directly in front of the two-foot wide passageway leading in to the refuge of boulders, they were completely invisible.

In silence, they heated their dinner over Gracie's tiny stove—the remaining packet of chicken noodle soup spiced with a little bottle of Tabasco from the MRE. They topped off a quarter each of the flat, but still tasty peanut butter sandwich with the packet of stale Skittles, which Rob painstakingly divided in half.

In silence, they crawled into the shelter. By the dim light of her headlamp, Gracie checked and rebound Rob's ankle with the elastic bandage.

In the dark, they climbed into their respective sleeping bags and lay down side by side, the trekking poles and Gracie's bared hunting knife between them.

**R**ALPH stood at the edge of the Aspen Springs Trail and watched the recovery team retrieve Steve Cashman's body from the depths of the canyon.

The all-encompassing cloud had lifted, but an unbroken layer of slate gray stratus clouds still obscured San Raphael and the surrounding mountains, and brought with them an early dusk.

Ninety minutes earlier, two EMTs had rappelled down the high-angle cliff to where the battered body lay at the bottom. They had radioed back the positive identification as a Timber Creek SAR member. Male.

Until that moment, Ralph hadn't realized how profound his terror was that Gracie might be dead. The report that the body was Cashman's elicited shock and a deep sadness. But his relief that it wasn't Gracie so overwhelmed him that he sagged down onto a rock before his knees gave way.

From a vantage point up the trail, Ralph watched the somber setup of the ropes system and the long, tedious process of hauling the litter containing Cashman's body up the side of the mountain to the trail.

The grim irony that Cashman had pushed to do a technical ropes body recovery only two days before wasn't lost on Ralph. Cashman had gotten a body recovery all right. His own.

How the hell had Cashman fallen from the trail? Ralph wondered. For all his flaws, the man was a mountain goat. If Cashman and Gracie had located one or more of the MisPers and one of them had been injured, Gracie, as the EMT, would stay behind with her patient or patients, and Cashman would hike out to radio in for a relief team.

But Steve had hiked almost all the way back to the CP. Why hadn't he called in earlier, as soon as he emerged from the dead spot?

Ralph grimaced. Cashman hadn't called in because he was Cashman. Publicity hound. Glory seeker. He wanted to be the hero. He had big news and wanted to deliver it in person. And that decision had somehow cost him his life.

As three members of the recovery team daisy-chained the last of the anchor webbing, and inventoried and packed away the heavy steel carabiners and rigging plates and Prusik-minding pulleys, four other team members carried the Junkin litter containing Cashman's body encased in a white plastic body bag, out to the trailhead parking lot and the ambulance that waited there.

Now the only thing that remained for Ralph to do was visit Wanda, Cashman's wife, who by this time had received the news that she was a widow and their little girls had lost their father.

But Ralph's thoughts hadn't gone there yet. By the light of his headlamp he regarded the scarred radio microphone resting in his open palm. While neither Cashman's GPS nor the HT itself had been recovered, the microphone had survived the four-hundred-foot fall into the canyon clipped to Steve's parka, the microphone that told Ralph with a certainty that chilled the blood in his veins that Gracie was out there essentially alone. Without a radio.

A cold, delicate touch brushed the back of Ralph's neck. He tipped his head back and looked up. White flakes, large and fluffy, floated down from above.

It was snowing.

# CHAPTER
## 57

**MILOCEK** sat at the base of the outcropping with his back against a granite boulder. He drew cigarette smoke deep into his lungs, then exhaled it through his nostrils.

The day ebbed toward evening with the flat layer of leaden clouds casting a pall across the entire canyon. The air was damp and chilled him to the bone.

Climbing up from the creek, he had resumed his search for any sign of a trail, but had found nothing. Except for the one instance of hearing what he was certain were human voices, he had heard anything.

When it had grown too dark to see, he climbed back up to the trail. He would resume the search the following day.

Milocek rarely second-guessed his own actions. But he cursed himself now. He never should have taken that first swig of brandy. He had dropped his guard, lost control. Killing the interfering man on the outcropping had been an impulsive act, the mark of an amateur and a fool.

He considered again if, when the woman recognized him,

he should have simply returned to his car and driven out of the country.

But he knew exactly what would happen if his identity were revealed. Manhunt. Capture. Imprisonment. Extradition. Tribunal. Execution. The decision to salvage the situation or die trying had been the right one. The only one.

But he wasn't giving up the fight yet.

Milocek's gloved hands balled into fists. He ground his back teeth until they squeaked.

Rob and the woman searcher were down there in the canyon. He could feel them. Smell them. Taste them.

Something wet and cold touched Milocek's face. He looked up.

It was snowing.

T was snowing. Hard.

Encased in her sleeping bag, Gracie stared at the powder-puff flakes dancing an ominous ballet of nature before the shelter entrance. Six inches of snow already hung on the surrounding boulders and the bushes and trees beyond, rendering the landscape a monochromatic palette of dark and light.

In the protective cove of granite boulders, the little shelter lay immune from the worst of the storm. Beyond, the moaning, blustering demon of wind blasted the snow into a swirling wall of white. Occasional icy breaths stole into the shelter through layers of fleece and straight to the skin.

Overnight Gracie and Rob's passive wait for relief had turned into an active fight for survival. All of life's other problems were shoved to the background. All self-doubt was erased. All Gracie's thoughts, all her energy laser-beamed into a single goal: Stay alive.

Years of training kicked in and Gracie mentally ticked off everything she could remember about survival theory.

Survival is a state of mind. Think positive thoughts. A positive mental attitude is number one on the list for keeping oneself alive. Despair was one sure marker on the slow route to death.

The snow also brought a curious sense of relief. While the storm meant no rescue for the time being, its protective layer also provided a respite, albeit temporary, from Joseph, if the man hadn't hiked out at the first sign of snow.

It was a given that while it snowed there would be no aviation evacuation. And it was a real possibility that the Command Post would elect to endanger no additional lives and pull any existing teams in from the field. The one thing that was a certainty was that she and Rob were stuck for the duration.

As quietly as possible, Gracie unfolded the map. First she pinpointed their location. Then she calculated approximately how far it was from the shelter down to the creek and up the other side of the canyon to the trail, from there to the parking lot. With the snow, she was fairly certain the Command Post would have been moved to a lower elevation, possibly the Coon Creek Jump-off, the junction of two forest service roads five miles back down the mountain. If not there, then the Sandy Flats Visitor's Center a mile or so down the main highway, the nearest location suitable for a large SAR operation. All told, the distance from the shelter to where Gracie could guarantee there would be a live person was more than ten miles.

Her eyes slid over to where Rob slept, the drawstring of his sleeping bag pulled so tightly around his head that only the top half of his face was visible.

Gracie was confident she could make the ten miles, even in the snow. But she couldn't take the chance that Rob might not.

They would stay right where they were and wait it out. Someone would eventually come. Search and Rescue never abandoned its own. Ralph would never leave her out there.

Not to mention the fact that the man who lay sleeping only inches away from her was literally worth his weight in gold. As soon as the storm blew past, the entire country would be out looking for them.

All they had to do was stay alive that long.

RALPH stood beneath the overhang of the visitor's center and watched through the oblique curtain of snow, alpine teams preparing for their snowcat rides up to the Aspen Springs Trailhead. His face was unshaven, his eyes red-rimmed from too few hours of trying to sleep on the hard floor of the visitor's center along with half a dozen other searchers.

The previous evening, as conditions deteriorated on San Raphael, the Deputy Incident Commander assigned to the twelve-hour night shift had pulled the remaining few teams of ground pounders in from the field. At 0600, newly reorganized and equipped alpine teams—all trained and certified in winter travel and survival—had arrived for deployment. In spite of Ralph's heated protests, a refreshed Incident Commander Nels Black had assigned only one team of three men and one woman to search specifically for Gracie.

Ralph knew the San Raphael Search, as it was now called, had not officially shifted focus. The rest of the world was interested only in one thing—bringing Rob Christian out alive. Yet for every searcher present, regardless of his or her assignment, locating the original MisPers had become secondary, replaced by a single, all-encompassing goal: find and save one of their own.

If Gracie was injured and off the trail, the chances were infinitesimal that searchers would locate her in this weather. But Ralph empathized with the gut-wrenching compulsion to try. He needed to be out there, too, searching for Gracie, doing everything physically possible to find her, to bring her safely in. He inwardly cursed his injured knee that left him grounded, helpless, watching from the sidelines.

Ralph stared at the small groups of SAR members from Timber Creek and other county teams checking and organizing their equipment carabinered and strapped in place on packs and climbing harnesses—ropes and climbing hardware, ice axes, snowshoes, snow pickets, crampons. The only visible manifestation of the turmoil beneath the surface was the muscle working in his cheek.

Gracie was still alive. She had to be. When pushed, she could be as ornery as a bull at a Rocky Mountain Oyster Festival.

"Hold on, Gracie girl," Ralph whispered.

# CHAPTER
## 60

**S**NOW now fell so thick and fast in the canyon that tracks Gracie and Rob made earlier that morning attending to nature's call were visible only as shallow concave ovals leading from the shelter. The wind had grown into a moaning, blustering demon of wind, sending blasts of bitter air howling and shrieking down the canyon and tormenting the flimsy plastic shelter.

There was no way to predict how long the snow would last. Storms in Southern California rarely lasted more than a single day, but they could be brutal nonetheless. A few years before, a single storm had dumped three feet of snow overnight on Gracie's cabin at seven thousand feet, several thousand feet lower in elevation than she and Rob were at now.

Upon awakening, Rob's initial reaction to the snow was similar to Gracie's—awe at the fierce beauty. But as the severity of their predicament gnawed its way into his consciousness, his fascination had grown into concern. He asked myriad questions—how long will the storm last, how much snow will fall, how does this affect the rescue, how long are we stuck here? To all of which Gracie provided the same answer: "I don't know."

Gracie and Rob lay side-by-side in their respective sleeping bags. What remained of the candle stub bathed the interior of the cramped shelter with a honey-colored light. Flickering with each gust of wind, the flame sent shadows dancing throughout the tiny space.

While Gracie forced her body to remain motionless, her mind was still active, darting from thought to thought.

*Had* the Command Post been moved down the mountain? Snow would make the narrow, winding road to the trailhead parking lot impassable to all vehicles except snowmobiles and snowcats. How much would that slow down any relief team? Had they pulled teams in from the field? Even alpine? Would she and Rob have to wait until the skies cleared and be airlifted out? What was Ralph doing? How much sleep had he had? How many cigarettes had he smoked? How high was his blood pressure?

Of all the worst-case scenarios Gracie could have conjured in her mind, snow would have been close to the top of the list. Not only would it change the nature of the search, requiring a major shift in personnel and logistics, it introduced a host of complications and hazards for any teams in the field, not to mention for her and Rob. The only thing she could think of that would make their situation worse would be if she were injured in some way.

Or if they were caught in an avalanche.

A spear of terror plunged through Gracie's stomach. Mountaineers more experienced than she had been killed while sleeping in their tents when it snowed during the night and an early morning avalanche roared through their camp and took them all out.

Gracie clawed out of the sleeping bag and threw on her boots. Leaving Rob openmouthed behind her, she scrambled outside, sighing in relief only when she reconfirmed that the mountainside above the shelter was thick with trees and boulders and held no signs of previous slides.

Back inside the shelter, she crawled into her sleeping bag, quickly zipping it all the way back up to her chin.

"What was that all about?" Rob asked.

"Nothing," Gracie answered, blowing him off, but hoping he wouldn't take offense.

A strong gust of wind blustered into the haven of boulders setting the plastic shelter to riffling and flapping above their heads and straining against the anchoring rocks. Gracie held her breath, shoulders drawn up to her ears, eyes skyward, then exhaled when the shelter held and the wind ebbed back to a whisper.

She looked over at Rob. In the dim light, his face appeared washed out and pale, the tip of his nose as if it had been dipped in pink paint. "You doing okay?" she asked. When he didn't answer, she propped herself up on an elbow so she could see his face better. "Rob?"

He lifted bleary eyes to hers.

"Are you okay?"

"I'm going to turn that around and ask you that same question. Are we okay?"

"In terms of . . ."

"Are we going to make it?"

"You mean make it through this? The snow?"

"Yes."

"Hell, yes! We are going to make it!" She sat up, hunching the sleeping bag over her shoulders and holding it closed at the neck. "Keeping warm and dry is our number one priority. We have lots of water. Our food and fuel levels aren't so hot. I'm not that worried about food anyway." Now was not the time to tell Rob they could survive for weeks without food if they had to.

The look on Rob's face told her he wasn't convinced.

"We are going to get out of here, okay? They are going to come for us. Could be today. Could be tomorrow. But they are going to come for us. We just have to hunker down and wait it out. Which is exactly what we're doing."

After a moment, Rob asked, "Do you believe in God?"

Gracie was silent, unsure of how much of her soul she wanted to bare. Finally she said, "In spite of my ultraconservative, right-wing upbringing, yes, I do believe in God." She looked over at Rob. "How about you?"

He nodded.

They sat quietly again until Rob said, "Do you believe in prayer?"

Gracie nodded. "I pray. Not often enough. Mostly when I'm thankful for something. I try not to just ask for things." She frowned. "Never could figure out why sometimes it seems to work and sometimes it doesn't."

"Maybe this is one of the times it'll work," Rob said softly.

"Maybe." Gracie squeezed her eyes closed. *Please, God,* she prayed, *help me to be strong. Help me to keep Rob . . . and me . . . alive. And please let don't let Cashman have gotten hurt in some way.*

Quite certain that bargaining never worked with the Supreme Being, she added anyway, *If you get us out of this, I'll do my level best to be a better person. I'll be nicer to people. I'll be nicer to Cashman. Well . . . I'll try to be nicer to Cashman.*

Satisfied that that was plenty of sacrifice to placate Him or Her, she signed off with: *If I think of anything else, I'll get back to you.*

RALPH slouched in a chair in the reception area of the visitor's center and stared with unseeing eyes at the members of the alpine teams who stood in the kitchen—cheeks flushed pink with cold, snow melting on hats and parkas—sipping cups of coffee and hot chocolate.

The alpine teams had never made it to the trailhead. Three miles in from the main highway, they had found the National Forest Service road that climbed up to the Aspen Springs Trail blocked by a massive snow slide. The road was impassable even to the snow cats in which the teams rode. They had been forced to return to the Command Post until a new search plan could be formulated.

Contracting for a plow to clear the road would take hours, if not days. According to the National Weather Service, the long, narrow storm cell would leave the area by the following morning. The most prudent course of action for the search would be to wait until then when aviation could be deployed.

Ralph blinked, then blinked again as it hit him for the

first time since the search began that Gracie might not survive the storm. And with that came the stunning realization of how integral to his life she had become. She was the only bright spot in the darkness. If Gracie didn't survive the storm, the precarious house of cards that was his life would collapse.

Ralph pushed his glasses up on his head and rubbed his face with his hands. He shoved aside the dismal thoughts with a physical effort. If he didn't do something constructive to occupy his mind, he was going to blow a gasket.

He picked up the clipboard resting on the arm of the chair, his own clipboard containing the original Command Post sign-in sheets, notes, and radio log, and the personnel and background information of all of the MisPers—the same clipboard he had unearthed that morning from beneath a pile of three-ring binders on one of the Command Post tables.

After the alpine teams had left for their ride up to the trailhead, Ralph had studied the headshots of Rob Christian and Tristan Chambers and the information about them gathered from the production company. He had just turned to Diana Petrovic's when the alpine teams had returned with the news of the snow slide.

Now he turned back to the missing woman's information. Petrovic, Diana. Height: 5'0". Weight: 97 pounds. Hair: brown. Eyes: brown. DOB: 9/15/85. One infraction on her driving record—a speeding ticket in L.A. County three years before. Background check showed no criminal record.

Ralph studied the headshot of the actress. She was attractive as was to be expected. Hair and sparkling eyes, both listed as brown on the driver's license, looked black in the photo. She wore bangs pushed off to the side and her straight hair shoulder-length.

Petrovic sounded what? Russian? Eastern European?

He flipped to the next pages. Van Dijk, Joseph A. Height: 5'9". Weight: 205 pounds. Hair: gray. Eyes: blue. DOB: 2/17/54. Clean as a whistle. No driving record. No criminal record.

Ralph turned to the man's driver's license picture. He squinted at the tiny photo and wondered why the picture hadn't been blown up further when it had been photocopied.

Squared jaw, fleshy cheeks, thick neck. In the photo, Joseph Van Dijk was bald. Or at least his head had been shaved.

Ralph looked more closely at the picture.

He couldn't be certain because the man's head was turned very slightly to the left—possibly deliberately, but it appeared as if Joseph Van Dijk was missing an ear.

# CHAPTER
# 62

**GRACIE** had blown it. Big-time.

Inside the shelter, she and Rob lay in their sleeping bags, heads on their crunchy pillows. Outside, the wind howled and moaned and shook and flapped the plastic above their heads.

Rob appeared to be sleeping. At least his eyes were closed. And he had barely moved in thirty minutes.

Gracie, on the other hand, had been puzzling over the realization that, in spite of everything, she was feeling an incongruous sense of contentment. It had been a patriarch's age since she had felt remotely comfortable around a man other than her teammates, especially in anything resembling a prone position—multiple layers of fleece, down and poly-propylene between them notwithstanding.

Until it hit her like a charge of dynamite—without her being aware of it, her feelings for Rob had moved into the mine-filled realm of the personal. He was no longer some nameless someone from whom she was clinically detached, uninvolved, emotionally remote. The man lying beside her was a living, breathing human being of whom, she realized with another jolt, she had grown quite fond.

Anxiety rose up to lodge a fist behind her sternum. The reality that she held Rob's life in her own feeble hands suffocated her with a physical weight. If he died, she would never be able to live with herself.

"Tell me about your life." Rob's soft voice barged in on her thoughts.

"I thought you were sleeping," Gracie said. "Are you warm enough?"

"Enough. Where did you come from? Your family. Things like that." He asked the questions offhandedly, like one would if one was used to everyday personal conversations.

"I don't want to talk about that," Gracie said, eyes focused back on the shelter ceiling.

"I want to know."

"Why?"

"Because I'm interested."

"Nothing to tell."

"Liar."

She turned over and propped her head up on her hand. She studied Rob through half-closed eyes, feeling as if she were teetering on the edge of a crevasse, arms windmilling, and she had to decide whether to leap across the abyss or remain safely where she was.

*Come on. If I can jump out of a helicopter, I ought to be able to do this.* "Born and raised in a small blue-collar town in the middle of Michigan," she said.

Rob sat up inside his sleeping bag. "Michigan. Detroit, right?"

"I'm impressed."

"Never been there."

"Congratulations. Nah, that's not fair. Parts of the state are gorgeous. It's the cities I can't stand."

"Ever been to London?"

"No."

"New York?"

"No. I told you, I hate cities."

"How can you hate cities you've never been to?"

"I've never stuck a red-hot poker in my eye either. I don't have to do it to know I won't like it."

"Why don't you branch out a little from your placid, uneventful life? Do something adventurous for a change. Come to New York for a visit."

"There are three chances of me ever going to New York City," she said. "Slim, fat, and none."

"Cheeky, aren't you?"

"Cheeky. You asked me a question, so let me answer."

"So answer already." He grinned. "I'm tired of waiting for you."

She shot him a look. "*Reader's Digest* condensed version. Morris. Stepfather. Executive. Workaholic. Evelyn. Mother. Racquet Club wife." A half brother and half sister from her mother's first marriage. She glossed over a childhood filled with symphonies, theater and ballet lessons. U of M. Budding career in advertising. "You can't find this interesting," she said with a grimace.

"I consider myself a student of human nature." He looked pointedly at her. "So you're the youngest?"

"Yep."

"What about your little sister?"

"What little sister?"

"The one you sold into slavery for that sleeping bag?"

"Huh, yeah. That little sister. Oops."

"Uh-huh. What other lies have you told me?" he asked, eyes crinkling.

Gracie inhaled to protest, but clapped it shut again because at that moment Rob looked so beautiful it was surreal.

"What about men?" he asked. "You said you were engaged. What happened?"

"Burned. No, chewed up and spit out is more like it.

That's all I'm going to say. Your turn. I want to hear every
boring detail straight from the horse's mouth."

Rob stretched out full length on his sleeping pad, resting
his head back on his pine-needle pillow. "My life's not
nearly as interesting as yours."

"Nice try," she said, turning over onto her back again.
"Spill it."

As the snow piled up outside the shelter, Gracie listened
as Rob presented to her a compendium of his life, which
boiled down to born and raised in London, fifth out of nine
children, two boys and seven girls. "My way of getting attention in such a big, noisy crowd was to act out, be the ham.
I was a royal pain in the arse."

"I can't imagine."

"Eventually university. Cut to present day. Currently rent-
ing a flat in New York. Upper West Side. Great restaurants
and pubs and bagel shops and newspaper stands. But quiet
on my street."

"Mmmm," was all Gracie could muster.

"There's an energy about the city. A vibrancy. You need
a whole different set of skills to survive there."

Gracie looked over at him.

"It's true," he said.

"Like I said before, three chances . . ." As if to punctuate
the point, Gracie's stomach rumbled audibly.

Rob smiled. "I heard that."

"I'm hungry."

Holding her eye, Rob drawled, "I'm so hungry, I could
eat a sow an' nine pigs an' chase the boar half a mile."
Before Gracie had time to roll her eyes, he sat bolt upright.
"Hold on! I had a rucksack!"

"Keep your voice down!" Gracie hissed.

Rob dropped his voice back to a whisper. "A . . . a backpack. I completely forgot about it. I was carrying leftovers
from the lunch. Must have lost it when I fell."

"Could I find it?"

His face fell. "Bloody hell, I don't know."

"That's all right. I can backtrack up to it." She scrambled out of her bag and grabbed her Gore-Tex pants, lying flat on her back to pull them on.

Rob watched her slip her radio chest pack over her head and clip it in place. "I want to go with you," he said in a deep voice.

"I don't want you re-injuring your ankle."

"I don't like you going out there alone. It's not safe."

"I'll be careful," Gracie said, wishing she felt as confident as she sounded. "I'm taking the pack. Block the entrance with my sleeping bag." She grabbed her mountaineering boots. "If something happens and I don't come back—"

Rob's eyes widened. "Don't say that!"

"If something happens," she said, "stay here. Do not— Are you listening to me?"

"I'm listening."

"Do not try to hike out. You have the most important things—shelter and water. A person can survive for weeks without food." At Rob's panic-stricken face, she quickly added, "Not that there's any way this is going to last that long. As soon as this storm breaks, they'll send aviation in. Describe the rucksack."

"Blue. Dark blue. Black straps."

"Pass me my crampons."

As she Velcroed her gaiters over her boots, he retrieved the steel spikes from the little storage area at the back of the shelter and handed them to her. "Nasty-looking things."

"Very useful for walking on ice and slippery slopes," she said, fastening them to the outside of her pack. "Ice axe."

He held it up. One end of the axe head—the adze—was flattened to a cutting edge; the other end, the pick, well-honed to a sharp point. The three-foot metal shaft itself ended in a spike. "Another nasty-looking thing." He turned it in his hands. "What's it for?"

"Mostly a sort-of walking stick in the snow." Taking it

from him, she gripped the shaft in one hand, placing the other on top of the axe head, the pick facing forward. "But if I fall, I jab it into the snow like this and, theoretically at least, slow myself down. It's called self-arrest."

"And you've done this?"

"In trainings. It's really hard."

"Bloody remarkable."

"Takes a lot of upper body strength and a lot of practice to become really proficient. I'm not very good."

Rob watched as she stuffed her arms into her parka sleeves and stretched a balaclava over her head, followed by the helmet, then flipped her hood up on top of everything.

She turned to crawl out of the shelter, then stopped. She pulled up her jacket, unsheathed the hunting knife and laid it carefully on the sleeping bag next to Rob.

"What's that for?"

Her eyes lifted to meet his. "Just in case."

She heard Rob curse under his breath as she turned again to leave. He grabbed hold of her arm to stop her. "Gracie," he said in a low voice. "Be careful."

"I always am."

She tried to turn away yet again, but he held on to her arm. "Gracie."

She turned back.

He looked her right in the eye. "Be careful."

She looked steadily back. "I always am."

Gracie tossed her mostly empty pack ahead of her into the snow and crawled out of the shelter.

# CHAPTER

# 63

**G**RACIE climbed up the side of the mountain, her body falling into a natural rhythm to conserve energy. Breathing in through her nose, she planted the end of her ice axe, kicked a step in the snow and placed her foot until her crampons grabbed. Then, while breathing out through her mouth, she pushed up, straightening her leg and momentarily resting the muscle. Then she took another breath and another step. Another breath. Another step.

Every few minutes, she stopped to catch her breath or unzip the underarm zippers of her parka. She glanced around, squinting her eyes against the blowing snow, taking note of landmarks—an oddly shaped boulder, a fallen log, a tangle of manzanita—anything that would help her negotiate her way back to the shelter. Before she had left the shelter, she had set her GPS to track. But she never relied solely on technology. Technology often failed. The thought of not being able to find her way back to Rob chilled her bones in a way the weather couldn't.

The wind grew even more ferocious as she worked her

way up. It pelted her face with icy slivers and whipped the air from her lungs. Her breathing grew more labored. Gradually all thought ceased until nothing existed but: Breathe in. Plant the ice axe. Step right. Straighten the leg. Breathe out. Plant the ice axe. Step left. Straighten. Breathe in.

She stopped again, chest heaving, the exposed skin on her face burning with the cold. She could see not far above her head, the jumble of boulders that formed the base of the rock promontory.

Thank Almighty God.

Gracie turned around in a circle, eyes half-closed against the wind, searching the hillside for any sign of Rob's knapsack. But no blue cloth stood out against the snow.

Gracie climbed up past the rock outcropping and hauled herself up onto the trail. As she straightened, a freight train of wind slammed into her, almost tipping her over. She staggered to regain her footing and braced herself against the wind as if against a solid wall. Then she tottered, zombielike with arms outstretched, across the trail and wedged herself into a narrow crack in the rock to catch her breath.

Gracie's body was sweating even as her cheeks and fingers stung with cold. Any moisture on her skin would quickly sap away the heat her body produced and she would soon be shivering. She unzipped her parka a couple of inches, flapped freezing air inside onto her bare skin, then zipped it back up.

Her eye caught on a streamer of neon orange flagging tape whipping crazily in the wind a few feet up the trail from where she stood. Was that there the first night? She didn't remember seeing it when she had aimed her flashlight up the trail. Flagging tape was the kind of thing she would have noticed. She hadn't walked very far past the point where the prints had left the trail. Cashman had, but she was confident he hadn't tied it there.

The only logical explanation for the orange tape was that a search team had hiked up the trail, marking their progress along the way.

Gracie's spirits hit bottom.

The search team had bypassed the rock outcropping and continued on up the trail. They hadn't known Gracie and Rob were down in the canyon, which meant they hadn't received the GPS coordinates of the bivouac. The possibility was zero that Cashman had reached the CP and told someone where she and Rob were.

Cashman had never made it back to the Command Post.

No one knew where they were.

Another thought slammed into her. She leaned out from the crack in the rock and looked down the trail, searching for a flash of the neon green flagging tape Cashman had tied when they first descended into the canyon. The wind bit at her face and whipped tears from the corners of her eyes back into her hair. She squinted so her eyelashes blocked most of the blowing snow. No neon green stood out against the white surroundings.

Gracie ducked back into the shelter of the crack.

There was no question in her mind that Cashman had flagged the spot where they left the trail. She distinctly remembered him tying several lengths. A quick check of her GPS confirmed she was in the right place.

Flagging tape was tough. It required a concerted, deliberate effort to remove it. A search team bypassing the outcropping without blowing whistles or shouting or following their trail down the side of the hill meant only one thing—someone had removed the green tape with the express purpose of preventing the searchers from finding her and Rob.

The hair on Gracie's arms prickled as she was struck by the feeling that someone was watching her.

*Get off the trail! Go down! Now!*

# CHAPTER

# 64

**G**RACIE could barely see her feet in the gusting snow.

The feeling of eyes watching her had disappeared as soon as she had thrown herself down on the edge of the trail and pushed off the side.

Now she concentrated on working her way down the steep slope past the giant up-thrust of rock that formed the outcropping. She fought the impulse to hurry, firmly planting her ice axe, and then each boot onto the steps she had made on the way up. Stepping with her knees bent, she leaned forward on her ice axe so her feet wouldn't fly out from under her. One false step, one misplacement of her ice axe, one caught crampon, and, courtesy of her slick, waterproof parka and pants, Gracie would find herself on an E-ticket ride to the bottom. Or worse—face-planting into a tree trunk along the way. The old adage "It's not the fall that'll kill you. It's the sudden stop at the bottom" almost made her smile beneath her balaclava.

At the base of the outcropping, she stopped in the shelter of the tumbled boulders to drink deeply from her water bottle and look around again for Rob's knapsack. As she twisted the cap back on, she scanned the mountainside below her. What she could see of the pines and firs, bushes and rocks appeared undisturbed by anything other than nature's fury.

She looked down at the ground around her feet. Beneath the snow, she recognized the signs of a second path diverting from the main track and running along the bottom of the outcropping.

Was that something she and Cashman had missed in the dark when they descended what seemed like weeks ago? Or had it been made after that? Her consternation grew when she remembered that Cashman had passed that way three more times, twice on the first night, the third time the previous morning and had noticed nothing. At least he had made no mention of it to her.

She resigned herself to the fact that she was probably expending valuable energy for nothing when she was already running below empty and trudged along the base of the promontory.

Fifty feet in, she stopped and looked up.

The body had been shoved up beneath a protective lip of granite where no snow had been able to accumulate. What was visible was thankfully not the face, but the back of the head, the torso, the lower portions of both legs, and one arm with a bare hand.

Bright red jacket. Bright yellow shirt. White-blond hair. Reeboks.

Gracie's brain plucked the details from the Lost Person Questionnaire.

She had found Tristan Chambers.

THERE was no need to check for signs of life. The body had been wedged back into the rocky crevice with the arms and legs tucked around it like so much limp spaghetti. Portions of the shirt and jacket appeared black, and the hair was matted with what was probably dried blood.

The body was confirmation that what Rob remembered about someone dying was, in actuality, fact. At least as far as Tristan was concerned, there was no more uncertainty. No more speculation. No more what-ifs and maybes.

Gracie felt the noose tighten around her neck.

She needed to get out of there. Fast. She needed to get back to where Rob waited alone, unsuspecting, unprotected.

Conscious the area was a crime scene, Gracie touched nothing on the corpse itself. She planted her feet firmly in the snow, pulled out her GPS again, and took a waypoint, labeling it DB. Dead Body.

Death was never pretty. Gracie never got used to it. The smell of fresh blood or decomposing flesh always made her insides roil. Tristan's body was frozen solid. At least there was no discernible smell. She took in deep, frigid breaths to keep down what little food she had eaten that day.

But as soon as she turned to make her way back along the base of the rock outcropping, her mouth filled with saliva and the familiar metallic taste. She dropped to her hands and knees, and vomited into the snow.

Gracie's body shook uncontrollably and her teeth chattered so violently she couldn't keep her mouth closed. Her head hung almost to the ground. She took in deep, heavy breaths to the bottom of her lungs, willing back the vomit that threatened to rise again in her throat. Tears dripped unheeded onto the snow.

*Get going. Put your feet under you and stand up.*

She spat out the sour taste and wiped off her mouth with a handful of snow. Then, leaning on her ice axe to steady herself, Gracie stood and looked up right into a pair of deep-set blue eyes.

GRACIE yelped and stumbled backward.

The man lunged forward, grabbed the front of her parka, and lifted her off the ground as effortlessly as if she were a hummingbird. "Where is he?" he rasped, his face so close she inhaled his foul breath into her lungs.

Fear shot adrenaline through Gracie's body. She grabbed at the man's hands, trying to peel back his fingers. Her hands slipped. She grabbed on to his forearms and tried to twist free.

The man tightened his grip and locked his elbows together so that his fists pressed up under her chin. His knuckles dug into her larynx.

She couldn't breathe.

She opened her mouth and tried to speak, but no words came out.

She was strangling. Her vision dimmed. Her world shrank into the all-consuming need to free herself and take in a breath.

"Where is he?" the man growled again and shook her until her teeth rattled.

Gracie's feet flailed around trying to gain purchase on something, anything, so she could push herself up and draw breath.

*Do something or you're dead!*

Gracie swung her foot back and kicked the man squarely in the shin with the steel points of her crampon.

The man grunted and bent forward.

Gracie's feet hit the ground. She coughed and sucked air into her lungs. Then she lifted her foot and stomped down onto his with all of her weight. Steel crampon talons plunged through boot leather, crunched bones, and sank deep.

The man roared with pain and fell back in the snow.

Gracie fell away from him onto her back and wrenched her foot free.

*Go! GO!*

Gracie plunged down the mountain in giant leaps. Propelled by adrenaline, she jumped, slid, fell, shoved herself back to her feet, jumped again. Twenty feet down. Thirty. Forty.

She was out of breath.

A split-second glance over her shoulder told her the man wasn't following. Not yet. She slowed a fraction and sucked more air into her lungs.

The man wanted Rob, no doubt to kill him. He would follow her to get to him. At all costs she had to keep him from doing just that.

She glanced back over her shoulder again. The trail she was leaving in the snow would be as easy to follow as a bulldozer's.

And there wasn't a damned thing she could do about it.

# 67

"**R**OB! Get up!" Gracie dived into the shelter and began stuffing her sleeping bag into her pack. "We have to get out of here! Now!"

Rob sat up in his bag, groggily wiping his face with his hands. "Good. You're back. Did you find the rucksack?"

"Get up!" Gracie yelled. "We have to get out of here!" She tossed his boots over to him. "See if you can get these on."

When Rob hesitated, she bellowed, "Move, dammit! We have to get outta here!"

That did it. Without another word Rob kicked his way out of the sleeping bag.

**GRACIE AND ROB** abandoned the plastic shelter and raced down the hillside—a minefield of fallen logs and loose rocks lying in wait beneath the snow to capture feet and snap ankles. At the creek, they scrambled along the steep, frozen embankment where no snow had been able to grab hold and leave obvious sign of their passing. For a tedious, painstaking quarter mile, they paralleled the water, sliding down, grabbing on to roots and branches to haul themselves back up and continue on.

When the embankment grew too steep to traverse, they dropped down to the creek itself and moved from rock to rock to rock, a finger pointing, a foot stepping, slipping, grabbing, then stepping again.

Throughout it all, if Rob's ankle pained him, he kept silent.

Adrenaline spent, Gracie's arms and legs trembled like warm jelly. She willed back the nausea churning her stomach.

*Not yet. Don't crash yet.*

Her eyes darted behind them, down to her feet, over to Rob's, then behind them again, scanning the creek bed, peering through the gloom of falling snow for any sign of the hunter.

"THIS'LL do," Gracie gasped and slung her pack from her back.

Behind her, Rob sank to his knees in the snow. Hands on thighs, head hanging, he dragged air into his lungs in deep, ragged breaths. "What . . . we doing?"

"Building a snow cave." She freed her snow shovel from its lash strap and heaved her pack into a bare hollow beneath the spindly bottom branches of a nearby fir tree. "We need shelter."

On a north-facing slope a third of the way up the mountain on the other side of the creek, Gracie had found what she was searching for: a giant upsweep of snow drifting higher than their heads with enough consolidated snow for a snow cave.

There was no way to tell where her attacker was. He could still be where she had left him at the base of the rock promontory. Or he could be following their tracks. Climbing up from the creek. Closing in for the kill.

But none of that mattered if she and Rob died of hypothermia. With shelter, they had a chance. Without it, death was certain.

Rob put a foot beneath him and staggered back to his feet. He looked as if the slightest provocation would topple him like a felled tree. "I'm . . . help you."

Gracie opened her mouth to protest, but closed it again. They needed shelter and she couldn't do it alone.

Working side by side, Gracie and Rob dug directly into the side of the drift. Gracie thrust in her little plastic shovel and tossed snow off to the side. Rob scraped and scooped with the little square of closed-cell foam.

As Gracie worked, time expanded. Every second lasted a minute, every minute an eternity. Fear buzzed inside her head like a swarm of flies telling her to hurry, hurry, hurry. She prayed to Jehovah, Yahweh, Allah, Shiva, Kane, and every other god who might be listening, that she had incapacitated her attacker enough, slowed him down enough that the falling snow—once the enemy—would fill in their tracks, obscure their trail, allow them to melt into the thousands of acres of raw wilderness.

And that the man would slip and fall and break his fucking neck.

## CHAPTER

# 69

GRACIE wriggled through the tiny rectangular hole in the drift. She crawled up into the oblong interior of the snow cave where the lantern flashlight glowed warm and welcoming from its own little snow shelf and, in stark contrast to her jumping nerves, it was quiet and still.

Rob lay stretched out on his sleeping bench, watching Gracie as she turned to kneel in the narrow aisle between the two benches and stow her pack in front of the entrance. "I didn't believe it, but you were right," he said, his low voice sounding dead and flat in the enclosed space. "*Inside* the snow *is* warmer than outside the snow."

"Once we close it up, it'll be warm and reasonably snug inside," Gracie had whispered to Rob as she smoothed out the cave walls with the straight edge of her snow shovel. Her arms felt as heavy as cast-iron skillets. A thin line of sweat trickled down the hollow between her breasts even as her fingers and toes burned with cold.

When Rob said nothing in return, Gracie looked sharply

over at him, aiming the beam of her headlamp directly into his face.

He stood two feet away, carefully shaping and smoothing the domed ceiling with his hands. His entire body was shaking. His cheeks were sunken and the circles beneath his eyes had deepened to purple bruises. His eyes, light and reflecting the snow, looked like shadowed ice. He looked seriously ill.

"Okay, that's enough," Gracie said. "Get inside your sleeping bag. I can finish the rest by myself."

She helped him remove his boots and zipped him fully clothed inside his sleeping bag, which lay atop the sleeping pad and a thick cushion of fir boughs.

Outside, Gracie bricked up the remaining wall using blocks of snow she had cut out of the drift. When she finally knelt to cut out the small round entranceway with her shovel, her hands were so numb her fingers would barely close around the handle. Her frozen toes were nonexistent inside her boots.

She took several precious minutes to smooth out the snow in front of the cave, tossing broken sticks haphazardly across the entrance, mentally crossing her fingers that with time, more snow and a little smile from above, she and Rob would be rendered invisible.

Back inside the cave, Gracie pushed herself up to sit on her own bench and leaned her trekking poles against the wall next to Rob's head. She shrugged off her parka and picked at the buckles of her crampons with fingers that felt like refrigerated bratwursts. "Goddammit," she said with teeth clenched.

"What's the matter?" Rob asked. His low voice sounded flat and dead in the small space.

"I'm cold." In testament to her words, her teeth chattered audibly.

"Get in the bag here," Rob said. He unzipped the zipper

of his sleeping bag. "It's already warm. We'll put yours over the both of us."

Gracie loosened the laces of her boots and pulled them off with the crampons still attached. Without compunction, she stretched out next to Rob and slid her feet down alongside his. Rob zipped up the bag as far as it would go, then pulled Gracie's sleeping bag over the top of them. He wrapped his arm around her waist, pulling her close against his body.

They lay together, breathing in tandem, Gracie's head tucked up under Rob's chin, until finally the sublime heat his body generated radiated through the layers of clothing and into hers. Gradually she stopped shivering.

She sighed heavily and tried to relax her muscles. She was aware of the feel of Rob's body against her own, her back resting against the hard muscles of his chest, his arm tightly anchoring her body to his, his scent earthy and all male.

"Better now?" His voice was soft in her ear.

"Mmm."

"Warm enough?"

She nodded.

"What happened? Something happened out there."

Obviously Rob wasn't going to let her sleep without an explanation of why she had abruptly uprooted their peaceful coexistence in the plastic shelter and dragged him through the cold, wind, and snow with no stated objective or destination.

*If his life's in danger, he has a right to know.* "Up by the trail," she started. "I found . . ." She stopped. There was no way to say it that didn't sound like a bad horror movie. "I found a body."

"A body. A dead body?"

She nodded. "A dead body."

She felt him sit up. "Are you all right?" he asked. "I mean—"

"It was Tristan Chambers."

"What?"

"It was Tristan Chambers."

His arm tightened around her like a tourniquet. "Tristan? He's dead?"

"I'm pretty sure it was him. He . . . It . . . had on a bright red jacket. And a yellow shirt." She rolled over on her back so that she could look up into Rob's face. "I don't know how he died, but somebody stuffed his body up beneath an overhang."

Rob frowned. "What?"

"Somebody hid the body. I'm guessing it was the man I met up there."

"What man?" Rob's voice was deeper than Gracie had ever heard it.

She described the feeling of eyes watching her up on the trail, finding the body, the attack. She relived the terror, saw the deep-set eyes, the bared yellow teeth. Felt his fists digging into her throat as he lifted her off the ground. His rank breath filled her nostrils.

"Did he hurt you?" Rob's voice cut in, angry, dangerous.

"Not really," Gracie said, blinking away the vision. "Mostly scared the hell out of me. He's actually the hurting puppy. I stomped on his foot with my crampon."

Rob looked down at her, almost smiling. "Remind me never to scare the hell out of you."

"The guy's a tank. Not much taller than me, but really strong. With creepy eyes. Deep set and creepy."

"Joseph."

"I thought so. However Tristan died, accidentally or on purpose, Joseph must have hidden the body. I found it."

Rob wiped a hand over his face. "Jesus."

"I think it was Joseph who tried to kill you. Because you saw what happened. He's looking for you. He asked me where you were."

Rob absorbed the information, then his eyes traveled the

interior of the cave. "Are we okay? I mean in here? Can he find us?"

"I don't know," she answered. "The more time that passes, the better for us."

"The snow—"

"—will hide our tracks."

Gracie rolled on her side and felt Rob lie down behind her. His voice was a whisper. "I'm responsible for this. If it weren't for me . . ."

Gracie reached back, found his warm hand with her own, and drew his arm around her. "We're okay for now," she mumbled. "He's hurt. It's snowing. There are two of us. We have weapons. Talk about it later." Her eyes closed of their own accord. "I didn't find your pack. Your . . . rucksack."

"To be expected."

"We don't have any food left."

He put his mouth next to her ear and whispered, "We'll be fine."

"I'm sorry."

"Don't be ridiculous. Get some sleep."

Gracie heard him stretch up and turn out the lantern flashlight.

It was black and silent inside the cave.

Rob seemed to fall immediately to sleep.

But as exhausted as she was, Gracie lay awake, restless, chewing on a cuticle. Anxiety knotted her stomach. Thoughts spun around inside her head. What, if any, mountaineering experience did Joseph have? At what skill level? What were his chances of surviving the storm? Was he holed up somewhere like they were, waiting it out? What the hell happened up on the outcropping?

When after what seemed like hours, Gracie finally did fall asleep, she slept fitfully, dreaming of mutilated bodies and deep-set blue eyes.

IT was quiet in the Command Post motor home, the only sound coming from Nels Black and Ron Gardner, who stood in front of the large map of the wilderness area, talking in low, urgent voices.

Near the back, Ralph sat perched in a folding chair at a flimsy card table, a clipboard of papers and a half a cup of coffee sitting in front of him. A couple of other SAR members sat at a long utility table nearby sorting forms and maps into multiple piles.

Outside in the parking lot, an orange snowplow the size of small house scraped away the still-falling snow, pushing it into mounds higher than the visitor's center's roof.

With the temporary lull in the action, most of the search and rescue ground teams had gone home. The remaining few, mostly alpine team members on standby, were holed up in the visitor's center.

Ralph flipped cursorily through the pages from the MisPers background checks that Deputy Montoya had run the first night of the search.

Aside from a single driving infraction, there was no dirt on Rob Christian. Apparently he led the boring life of a mega–movie star. There was nothing on Diana Petrovic either. Tristan Chambers, however, had been picked up twice in London for assault: once at the age of nineteen and a second time at twenty-one. And Cristina Sanchez had been arrested for solicitation in L.A. two years earlier. There was nothing on her husband, Carlos. The information on the couple was moot anyway.

On the pages about Joseph Van Dijk, Ralph stopped, frowning.

The man had multiple aliases: Aleksandar Novak, Alex Novak, Goksi Kovac.

What the hell kind of spelling was Aleksandar? And what the hell kind of a name was Goksi?

Ralph thumbed back several more pages and stopped again.

Deputy Montoya had also run the MisPers' social security numbers through a federal verification database. Joseph Van Dijk's social security number had come back as a fake.

Ralph leaned back in his chair and mentally sifted through the pieces of information. Then he stood up abruptly, tipping his chair over on the carpet. He grabbed up the clipboard, walked over, and sat down at one of the Command Post computers. He Googled the name "Joseph Van Dijk." No results. He typed in "Aleksandar Novak." Nothing. He tried the single word "Aleksandar." Several listings appeared, the third for Aleksandar Veljic, a retired Serbian basketball player.

He typed in "Goksi Origin." The very first listing told him it was a nickname for the Slavic name Goran, used in several Eastern European countries.

He thought for a moment, fingers poised above the keys. Then he typed in "Petrovic." Several listings down was a site describing the name as Croatian and Serbian.

Ralph stretched back in the chair, thought for a moment,

then shuffled through the stack of papers again and pulled out the original Lost Person Questionnaire. He scanned the pages until he found a note Gracie had scribbled in a side margin: "Per Eric: JVD-slight accent, poss. E. Eur."

For more than thirty minutes, Ralph searched the Internet using various combinations of "criminal record" and "alias" and "Serbia" and names like "Goksi" and "Aleksandar." He opened tangential sites, hit dead ends, backtracked. He didn't know exactly what he was searching for; he simply followed the meandering threads of information until one of the pages he opened contained a link to the Interpol website.

Ralph clicked on the site and spent several minutes opening and reading the various pages. Structure. News. Drugs and Criminal Organizations. Under Fugitives, he searched through the Wanted pages and the listings for the United States under National Wanted Websites. Another dead end. He hit the Back button and stared at the National Wanted Websites home page, wondering where he should look next. His eyes focused and he read what he had been staring at: the listing directly beneath the United States listing: United Nations International Criminal Tribunal for the Former Yugoslavia.

Ralph clicked on the site.

He scanned the first page, scrolling down until, at the bottom of the page, something caught his eye—a little blue box reading simply: "Fugitives: Facing Justice" and two names. Ralph homed in on one: Goran Lucovic.

He clicked on the window.

The page that opened contained the pictures of two men. Goran Lucovic was no one Ralph recognized. He peered at the picture of the other man, old, grainy, in black-and-white. He couldn't be sure.

He searched further until on the right side of the screen, a Wanted poster appeared.

Ralph clicked on the poster.

At the top of the page, large red letters blared UP TO

$5 MILLION REWARD. In the bottom right corner was a circular seal from the United States Department of State Diplomatic Security Service. Along the right side of the page ran several paragraphs of type, which Ralph scanned. His mind registered only certain words and phrases: *United Nations . . . Criminal Tribunal . . . torture . . . rape . . . murders of thousands of innocent civilians.*

On the left side of the page were color photos of three men.

The larger, top picture was of Slobodan Milosevic: "Wanted for crimes against humanity."

Below were pictures of two other men, "Wanted for genocide and crimes against humanity." The man on the right was Goran Lucovic.

The man on the left was thinner and clean shaven with a full head of hair. Square jaw. Deep-set eyes. And only one ear.

The man on the left was named Radovan Milocek.

The man on the left was Joseph Van Dijk.

GRACIE jerked awake and stared out into the absolute darkness of the snow cave.

Had she heard something outside?

She lay without moving and listened.

A full minute passed. Then another. She heard nothing but Rob's soft breathing.

It was probably nothing she decided and checked her watch. She had slept for more than four hours.

Feeling creaky, but rested in spite of her fitful sleep, she slipped out of the sleeping bag, whispering, "Go back to sleep," when Rob mumbled, "What are you doing?"

She pulled on her parka and boots in the dark, grabbed up a trekking pole, and pulled the pack from the doorway. Crouching down, she pawed away the heavy snow that had piled up over the entrance and peered through the hole into the darkness outside.

She could see nothing.

She wormed out of the cave, pulled the pack into place behind her, and stood up in the knee-deep snow.

For five full minutes, Gracie stood just outside the entrance of the shelter and listened.

There was no sound. The wind had died completely. There was no movement, but ethereal snowflakes floated down to land softly on her upturned face and cling to her eyelashes. Overhead, a single star, steady and bright, peeked out through an opening in the clouds.

The storm was passing.

CHAPTER

# 72

"I'M thinking about quitting," Rob said.

He and Gracie sat on their respective benches, drinking scalding brown water brewed with the last of the fuel from the last tea bag. The little lantern flashlight filled the cave with a muted, golden light.

Upon waking, Rob had declared himself "aces up" ("I can't help it. It just comes out."). Gracie noted with relief that he did in fact resemble a human being and not the walking zombie of a few hours earlier.

Gracie and Rob were engaged in comfortable and consciously distracting mundane banter when he had tossed out that thunderbolt.

Gracie blinked at him. "Quitting what? Smoking?"

"Acting."

"Acting."

"Sometimes I despise it."

"You're an actor," she said, reminding herself to breathe.

"I'm aware of that," Rob said, head bowed. "But I feel like I've sold my soul to the devil. I've gotten caught up in the trappings." The pain in his voice was palpable and Gracie felt her insides wrench. "I've lost touch with what really matters. Sometimes I don't even know who I am anymore. Bloody hell, even that sounds like a line of dialogue."

"Why do you do it if you don't like it that much?"

"But I do! Love it even. I love the process. The audience. It's the accompanying baggage I've had my fill of. The frenzy. The . . . the clutching. The suffocating loss of privacy. The lack of integrity."

"The money?"

He smiled with irony. "That's the trade-off, isn't it? If you don't take the good with the bad, if you complain at all, you're a spoiled, ungrateful sod. Some days I would trade it all for a moment's peace. For the ability to trust a friend." He stared down at his hands. "Some days I feel the whole bloody profession is irrelevant in today's world. Wars are being fought. Millions of people live in poverty. Die of starvation. What's my contribution to solving the mess? Reciting a couple of lines and getting paid obscene amounts of money?"

Myriad responses flooded Gracie's mind, then she said, "I read an article once about an artist who couldn't paint for a long time after 9/11. In light of all that happened, she felt it was irrelevant. But after a lot of soul searching, she finally decided that not only was it not irrelevant, it was imperative. The world needed the positive and the beautiful to balance out the killing and the evil and the hatred." She looked over at Rob to confirm that he was even mildly interested.

His eyes were laser-focused on her. "I'm with you."

"This woman also decided," Gracie said, "that what she painted from then on had to count for something and that she needed to identify exactly what it was she wanted to accomplish. Did she want her paintings to heal? Help people escape? Stir them to action? Enlighten?" She clenched her hands together to hide their trembling. "Maybe if your acting were the means to an end, a . . . a springboard to a loftier goal . . . like save the rain forest. Teach at-risk kids responsibility. Build wells in the Sudan."

Rob nodded slowly. He glanced up, caught her watching him, and winked at her.

Gracie let out a breath she didn't realize she was holding and smiled back at him.

They sat in silence again until Rob said, "Tell me something nobody else knows." Gracie stared at him for several seconds, then, letting the sleeping bag fall from her shoulders, she pulled up the shirts on her left side and turned so that he could see her ribs.

Rob leaned forward and squinted at the small round scar just above the waistband of her pants. "What is that?"

Gracie pulled her shirts back down. "Burn scar."

Rob's eyes shot up to hers. "Where the hell did you get that?"

Gracie cleared her throat. "Morris's . . . my stepfather's cigar. He used to hit us . . . Lenora, Harold, and me. Usually with a belt. Always on our backs so no one would know. When he came at us, I always ran way out behind the house, climbed up to the top branches of this big old apple tree, and stayed there. Sometimes for hours. I felt safe there. He caught me once when I was nine. Guess he wanted to make it count."

"Jesus, Gracie," Rob whispered. "No one ever . . . he never went to jail?"

Gracie shook her head. "Mother wouldn't allow it."

"Jesus," Rob whispered again. He leaned over and encircled her wrist with his fingers.

Gracie stiffened. "What?"

"Sit next to me."

She allowed him to draw her across the aisle and sat next to him.

He tucked her sleeping bag around her. "Keep talking."

Gracie cleared her throat again. "We never knew what would set Morris off. A-minus on a test. Wet towel on the floor. Didn't take me long to grow into a turtle. Fly below the radar. I got straight A's. Went to U of M. Dated the moronic sons of his friends. Took the job he wanted me to when what I really wanted to do was go off somewhere and study wolves. One day after work, I stopped by the house to see how my mother was doing. Her arm was in a cast. Morris had broken it."

"Bastard."

Gracie stared straight ahead. "It's like watching it on tape. Not like me doing it at all. Morris was watching the news. I took a shotgun from the gun cabinet, grabbed a handful of shells, loaded two, walked into the den and blew two huge holes in the wall right above his head. Two right in a row. Boom. Boom."

"Gracie!"

"It didn't hurt him. Well, not really. He got hit with a couple of pellets." She stifled a giggle. "I told him if he ever laid another hand on my mother or anyone else again, I'd aim lower."

Rob gaped at her.

"It blew the toupee right off his head." She barked a laugh. "He sat there in his chair, drink in his hand, big bald head covered with plaster dust, pictures all crooked, and his toupee sitting on the back of the chair like a furry little rat. It looked so funny, I laughed. I swear he was more pissed off about me laughing at him than anything else. But he had to sit there and do nothing because I still had the shotgun and I'd already reloaded."

"Bloody . . . !" Rob rubbed his hands down his face and chuckled. "So nobody called the police? Even then?"

"Are you kidding? What would the neighbors think? Evelyn picked the pellets out herself. They plastered up the wall and no one ever found out. As far as I know, Morris never hit her again."

"Bloody bully."

"If not for him, I might still be living in Detroit. . . ." Gracie said. "Evelyn sided with him. Even then. She

screamed at me to get out and leave them alone. So I—"
Gracie sat up and rubbed her eye with the heel of her hand.
"Sorry. I shouldn't—"

"Don't be stupid," Rob said. "So you what?"

Gracie relaxed again. "Quit my job. Sold my house. Drove
out here. Worked jobs that they considered beneath my station. Pizza delivery, waitress, cashier, um, pizza delivery."

"That'll show them."

"I know, right? He sent me a certified letter telling me
he'd written me out of his will. I'm persona non grata, men-
tioned as little as possible within the family. Outside the
family, never at all. Next to Jimmy Hoffa, I'm the best-kept
secret of southern Michigan."

"How long ago did all this happen?"

"Eight years? Nine? I can't seem to get back on track."
She looked over at Rob. "I can't believe I'm telling you this.
I've never told anyone. Not even Ra . . . not even my best
friend."

"Nine years is a long time."

"I know."

Rob grinned at her and shook his head.

"What?"

"You're something else." He leaned toward her, lifted her
chin and kissed her. His lips were soft and warm.

Gracie shrank back, trying to read his eyes in the dim
light.

What was she doing? She had just met Rob. She knew
almost nothing about him. When was she ever going to
learn?

She smiled and leaned toward him.

Rob pressed his lips to hers again, a long lingering kiss,
mouth open, tongue touching hers.

Feelings that had lain dormant for years reignited and
roared to the surface, blasting to tiny bits any semblance of
self-control and spreading a warm glow throughout her
entire body.

Gracie pulled away.

Rob looked into her face. "What is it?" His voice was almost a caress. "Too fast?"

She shook her head. "It's not that."

"Then what?"

"I can't compete."

"With what, love?"

"Those perfect Hollywood starlets."

He snorted. "Give me a . . ." He stopped when he saw her face. "Gracie, love, it's all surface crud anyway. Like that addition to my vocabulary? Thanks to one Grace Kinkaid."

"Terrific."

He dipped his head to look into her eyes. "Besides, I think you're beautiful."

A blush crept up her cheeks that she hoped he couldn't see. "No, you don't. No, I'm not."

"Why can't you just accept the compliment? You are. Very beautiful." His voice changed. "In a highly appealing, grimy, slightly gamey sort of way."

She sat up straight in indignation. "I told you I wanted a bath."

He lifted her hand, drew off her glove and kissed the bare palm.

A shiver ran up Gracie's neck that she knew wasn't from the cold.

"You don't have to compete." He leaned closer to kiss her neck. "And, I reiterate . . ." He lifted the flap of her hat and kissed her ear lobe. "You are beautiful."

"This is that rescuer complex thingee."

"Eloquently put. You'll sweep me off my feet."

"You're hurt." Grace's protests sounded wimpy-assed even in her own ears.

"Be quiet," he said, tracing the length of her body with his fingertips, his feather touch raising the hair along her arms and other places.

"You're seducing me."

"Will you shut up?"

Then he kissed her again, deeply, his tongue seeking hers, his hands entwined in her hair, pulling her down on the bench and dragging the sleeping bags over the top of both of them.

Gracie closed her eyes, refusing to think, refusing to face what would come after, shutting out the rest of the world. In the sanctuary of the cave, no one but the two of them existed. She immersed herself in the moment, submitting herself wholly to his touch, his scent, knowing nothing but the taste of his lips and the feel of his body on top of hers.

# CHAPTER
## 73

**M**ILOCEK groaned in pain as he drew his cotton sock, saturated and stiff with half-frozen blood, from his injured foot.

He sat on a prickly mat of evergreen boughs at the base of a massive fir tree; the bottom branches drooped low, keeping the ground beneath dry and virtually clear of snow. The little tipi fire he had built of broken twigs and fir needles snapped and popped and cast a halo of orange light throughout the tiny enclosure.

Milocek's nose and cheeks were numb. His fingers burned with cold. He snugged the wool blanket up tighter around his shoulders and bent to examine his foot.

The spikes the woman searcher wore on her boots had sliced through the tendons and ligaments of the instep and broken at least one, maybe more, of the small metatarsal bones. The skin was mottled red and purple with bruising. Blood dripped from the wound onto the hard-packed dirt.

Milocek had followed the woman down the side of the mountain. Boiling with rage, he wanted to kill her, needed to kill her. But he managed only fifty feet when the ferocious pain in his foot had forced him to stop.

Now huddled in the shelter of the giant fir, he dragged Rob's knapsack toward him, unclipped the buckle of the top flap and pulled out the remnants of the gourmet brunch prepared for the hikers by the hotel.

Pushing up his pant leg, he dabbed clean the twin punctures on his shin with a salmon-colored cloth napkin. With his knife, he slit a second napkin into a single long strip and, with the gentle care of a mother, used it to bind his foot.

He wolfed down the discarded crusts of a shrimp-salad sandwich and finished off a bag of kettle chips in between swigs of water.

Then he added several more twigs to the tiny fire and lay down with his head on the empty knapsack. He drew his knees up to his chest to preserve his core heat and dragged long, heavy evergreen boughs up over himself.

His eyes closed.


**SCREAMS INSIDE MILOCEK'S** head snapped him awake. His mother's. Those of girls and women dragged away by his men. Diana's—muffled by his hand, cut short by his blade.

He threw back the blanket of evergreen boughs and sat up. Digging into a jacket pocket, he pulled out a crumpled pack of Camels, shook one loose, grabbed it with cracked and peeling lips, and lit it with his lighter. He drew the smoke deep into his lungs and exhaled it through his nostrils in two thin streams.

The little fire had died to glowing embers. He snapped off dead branches from the tree trunk behind him and added them, with a handful of needles to the fire, watching as the flames devoured the dry fuel.

Milocek had started young. At the age of eight he had killed a squirrel in a fit of rage after watching helplessly as his drunken father beat his mother unconscious and smashed his little sister's eye socket, leaving the girl partially blind and permanently disfigured. As the young Radovan gutted the squirrel, he anticipated the satisfaction he would feel when he plunged a kitchen knife deep into his father's neck.

As the boy grew, he sharpened his skills on larger animals—a stray dog, a wild pig—until each evisceration was accomplished with precision. He learned to savor the sound and feel of the blade slicing through tissue and bone, the rich smell of the open cavity, the brilliant blood still pumping freely until he stopped it with a flick of his blade.

The day he watched his father smash his mother's skull with a shovel, splashing her brains across the gray wood of the barn, Radovan slit the throat of his mother's killer, nearly severing his head from his body with the finely honed knife he kept hidden beneath his shirt. The boy field-dressed the carcass and hung it from a meat hook in the barn. He set fire to the tinder-dry straw in an empty stall, then walked away forever, the smell of woodsmoke and burning flesh filling his nostrils.

He was fourteen.

As an adult, Milocek had killed countless men, taking great pleasure in the slow blade. He had allowed his men to take women, young and old, to do with as they pleased. But he had never participated, operating within the confines of his own strict code of conduct.

Dispatching the man rescuer had been too easy, as effortless as snapping his fingers, robbing him of much of the thrill that accompanied the kill. Diana had been weak, submissive. There had been no challenge in taking her life. No joy.

But the woman searcher was strong. A fighter. A worthy adversary. He had underestimated her. But he never made the same mistake twice. He would find her and he would kill her. He shivered with the thought of drawing his blade across that long, slender throat and watching the life sparkle die in her eyes.

Milocek looked down at his foot. The blood had already soaked through the cloth bandage.

He needed to stop the bleeding.

He unwound the damp binding from his foot, then drew out his knife and held it to the fire. He pinched the edges of the wound together and, growling like an animal, pressed the flat of the steel blade against the skin.

His dry lips cracked and bled as he smiled and breathed in the scent of sizzling flesh.

# CHAPTER
# 74

**THE** glowing dial of Gracie's watch told her it was 5:23 A.M.

In the darkness, she could hear Rob breathing softly, rhythmically in sleep.

In spite of the specter of fear hovering just beneath the surface, she felt curiously light, as if her body could float on a puff of air.

At first, her and Rob's lovemaking had been ferocious, their thirst for each other insatiable. Gracie forgot all else in total immersion of the moment. Rob's touch was an unself-conscious exploration, testing, teasing, then generous, awakening in her the desire to discover and give selflessly in return. Closure was dizzying, fast, mutually satisfying.

The second time was a slow, delicious feast for the senses. A murmur. A laugh. A gasp. A groan of pleasure. Rob's silken fingers gliding beneath her clothes, searching, cajoling. Down Gracie's back, her arms, over her hips. The earthy perfume of his skin. The sweet taste of his lips, his tongue, the whiskered skin of his jaw and neck, the mat of chest hair running in a dark line to his navel. And the perfect warmth of his mouth on hers.

Gracie reached back and above her head and turned on the little lantern.

Rob didn't stir.

She studied his face, serene with sleep. The long dark eyelashes, shining hair tousled and curling. He was without a doubt the most physically beautiful person she had ever seen. But it was his mind, his gentleness, his sanity, his surprising normality to which she was drawn.

Too good to be true, Gracie told herself with an internal sigh. She had found out the hard way that someone that good looking was most likely a super-sized prick. Time no doubt would reveal Rob's dark side, an underbelly. He probably drank too much. Or was into heavy drugs. Or gambled too much. Or was abusive—verbally, emotionally, physically. Or he possessed a secret, dark and terrible, like Mr. Rochester in *Jane Eyre*, although she doubted he harbored a mad wife in his New York attic.

Still, she thought with a smile, I have no regrets.

Ralph's blue-gray eyes appearing in her mind's eye submersed her in a wave of remorse and jarred her fully awake. She deliberately pushed the thought aside, knowing she would have to deal with that—with Ralph—later, if . . . when she and Rob made it out of there.

She studied Rob's face again, cementing every line, every aspect to memory, savoring every second, knowing it would inevitably end.

Sadness rose to choke her throat. She reached out and touched his hair with her fingertips.

Rob's eyes opened and looked into hers.

She pulled her hand back. "Sorry," she whispered.

He drew her to him, brushing his lips across hers. "I'm not."

# CHAPTER

# 75

GRACIE stood outside the snow cave, thigh-deep in pristine powder snow. Her breath wafted around her in diaphanous clouds of vapor. Overhead the predawn sky was clear, cloudless, the stars retreating. A blush of pink in the east heralded the new day.

All around, trees and boulders were heavily laden with snow, as if they had been dipped in white frosting. Far above her head, skyscraper peaks, white and perfect, rose up and up, reclaiming their dominance against the flawless sky. The silence was absolute.

Along with the clearing weather had come the cold. The air, free of scent, prickled the inside of Gracie's nose and cut into her lungs with every breath.

She tipped her head back and stared up into the alabaster sky.

It was over. She had done it. She had kept them alive.

With the thought came no elation, no relief, no sense of a job well done. Only the knowledge that the nightmare was ending along with an all-encompassing exhaustion of body and mind and an overwhelming loneliness.

She heard Rob crawl out of the cave behind her and scrunch through the snow to stand so closely behind her that wisps of his breath floated over her shoulder.

"Incredible," he breathed.

Gracie smiled back up at him. His eyes were dark and bright and alive.

"The best thing about a winter storm is what comes after," she whispered back. "This—all of this—is what I live for."

"This is what we all should live for," he said.

# 76

GRACIE drove the ice axe into the snow with both hands and dropped to her knees. She covered her mouth and nose with her mittens and breathed in the warmed air. Her eyes roamed the surrounding landscape, the incline above, the canyon below, the rocks, boulders, bushes, trees. No movement caught her eye. No unnatural splash of color drew her attention. No sign of Joseph made her heart stop. All was silent and still.

With the clearing skies, Sixty King, the Sheriff Department's helicopter, would fly at first light to look for them. Believing as Gracie did that Cashman had never reached the Command Post to relay their location, logic told her that the helicopter's initial route would be to follow the Aspen Springs Trail in from the trailhead parking lot.

But unless Gracie could somehow draw the flight crew's attention, they might very well miss the ant wearing an orange Search and Rescue parka among the thousands of trees.

Gracie and Rob had argued in heated whispers about the risk of her climbing up to the trail alone with Joseph possibly having survived the storm and out looking for them. Gracie had finally pulled rank and ordered him to stay behind to pack up the rest of the gear. Now she was slogging her way up to the trail for what she hoped was the last time in her life. Once she was out in the open, she would wave her arms, blow her whistle or, when the sun crested the eastern ridge, signal with her mirror, whatever it took to make herself noticeable.

The climb grew into endless torture; a marathon of will-power. Gracie's nearly empty reserve of energy quickly dwindled to nothing as she plowed through the snow calf-deep in places, waist-high in others. She propelled herself upward with her arms like a swimmer in high surf. She was an automaton, her body moving of its own volition. She plunged in her ice axe, stabbing the hillside with her crampons to seek purchase in the snow. Stumbling, falling, pushing herself back to her feet, she clawed her way up out of the canyon.

Now she rested on her knees, allowing the pain in her chest to diminish. She sat back on her heels and looked up. High above, the trail—invisible through the trees—wound along the mountainside, unattainable as perfection. Higher still, snow-covered mountain peaks glowed pink with the first rays of the morning sun.

*Move*, Gracie told herself. *With the sun comes Sixty King. Get out from under the trees and into the open.*

Her body refused.

She tipped her head back and prayed. *Please, God, give me strength. Help me get up to the trail.*

But when she opened her eyes to the mountains rising up before her, she knew she couldn't go another step. She was played out.

**SHE FELT IT** first as a shimmer in the air, an indistinct pulse barely distinguishable from the beating of her own heart, growing until finally she heard it: an unmistakable *whumping*—the staccato rhythm of an approaching helicopter.

Sixty King.

She would be invisible under the cover of the trees. "Oh, God!"

The throbbing grew louder. Gracie blew long, hard blasts on her whistle until black spots kaleidoscoped before her eyes. She waved her arms until Sixty King roared overhead like a giant prehistoric beast, its wake whipping the snow into whirling dervishes of white.

The helicopter disappeared over the tops of the trees. The *thump* of the rotor blades faded to a throb, then silence.

They hadn't seen her.

"They'll come back!" Gracie croaked. "They'll circle around and do another sweep."

A final burst of adrenaline pushed her up the mountain. She climbed, fell headlong in the snow, forced herself to her feet. With muscles straining, arms flailing, grabbing, hauling, she drove herself up to the trail.

With a grunt, Gracie fell full length into the deep snow on the trail.

She allowed herself no time to recover her breath. Instead she pushed herself to her feet and waded up the trail in the direction the helicopter had flown. But she had taken only a few steps before she stumbled to a stop, unable to see. Weaving on her feet, she sucked air into her lungs until her vision cleared.

Dread wrapped cold arms around her. She lifted her eyes. On a ridge high above her head, a cornice of snow curled elegantly against the cerulean sky. Turning around slowly, she looked down to where below her a vast white scar slashed the canyon wall.

She stood dead center of an avalanche trough, its concave chute lying in wait for her to brush its hair trigger and release the slide.

Gracie forced her fast, shallow breathing to slow and deepen until she could listen, ears attuned to any sound signaling an instability of the death trap on which she stood, a collapsing of the layers that preceded the violent onslaught.

Dread crystallized to horror as only a hundred yards below, Rob waded out from among the trees and onto the snow field. He had followed her up the mountain after all. Drawn out by the sound of the helicopter, he stopped and looked up.

Oh, shit. Oh, shit. Oh, shit. Gracie swung her arm wide. "Move back!" she yelled. "Go back!"

Rob cupped his hands around his mouth and yelled something indecipherable back.

Gracie crept on eggshells to the edge of the chute, into the safety of the trees, praying all the while that Rob would recognize the danger and do the same.

An agitated Steller's jay, blue feathers brilliant against the snow, hopped from limb to limb in a nearby pine, jarring the quiet with its loud squawking.

Had Rob understood her frantic gestures? Gracie craned her neck, trying to see if he had backed away from the chute. But trees now blocked her line of sight. She stood on tiptoe, not quite able to see—

A scrunching of snow snapped her eyes back down the trail.

Joseph.

Twenty feet away. Limping toward her. Fast. The curved knife in his fist, blade out for the stab and slice.

Time slowed to a crawl.

Gracie's heart thudded in her chest. Every aspect of the man's face appeared in crystal-clear high definition. Eyes shadowed in their sockets. Lips—dried to white, cracked, bloodied—pulled back into a ghoulish grimace of yellowed teeth. Pale, frostbitten splotches on nose and cheekbones.

The curving silver knife blade.

He was ten feet away.

Eight.

Six.

Gracie planted her feet, blew out a long breath, and watched him come.

His arm swung back for the strike.

Gracie swung her ice axe like a scythe and planted the sharp pick deep into the soft flesh of Joseph's cheek.

Bones and teeth crunched.

Joseph slid to his knees at Gracie's feet, slapping both hands to the wound and spattering bright blood in an arc around them. The knife shot out of his hands and disappeared into the snow.

Gracie turned to run.

Joseph lunged up, grabbed her around the waist from behind, and heaved her over the side of the cliff.

**G**RACIE fell, arms and legs and mind whirling.

She hit a rock. Bounced off. Tumbled down.

*Stop yourself before it's too late!*

She heaved herself over onto her stomach and jammed her ice axe into the snow. The pick bounced off and slammed the adze back into the padding of her chest pack.

She stabbed the pick in again with all her weight behind it. It buried and caught.

Her body's momentum pulled the handle out of her hands. The strap on her wrist yanked her up short. Her shoulder wrenched. Pain exploded through her upper body.

The axe pulled loose.

She slid down on her side. Hit another rock. Her parka's slippery shell propelled her like a rocket. She picked up speed.

*This is really it. I'm going to die.*

She smashed through the top branches of a bush sticking out of the snow, ricocheted off to the side, and spun around like a top.

The slope leveled off a fraction and Gracie felt her body break through a thin crust of snow beneath the powder. She punched through the crust with both elbows. She stopped spinning and slowed down.

Not slow enough.

A granite boulder jutting up from the snow field rushed up to meet her.

Gracie planted her crampons.

She catapulted head over heels and slammed to a stop.

# CHAPTER

# 78

*CRIMSON. Vermillion. Red.*
*Bright red.*
*Blood red.*
*Blood.*

Gracie's eyes were open and focused before her brain fully comprehended that what she saw was her own blood saturating the snow around her head like a macabre snow cone.

Her other senses seeped back—the taste of blood filling her mouth, cheek on fire with cold, heart beating a bass drum in her chest. An overall ache permeated her body.

She lay on her side, curled in a fetal position, lodged among the leafy branches of a manzanita bush, and half-buried in the snow. Her head faced downhill.

*Decidedly uncomfortable*, she thought. *And really hard to breathe.*

She tensed her muscles to move so she could draw in a full breath. Pain shot through her right shoulder so piercing that she cried out. She froze, sucking in air through clenched teeth until the pain eased. "Guess I'll stay right here and not move," she mumbled into the snow.

Seconds slipped away as Gracie sipped air into her lungs.

She moved her eyes a fraction to focus on a black Gore-Tex mitten lying inches from her face. Her mitten. Her hand.

Gracie sent the message to wiggle the fingers and was relieved when they actually responded. She lifted her hand off the snow. No pain. No perceptible wrist injury. Again, relief.

Where her left hand with its corresponding arm was and in what shape, she had no idea. Beneath her somewhere. But she could neither see nor feel it. For all she knew, it lay back up on the trail.

The trail.

She had fallen from the trail. How in the world had she done that? She remembered the fall itself only in whirling vignettes, a vertiginous jumble of arms and legs and mind and pain. But nothing about how or why.

Her cheek was numb. Not a good thing. And her chest was so compressed by her own weight, it was impossible to draw in a decent breath.

Time to try to move again.

She sent the message to lift her arm, but the resulting movement brought on another paroxysm of pain that she cried out and lay still again.

How about the legs?

She tried her feet, one at a time, then both legs together. Her hips and knees were bruised and sore, and one calf stung like a yellow jacket, but she could endure the pain of moving them. Slowly, with gravity's help, she swung her legs around, pivoted her torso and, with a crackling of branches, slid off the bush and onto the hillside. She eased onto her back, straightening her body so that she lay with her feet facing downhill, knees bent, crampons holding her in place.

At least she could inhale more than a millimeter. Except

now, blood filled her mouth and pooled at the back of her throat. If she swallowed too much, she would eventually throw it back up, which in her current state she considered a fate worse than death. She tried to spit out the bloody mouthful, but it drooled down the side of her cheek and into her ear.

*Lovely.*

One by one, she moved various parts of her body, testing, assessing, until she isolated the most significant injuries. She had torn ligaments somewhere and broken something in her right shoulder, maybe the clavicle, maybe the scapula, maybe both. The sharp pain in her calf was most likely a puncture from a crampon point. Her chest and right wrist were notably sore. She felt blood on her face from a cut somewhere around her left eye. With her tongue she could feel the source of the blood in her mouth—a slice, inches long, on the inside of her cheek.

Not great, but nothing life threatening.

At least not yet.

A sound drew her eyes to the slope above.

At the edge of the avalanche chute, someone was making his way down the mountain in a barely controlled glissade. Black jacket. The side of his face red with what looked like—

Joseph.

A rush of images flooded back. She knew exactly where she was and why.

Joseph had thrown her over the side. He had watched her fall. He had seen her move. He knew she was still alive. He was leaving nothing to chance.

*He's coming to finish the job.*

Gracie cradled her injured arm with the other and rolled over. She pushed herself up to kneel on the ground, then wobbled to her feet.

She looked up.

Joseph was moving faster now, sliding down through the deep snow.

She could see no weapon. He probably didn't need one.

Gracie took a step and slipped, landing hard on the snow. Starbursts of pain flashed before her eyes as the broken ends of bone ground against each other, tearing more tissue.

She wasn't going to escape.

From where she lay, Gracie watched Joseph come until he slid to a stop in the snow beside her. He looked down on her, his mouth pulling back into a ghoulish grimace, red with blood. The wound in his cheek gaped like a second mouth, exposing teeth and bone. He sank to his knees beside her.

Rob flew out of the trees like an eagle diving for the kill and swung a thick pine branch directly at Joseph's head.

The branch landed on a forearm raised in defense and burst into a thousand fragments. Joseph fell backward into the snow.

Rob's own momentum overbalanced him and he pitched forward. He grabbed on to a rock to keep from sliding down the hill, then scrambled up as Joseph pushed himself to his feet.

The two men faced each other.

The wolverine and the panther, Gracie thought absurdly.

Then Joseph lunged forward to tackle Rob around the waist.

The two men fought. Gouging, biting, clawing, kicking, ripping. Eyes, ears, throat, knees, testicles, all fair game. Ugly, primitive, brutal. Both men grunted, yelled. Fell, slid down, then surged up again.

Blood sprayed, Jackson Pollock red across white snow.

The reality that Joseph was going to kill Rob slammed into Gracie.

*Do something!*

The ice axe still dangled from its strap on her injured arm. She slipped it off her wrist and, with her left hand, dug the pick into the snow and dragged herself up the slope. With every dig of the axe, she gained a foot. Another. Another.

Only feet above her, the men broke apart.

Joseph stumbled backward, fighting to remain upright. He gulped in air like a drowning man rising to the surface. His damaged arm hung limply at his side. His one good ear was torn and bleeding. The gaping hole in his cheek dripped blood onto the ground.

Rob knelt in the snow, head hanging, eyes lifted toward Joseph, mouth a smear of bright red. He dragged air into his lungs. One eye had ballooned closed. A cut on his cheekbone spilled blood down his face.

Joseph lunged again, hitting Rob with a body slam that knocked them both into the snow with Joseph on top. His hands encircled Rob's head, thumbs digging for the eyes.

With a yell, Gracie surged upward and buried the pick of her axe into the muscle of Joseph's calf.

The man's bellow of pain was lost as a crack echoed throughout the canyon. He rolled off Rob and grabbed around at the axe handle, trying to pull the pick loose.

Rob threw himself toward the edge of the chute, picking Gracie up by her parka along the way. He flung her down next to the manzanita bush, dove on top of her, and held on.

High above, the entire hillside shifted and the mountain released its hold. The giant slab broke free, instantly a roaring slide of churning snow. Shaking the ground, it swallowed Joseph and swept him away. A glittering white plume flowered high into the air. Beyond it, a tiny speck grew larger, rotor blades pulsing, soundless against the roar of nature's fury.

Sixty King.

GRACIE and Rob sat perched on the side of the mountain, Rob's arm cradling Gracie close.

Sixty King hovered overhead. They watched a Sheriff's Department medic being lowered at the end of a cable, dangling like a spider on a filament of silk.

"You're going first," Rob said, sounding like his mouth was full of cotton balls.

"No, I'm not," Gracie answered through a mist of pain.

"You're in no shape to argue."

With the demeanor of a cranky old lady, Gracie submitted to being treated first. Her right arm and shoulder were strapped in place. Butterfly bandages closed the cut encircling the outside of her eye and the deep puncture on the back of her leg. A wad of gauze stuffed inside her cheek soaked up the blood.

And even though shock had set her body to quivering like a plucked harp string, she insisted in a loud voice on stepping into the litter of her own volition. She carped and crabbed as she was strapped in, or, as Rob archly informed her, "Packaged."

When she was ready, black webbing crisscrossing her body and holding her in position, the clear acrylic head shield ready to be lowered, Rob slowly dropped to his knees and kissed her gently on the mouth. Then he fell back and watched as the shield was clamped in place.

Sixty King swooped back. The rotor blades whirled the powdery snow into a blinding white tornado that, even with the shield lowered, pierced Gracie's cheeks with a thousand tiny ice crystals.

She watched with a critical eye as the medic clipped the litter rigging onto the cable that had been lowered and tightened the quick-link closed. Her eyes slid back to Rob, who flashed her a lopsided smile.

Then she felt a tug on the cable and was swept up and up into the air.

"**D**AMN, Kinkaid! You look like shit!"

"More like death warmed over."

"Shit warmed over."

Gracie looked down the length of her body to her teammates standing in a cluster at the end of the hospital bed. "Gee, thanks, guys," she said, fighting to talk intelligibly with a cheek swollen to the size of a baseball. Her unbandaged eye zeroed in on Lenny, who stood looking uncomfortable, one hand thrust deep in the front pocket of his jeans, a stack of newspapers held close to his side with an elbow. The other hand held what looked like an inexpensive Walmart bouquet of carnations, the bright orange sale sticker still stuck to the plastic wrap. "Those for me?" she asked.

The young man blushed, his own eyes sliding over to an enormous basket of pink, yellow, and white roses with brightly colored balloons, which sat on a table in the corner of the room.

"They're beautiful," Gracie said. "Carnations are my favorite."

Lenny grinned with relief and crept up to lay the bouquet on the rolling tray next to the bed.

Kurt stepped forward and gave her a light peck on her good cheek. "How ya doing, kid? How does it feel to be a hero?"

Gracie's eye moved over to where Ralph stood just inside the doorway leaning against the wall, arms folded across his chest. "Hey, Ralphie," she said.

"Hey, Gracie girl," he said and winked at her.

Gracie laid her head back on the crisp pillow and let the sound of her teammates' banter and joke-telling flow over her. Her eyes traveled from face to face to face. *I love these guys*, she thought. In spite of the fact that she felt like she had been flattened by a steamroller, and every square inch of her body was as sore as hell, in spite of the fact that only half of her face worked, she smiled with contentment. "Where's Cashman?" she asked. "I wanna whup his butt for leaving me out there."

Silence in the room. Gracie's words hung in the air. Her eye moved from one man to the next until Lenny piped up, "Hey, Gracie! You're everywhere!"

"I am?"

"Yeah! Look!" The young man plopped the pile of newspapers he had been holding onto the bed beside her. He held up the front page of the L.A. *Times* so she could read the headlines: WOMAN RESCUES ACTOR! with her own team ID picture and a headshot of Rob beneath. Lenny picked up another paper. "This one's from San Francisco. " 'They're Alive!' " he read. "And this one. You've been on TV, too! Here." He grabbed the remote from the bedside table, turned on the television hanging on the wall near the ceiling, and flipped through the channels. "Even . . . What's that one program . . . ?"

"*Entertainment Tonight*?" someone suggested.

"Yeah! *Entertainment Tonight*," Lenny said. "There!"

The same ID photo of Gracie and a different picture of

Rob filled the television screen. A woman's voice announced: ". . . Hiking party caught in a Thanksgiving Day snowstorm in the San Raphael mountains one hundred miles east of Los Angeles."

"It's friggin' awesome!"

A half-ton weight settled in the middle of Gracie's chest. "Turn it off."

"No, wait—"

Kurt reached up and pushed the Power button on the television. The screen went black.

A series of clicks out in the hallway drew everyone's attention toward the door where a man stood just outside the room, a camera pointed directly at Gracie.

"A camera!" she wailed and turned her head away.

Ralph and Kurt dived out into the hall with the rest of the men on their heels. The door swung closed and Gracie was left alone in the room. She listened to several minutes of scuffling, pounding feet, muffled voices, cursing, and receding footsteps until the door swung back open and her teammates ambled back in.

"He got pictures of me," she moaned. "Like this!"

"Not anymore," Kurt said, his head lowered and concentrating on deleting the pictures from the digital camera.

"Don't know how that joker got through security."

"There's security?" Gracie asked.

"Reporters are camped outside the front door downstairs," Warren said.

"And in front of your house."

"Oh, God!" Gracie's head sank back into the pillow.

"Guys," Ralph said and signaled with a barely perceptible nod of his head toward the door.

Kurt leaned over Gracie and whispered in her ear, "Don't let the assholes get you down."

The men trooped out of the room.

"Don't be getting a big head . . ."

"We'll be back . . ."

". . . a couple of days . . ."

". . . bring a bottle of Cuervo."

". . . have to smuggle it in."

". . . in a backpack."

". . . a water bottle."

The laughter and voices faded down the hallway.

Ralph closed the door after them. He walked over and sat down in the chair next to the bed.

Gracie studied his face. Even through the haze of pain-killers, it shocked her how haggard and old he looked, how drawn his cheeks were, how pronounced the lines on his forehead and around his mouth. And that he looked as if he hadn't shaved in a week. "You look like shit yourself, Ral-phie," she said.

He nodded and said, "I checked your house. I put up some crime scene tape to keep the reporters out."

"Thanks."

"Threw out the sour milk. And green sandwich meat."

Gracie rolled her one good eye.

"Your answering machine was full. You got an offer from a book publisher. And one from a movie company. Your mother left four messages."

"Of course."

"She sounded distraught."

"Of course."

"I think she's genuinely worried. I can call her back for you."

"I'll do it. Maybe tomorrow." Gracie closed her eyes. "Where's Cashman?"

Ralph picked up Gracie's hand in his cool, dry one. With his gravelly voice low and quiet, he described how Rob had been airlifted out to a landing zone at Aviation's headquarters. A private helicopter whisked him from there to an undisclosed L.A. hospital, where he was kept overnight for observation. Except for multiple bruises, his injured ankle, and two facial cuts requiring microscopic plastic surgery, he was declared to be in reasonably good condition considering his ordeal.

Ralph provided only vague generalities about Tristan Chambers and Diana Petrovic, and about Joseph Van Dijk, aka, Radovan Milocek, aka The Surgeon. There was ample time later to delve deeper into that nightmare.

And in the quiet of her hospital room, Ralph told Gracie that Steve Cashman was dead.

# 81

"I should have stayed home after all." Gracie said through teeth clenched against the pain of riding in a wheelchair over the uneven brick walkway.

"Almost there," Ralph said as he pushed the chair up the sidewalk leading to the church.

Across the wide gravel parking lot, in the lengthening blue shadows of tall pines, a phalanx of reporters and camera crews—held back by several lengths of yellow Sheriff's Department tape—snapped and filmed the funeral goers as they trickled into the church. A cluster of onlookers, mostly women, huddled to one side. Stationed at various points around the church grounds were several deputies and a security detail of burly men in suits and sunglasses.

"What the hell!" Gracie growled. "Groupies at a funeral? I want my stupid-ass life back."

"Almost there," Ralph said into her ear.

The wheelchair swept past a single deputy standing guard and in through the front door of the church. Gracie blinked to adjust her eyes as they passed from daylight into the darkness of the dimly lit narthex.

Just inside the door stood a small table covered with a white tablecloth on which had been arranged an eight-by-eleven portrait of Steve Cashman in uniform; his scratched and dented helmet; dress uniform shirt, recently ironed; and a coil of Steve's personal climbing rope. Flanking the entrance to the sanctuary itself were two members of the National Search and Rescue Honor Guard dressed in ceremonial uniform from black berets to charcoal gray shirts and white gloves to 10th Mountain Division ice axes.

"Don't stop," Gracie whispered over her shoulder to Ralph.

The late-afternoon sun through stained glass cast slanting streamers of color across a sea of orange shirts already seated inside—search and rescue personnel from all over the state, mourning their colleague killed in the line of duty.

"We should have come earlier," Gracie said through teeth still clenched so tightly together it was making her jaw ache. She stared straight ahead as heads swiveled and eyes tracked the wheelchair making its excruciatingly slow way down the center aisle to the front of the church. Ralph stopped beside the second row of pews, set the brake, and took the open seat at the end next to Gracie. On the other side of him, in a somber row, sat the eight remaining members of the Timber Creek Search and Rescue team.

In the front pew of the church, alongside Cashman's family and directly in front of Kurt, Rob sat looking straight ahead and appearing stiff in slicked-back hair, and a bright white shirt and black suit.

Throughout the ponderous service, Gracie fought the temptation to glance over at Rob. Instead she stared at the minister, barely hearing his monotone delivery or the eulogies given by her teammates, pondering why the hero label bestowed upon Cashman rang hollow in her ears and about why she didn't really feel anything about his being dead.

Even as Ralph and five other men from the team carried the casket bearing Cashman's body past her back up the aisle, with bagpipes playing "Amazing Grace" from the choir loft, Gracie's eyes remained dry, the neatly folded cloth handkerchief Ralph had placed on her knee before the service unused.

Immediately afterward, before anyone else in the sanctuary moved, two bodyguards whisked Rob out a side door and Gracie found herself being wheeled by Warren across the front of the sanctuary, through a different side door and into a small windowless room. Warren parked the wheelchair, set the brake, and left the room without a word. "What the—?" Gracie said to the closing door.

Gracie looked around the room—dark wood paneling, crimson carpet worn to threadbare, a small round table surrounded by four wooden chairs with a box of generic tissues placed dead center.

It was warm. And stuffy.

The door opened again and Gracie looked up.

A jolt of electricity hit her as Rob limped in.

He closed the door quietly behind him, then he turned and looked directly at her.

The two studied each other.

Gracie's heart was thumping so loudly she wondered if Rob could hear it from where he stood only six feet away. She took in every facet of Rob's face, the black eye and other contusions, the abrasions, the microscopic stitches on the cuts on his cheekbone and above his eye. He looked taller than she remembered. And cleaner. "You took a bath," she said.

The corners of his mouth twitched. "So did you."

"Such as it was." She almost shrugged, but remembered her broken clavicle in time.

Rob took a step toward her, bent forward and kissed her.

*Soft and warm*, Gracie thought. *That's what I'll remember about his kiss.*

Rob dragged one of the wooden chairs over, placed it an inch away from the wheelchair, and sat down.

Gracie looked over at him. "I don't want to hear a single word about how much like a lopsided chipmunk I look or how much like shit. And I didn't want this friggin' wheelchair, but it's the only way they would let me come."

Rob's dark eyes sparkled. "Haven't changed a bit, have you then?"

"Why the hell should I have changed?"

He smiled. "I don't suppose there's any way you'll let me whisk you away from all of this. Take you back to London with me."

"I don't suppose there is," she said and saw a flicker of something flash in the bright brown eyes. But whether a flicker of pain or of relief she couldn't decipher. "At least not with all the friggin' paparazzi following you—and me—everywhere."

The smile faded. "I'm sorry for that, Gracie. Truly sorry."

"Besides, I told you before. I hate cities."

"So you did." He cocked his head at her. "God, I love you."

Gracie jerked away from him as if she had been slapped, then grit her teeth as pain shot through her shoulder. "Don't," she said.

"Gracie." Rob gently lifted her hand and kissed her bruised knuckles, which sent goose bumps up her spine. "I need to tell you something," he said. "Will you hear me out? Please?"

She nodded and stared down at the orange buttons of Ralph's uniform shirt draped around her shoulders—the only one large enough to fit over the massive bandage on her shoulder and arm.

"I'm not in love with you," Rob said in a low voice. "Well, maybe I am, but that's not what I'm saying here." He bent to look into her face. "Look at me, love. Please."

Gracie dragged her eyes up to meet his.

"How can I say this? You've ruined me for good."

"Oh—" Gracie began.

"Let me finish, woman!"

"Don't call me *woman*," Gracie growled back at him.

Rob chuckled, bowed his head for a moment, then he said, "You've given me my life back. Or given me a new one is closer to the truth. People who live in cities and for cities—and I am one—get all caught up in the minutiae of life, the clutter and clamor and chaos."

"Nice alliteration," Gracie said.

Rob stopped.

"Sorry," she said. "Go on."

"But," he continued, "I feel like I'm fully awake for the first time in . . . forever. In my previous life, I lived in two dimensions. Now I live in three. Life seems simpler. More basic. Yet it's richer, more complex. If that makes any sense at all. I'm seeing things with renewed clarity. Experiencing my life, truly living it. Maybe for the first time. You are the one who brought me there."

The lump in Gracie's throat made it difficult for her to swallow back the impending tears.

"You and I come from different worlds that in all probability cannot mesh."

"Probably not," she whispered, and bit her lower lip to stop it from quivering.

"But I do love you," he said. "Everything about you. I love that you're doing something good in this world, especially saving my worthless English arse." Rob's eyes twinkled back at her. "I love your fearlessness. Your strength. Your absolute lack of pretense. I love your smile. Your incredible eyes."

A single tear slid down Gracie's cheek and dripped onto her uniform pants.

Rob leaned forward so that his mouth was right next to her ear. "Do not change," he said, his voice breaking. "Do you hear me? Do *not* let this world change you."

Gracie leaned over to rest her head against Rob's. "Yes."

"No matter what happens, Gracie," he whispered. "You'll always be with me. You'll always be a part of me."

"And you'll be a part of me," she whispered back, choking back a sob.

He pressed his lips to her hair. Then he rose and, with feet silent on the carpet, walked out of the room.

Gracie sat in the silent room, head bowed until gradually her body stopped shaking. Then she shuddered in a long, painful breath and blew it slowly out.

The main door opened, then closed. Gracie felt rather than saw Ralph sit down in the chair beside her.

She lifted her head and looked over at him.

Before Gracie realized what he was doing, Ralph leaned over and kissed her on the mouth.

She sat up, eyes wide with surprise. "What was *that*?"

"Whatever you want it to be, Gracie girl."

Gracie stared unblinking back at Ralph, her best friend, the man who made her feel warm and calm and safe, the one person who had never let her down, the one person who, she knew without a doubt, would always be there for her.

Gracie smiled at him.

The blue-gray eyes crinkled. "Ready to go?" he asked in a gentle voice.

"I'm ready."


**AN AUTOPSY OF** Cashman's body had revealed injuries consistent with a traumatic fall, the cause of which was undetermined. Tristan Chambers's death was attributed to massive internal injuries and blood loss due predominantly to a severed aorta.

No trace of Diana Petrovic was ever found.

The curved knife was never recovered.

Rob never regained full memory of what had transpired up on the rock promontory.

And somewhere in the depths of the canyon, the body of Radovan Milocek, "The Surgeon," lay buried in its frozen tomb until early summer and the melting of the last of the high-country snow.

The story of Rob Christian and Grace Kinkaid became yesterday's news, and Gracie's life reverted back to something resembling normal. Her contusions faded from purple and black to green and yellow. Her punctures and cuts healed to pink scars. Her clavicle and arthroscopically repaired shoulder ligaments mended.

The emotional bruises took longer to heal.

And eventually, months later, Gracie wept for Steve Cashman.

# ANNA PIGEON SERIES
## by Nevada Barr

*Borderline*
*Winter Study*
*Hard Truth*
*High Country*
*Flashback*
*Hunting Season*
*Blood Lure*
*Deep South*
*Blind Descent*
*Endangered Species*
*Firestorm*
*Ill Wind*
*A Superior Death*
*Track of the Cat*

penguin.com